AZAZEL

AZAZEL

Isaac Asimov

A FOUNDATION BOOK
Doubleday
NEW YORK   LONDON   TORONTO   SYDNEY   AUCKLAND

All characters in this book are fictional
and any resemblance to actual persons,
living or dead, is entirely coincidental.

A Foundation Book
Published by Doubleday, a division of
Bantam Doubleday Dell Publishing Group, Inc.,
666 Fifth Avenue, New York, New York 10103.

Doubleday, Foundation and the portrayal of the letter F
are trademarks of Doubleday, a division of
Bantam Doubleday Dell Publishing Group, Inc.

Library of Congress Cataloging-in-Publication Data

Asimov, Isaac, 1920–
Azazel.

1. Fantastic fiction, American.   I. Title.
PS3551.S5A9   1988   813'.54   87-32980
ISBN 0-385-24410-X
Copyright © 1988 by Nightfall, Inc.
All Rights Reserved
Printed in the United States of America
November 1988
First Edition

BG

To Sheila Williams,
the sweet managing editor of
Isaac Asimov's Science Fiction Magazine

Acknowledgments

"One Night of Song" appeared in the April 1982 issue of *The Magazine of Fantasy and Science Fiction* (F & SF). Copyright © 1982 by Mercury Press, Inc.

"The Smile That Loses" appeared in the November 1982 issue of *F & SF.* Copyright © 1982 by Mercury Press, Inc.

"To the Victor" appeared in the July 1982 issue of *Isaac Asimov's Science Fiction Magazine* (IASFM). Copyright © 1982 by Davis Publications, Inc.

"The Dim Rumble" appeared in the September 18, 1982, issue of *IASFM.* Copyright © 1982 by Davis Publications, Inc.

"Saving Humanity" appeared in the September 1983 issue of *IASFM.* Copyright © 1983 by Davis Publications, Inc.

"A Matter of Principle" appeared in the February 1984 issue of *IASFM.* Copyright © 1983 by Davis Publications, Inc.

"The Evil Drink Does" appeared in the May 1984 issue of *IASFM.* Copyright © 1984 by Davis Publications, Inc.

"Writing Time" appeared in the July 1984 issue of *IASFM.* Copyright © 1984 by Davis Publications, Inc.

"Dashing Through the Snow" appeared in the mid-December 1984 issue of *IASFM.* Copyright © 1984 by Davis Publications, Inc.

"Logic Is Logic" appeared in the August 1985 issue of *IASFM.* Copyright © 1985 by Davis Publications, Inc.

"He Travels the Fastest" appeared in the November 1985 issue of *IASFM.* Copyright © 1985 by Davis Publications, Inc.

"The Eye of the Beholder" appeared in the January 1986 issue of *IASFM.* Copyright © 1985 by Davis Publications, Inc.

"More Things in Heaven and Earth" appeared in a pamphlet, "Science Fiction by Isaac Asimov." Copyright © 1986 by Nightfall, Inc.

Contents

Contents

Introduction

In 1980, a gentleman named Eric Protter asked me to do a monthly mystery story for a magazine he was editing. I agreed, because I find it difficult to say No to nice people (and all the editors I have ever met have been nice people).

The first story I wrote was a kind of fantasy-mystery, featuring a small demon about two centimeters tall. I named it "Getting Even" and Eric Protter accepted and published it. It featured a gentleman named Griswold as the narrator and three men (including a first-person character who was me, although I never named myself) who were his audience. The four were described as meeting every week in the Union Club and I intended the series to continue to feature the tales of Griswold in the Union Club.

However, when I tried to write a second story involving the little demon of "Getting Even" (the new story was named "One Night of Song") Eric said No. Apparently a bit of fantasy was all right once, but he didn't want me to make a habit of it.

I therefore put "One Night of Song" to one side and proceeded to write the series of mystery stories with no fantasy admixture at all. Thirty of these stories (which Eric insisted be only 2,000 to 2,200 words long) were eventually collected in my book *The Union Club Mysteries* (Doubleday, 1983). I did not include "Getting Even," however, because since it featured the little demon it didn't match the rest of the stories.

Meanwhile I was brooding about "One Night of Song." I hate waste, and I can't endure leaving something I wrote unpublished if there is anything I can do to correct the situation. I therefore approached Eric and said, "That story, 'One Night of Song,' which you rejected—may I publish it elsewhere?"

He said, "Certainly, provided you change the name of the characters. I want your stories featuring Griswold and his audience to be exclusive in my magazine."

So I did. I changed Griswold's name to George, and I kept an audience of only one, the first-person character who was myself. That done, I sold "One Night of Song" to *The Magazine of Fantasy and Science Fiction* (F & SF). Then I wrote another story of the kind I now thought of as "George and Azazel stories," Azazel being the name of the demon. This one, "The Smile That Loses," was also sold to *F & SF*.

But I also have a science fiction magazine of my own, *Isaac Asimov's Science Fiction Magazine* (IASFM), and Shawna McCarthy, who was then the editor, objected to my having fiction in *F & SF*.

I said, "But Shawna, these George and Azazel stories are fantasies, and IASFM publishes only science fiction."

She said, "So change the little demon and its magic into a little extraterrestrial being with an advanced technology, and sell the stories to me."

So I did that, and since I was still crazy about the George and Azazel stories, I continued to write them, and now I can include eighteen of these stories in this collection *Azazel*. (Only eighteen are included, because without Eric's need for briefness, I was able to make the George and Azazel stories twice as long as my Griswolds.)

But again I didn't include "Getting Even" because that didn't quite have the flavor of the later stories. Having been the original inspiration of two different series, "Getting Even" had the sad fate of falling between two stools, and not fitting into either set of descendants. (Never mind, it's been anthologized and it may yet appear in the future in other guises as well. Don't feel too sorry for it.)

There are some points I would like to make about the stories; points you'll probably notice for yourself, but I'm a blabbermouth.

1) As I said, I omitted the first story I wrote about the little demon because it didn't fit. My beautiful editor, Jennifer Brehl, insisted, however, that a first story was necessary to describe how George and I met, and how the little demon first entered George's life. Since Jennifer, although a model of sweetness, is not to be withstood when she clenches her little fists, I wrote a story "The Two-Centimeter Demon," which does as she asks, and it is inserted as the first story in the book. What's more, Jennifer decided that Azazel is definitely going to be a demon and not an extraterrestrial, so we are back in fantasy. ("Azazel" is a biblical name, by the way, and Bible readers usually take it to be the name of a demon, though the matter is a bit more complicated than that.)

2) George is pictured as a deadbeat of sorts and I dislike deadbeats—and yet find George lovable. I hope you do too. The first-person character (really Isaac Asimov) is often insulted by George and invariably victimized by him to the extent of a few dollars, but I don't mind. As I explain at the end of the first story, his stories are worth it, and I make far more money out of them than I give to George—particularly since the giving is fictional.

3) Please be aware that the stories are intended to be humorous satires, and if you find the style overblown and "un-Asimovian," that is on purpose. Consider this a warning. Don't buy the book expecting something else, and then find yourself annoyed. And, by the way, if you occasionally detect the faint influence of P. G. Wodehouse, believe me, that's not accidental.

AZAZEL

The Two-Centimeter Demon

I met George at a literary convention a good many years ago, and was struck by the peculiar look of innocence and candor upon his round middle-aged face. He was the kind of person, I decided at once, to whom you would give your wallet to hold while you went swimming.

He recognized me from my photographs on the back of my books and greeted me gladly, telling me how much he liked my stories and novels which, of course, gave me a good opinion of his intelligence and taste.

We shook hands cordially and he said, "My name is George Bitternut."

"Bitternut," I repeated, in order to fix it in my mind. "An unusual name."

"Danish," he said, "and very aristocratic. I am descended from Cnut, better known as Canute, a Danish king who conquered England in the early eleventh century. An ancestor of mine was his son, born on the wrong side of the blanket, of course."

"Of course," I muttered, though I didn't see why that was something that should be taken for granted.

"He was named Cnut for his father," George went on, "and when he was presented to the king, the royal Dane said, 'By my halidom, is this my heir?' "

" 'Not quite,' said the courtier who was dandling little Cnut, 'for he is illegitimate, the mother being the launderwoman whom you—'

" 'Ah,' said the king, 'That's better.' And Bettercnut he was known from that moment on. Just that single name. I have inherited that name in the direct male line except that the vicissitudes of time have changed the name to Bitternut." And his blue eyes looked at me with a kind of hypnotic ingenuousness that forbade doubt.

I said, "Would you join me for lunch?" sweeping my hand in the direction of the ornate restaurant that was clearly intended only for the fat-walleted.

George said, "Don't you think that that bistro is a bit garish and that the lunch counter on the other side might—"

"As my guest," I added.

And George pursed his lips and said, "Now that I look at the bistro in a better light, I see that it has a rather homelike atmosphere. Yes, it will do."

Over the main course, George said, "My ancestor Bettercnut had a son, whom he named Sweyn. A good Danish name."

"Yes, I know," I said, "King Cnut's father's name was Sweyn Forkbeard. In modern times, the name is usually spelled Sven."

George frowned slightly and said, "There is no need, old man, to parade your knowledge of these things. I accept the fact that you have the rudiments of an education."

I felt abashed. "Sorry."

He waved his hand in grand forgiveness, ordered another glass of wine and said, "Sweyn Bettercnut was fascinated by the young women, a characteristic all the Bitternuts have inherited, and he was very successful with them, I might add—as we have all been. There is a well-attested tale that many a woman after leaving him would shake her head admiringly and say, 'Oh, what a Sweyn that is.' He was an archimage, too." He paused, and said abruptly, "Do you know what an archimage is?"

"No," I lied, not wishing to parade my knowledge offensively yet again. "Tell me."

"An archimage is a master magician," said George, with what certainly sounded like a sigh of relief. "Sweyn studied the arcane and hidden arts. It was possible to do it then, for all that nasty modern skepticism had not yet arisen. He was intent on finding ways of persuading the young ladies to behave with that kind of gentle and compliant behavior that is the crown of womanhood and to eschew all that was froward and shrewish."

"Ah," I said, sympathetically.

"For this he needed demons, and he perfected means for calling them up by burning certain sweet shrubs and calling on certain half-forgotten names of power."

"And did it work, Mr. Bitternut?"

"Please call me George. Of course it worked. He had demons in teams and shoals working for him for, as he often complained, the women of the time were mule-headed and obstinate who countered his claim to be the grandson of a king, with unkind remarks about the nature of the descent. Once a demon did his thing, however, they could see that a natural son was only natural."

I said, "Are you sure this is so, George?"

"Certainly, for last summer I found his book of recipes for calling up demons. I found it in an old English castle that is in ruins now but that once belonged to my family. The exact shrubs were listed, the manner of burning, the pacing, the names of power, the intonations. Everything. It was written in Old English—Anglo-Saxon, you know—but I am by way of being a linguist and—"

A certain mild skepticism made itself felt. "You're joking," I said.

His glance was haughty. "Why do you think so? Am I tittering? It was an authentic book. I tested the recipes myself."

"And got a demon."

"Yes, indeed," he said, pointing significantly to the breast pocket of his suit coat.

"In there?"

George touched the pocket and seemed on the point of nodding, when his fingers seemed to feel something significant, or perhaps failed to feel something. He peered inside.

"He's gone," he said with dissatisfaction. "Dematerialized. —But you can't blame him, perhaps. He was with me last night because he was curious about this convention, you know. I gave him some whiskey out of an eyedropper and he liked it. Perhaps he liked it a little too much, for he wanted to fight the caged cockatoo in the bar and began squeaking opprobrious names at it. Fortunately he fell asleep before the offended bird could retaliate. This morning he did not seem at his best and I suppose he has gone home, wherever that might be, to recover."

I felt a touch rebellious. Did he expect me to believe all this? "Are you telling me you had a demon in your breast pocket?"

"Your quick grasp of the situation," said George, "is gratifying."

"How big was he?"

"Two centimeters."

"But that's less than an inch."

"Perfectly correct. An inch is 2.54 centimeters."

"I mean, what kind of a demon is two centimeters tall?"

"A small one," said George, "but as the old saying goes, a small demon is better than no demon."

"It depends on his mood."

"Oh, Azazel—that's his name—is a friendly demon. I suspect he is looked down upon in his native haunts, for he is extraordinarily anxious to impress me with his powers, except that he won't use them to make me rich, as he should out of decent friendship. He says his powers must be used only to do good to others."

"Come, come, George. Surely that's not the philosophy of hell."

George put a finger to his lips. "Don't say things like that, old man. Azazel would be enormously offended. He says that his country is kindly, decent, and highly civilized, and he speaks with enormous respect of his ruler whom he won't name but whom he calls merely the All-in-All."

"And does he indeed do kindnesses?"

"Whenever he can. Take the case of my goddaughter, Juniper Pen—"

"Juniper Pen?"

"Yes. I can see by the look of intense curiosity in your eye that you wish to know the story and I will gladly tell it to you."

Juniper Pen [said George] was a wide-eyed sophomore at college when the tale I tell you opened—an innocent, sweet girl fascinated by the basketball team, one and all of whom were tall, handsome young men.

The one of the team upon whom her girlish fancies seemed most fixed was Leander Thomson, tall, rangy, with large hands that wrapped themselves about a basketball, or anything else that was the size and shape of a basketball, which somehow brings Juniper to mind. He was the undoubted focus of her screaming when she sat in the audience at one of the games.

She would speak to me of her sweet little dreams, for like all young women, even those who were not my goddaughters, she had the impulse to confide in me. My warm but dignified demeanor invited confidence.

"Oh, Uncle George," she would say, "surely it isn't wrong of me to dream of a future with Leander. I see him now as the greatest basketball player in the world, as the pick and cream of the great professionals, as the owner of a long-term, large-sized contract. It's not as if I ask for much. All I want out of life is a little vine-covered mansion, a small garden stretching out as far as the eye can see, a simple staff of servants organized into squads, all my clothing arranged alphabetically for each day of the week, and each month of the year, and—"

It was forced to interrupt her charming prattle. "Little one," I said, "there is a tiny flaw in your scheme. Leander is not a very good basketball player and it is unlikely that he will be signed up for enormous sums in salary."

"That's so unfair," she said, pouting. "*Why* isn't he a very good basketball player?"

"Because that is the way the universe works. Why do you not pin your young affections on someone who *is* a good basketball player? Or, for that matter, on some honest young Wall Street broker who happens to have access to inside information?"

"Actually, I've thought of that myself, Uncle George, but I like Leander all by himself. There are times when I think of him and say to myself, Is money really all that important?"

"Hush, little one," I said, shocked. Women these days are incredibly outspoken.

"But why can't I have the money *too?* Is that so much to ask?"

Actually, was it? After all, I had a demon all my own. It was a little demon, to be sure, but his heart was big. Surely he would want to help out the course of true love, in order to bring sweetness and light to two souls whose two hearts beat as one at the thought of mutual kisses and mutual funds.

Azazel did listen when I summoned him with the appropriate name of power. —No, I can't tell you what it is. Have you no sense of elementary ethics? —As I say, he did listen but with what I felt to be a lack of that true sympathy one would expect. I admit I had dragged him into our own continuum from what was an indulgence in something like a Turkish bath, for he was wrapped in a tiny towel and he was shivering. His voice seemed higher and squeakier than ever. (Actually, I don't think it was truly his voice. I think he communicated by telepathy of some sort, but the result was that I heard, or imagined I heard, a squeaky voice.)

"What is basket ball?" he said. "A ball shaped like a basket? Because if it is, what is a basket?"

I tried to explain but, for a demon, he can be very dense. He kept staring at me as though I were not explaining every bit of the game with luminous clarity.

He said, finally, "Is it possible for me to *see* a game of basketball?"

"Certainly," I said. "There will be a game tonight. I have a ticket which Leander gave me and you can come in my pocket."

"Fine," said Azazel. "Call me back when you are ready to leave for the game. Right now I must finish my zymjig," by which I suppose he meant his Turkish bath—and he disappeared.

I must admit that I find it most irritating to have someone place his puny and parochial affairs ahead of the matters of great moment in which I am engaged—which reminds me, old man, that the waiter seems to be trying to attract your attention. I think he has your check for you. Please take it from him and let me get ahead with my story.

I went to the basketball game that night and Azazel was with me in my pocket. He kept poking his head above the edge of the pocket in order to watch the game and he would have made a questionable sight if anyone had been watching. His skin is a bright red and on his forehead are two nubbins of horns. It is fortunate, of course, that he didn't come out altogether, for his centimeter-long, muscular tail is both his most prominent and his most nauseating feature.

I am not a great basketball aficionado myself and I rather left it to Azazel to make sense out of what was happening. His intelligence, although demonic rather than human, is intense.

After the game he said to me, "It seems to me, as nearly as I could make out from the strenuous action of the bulky, clumsy and totally uninteresting individuals in the arena, that there was excitement every time that peculiar ball passed through a hoop."

"That's it," I said. "You score a basket, you see."

"Then this protégé of yours would become a heroic player of this stupid game if he could throw the ball through the hoop every time?"

"Exactly."

Azazel twirled his tail thoughtfully. "That should not be difficult. I need only adjust his reflexes in order to make him judge the angle, height, force—" He fell into a ruminative silence for a moment, then said, "Let's see, I noted and recorded his personal coordinate complex during the game . . . Yes, it can be done.

—In fact, it is done. Your Leander will have no trouble in getting the ball through the hoop."

I felt a certain excitement as I waited for the next scheduled game. I did not say a word to little Juniper because I had never made use of Azazel's demonic powers before and I wasn't entirely sure that his deeds would match his words. Besides, I wanted her to be surprised. (As it turned out, she was very surprised, as was I.)

The day of the game came at last, and it was *the* game. Our local college, Nerdsville Tech, of whose basketball team Leander was so dim a luminary, was playing the lanky bruisers of the Al Capone College Reformatory and it was expected to be an epic combat.

How epic, no one expected. The Capone Five swept into an early lead, and I watched Leander keenly. He seemed to have trouble in deciding what to do and at first his hands seemed to miss the ball when he tried to dribble. His reflexes, I guessed, had been so altered that at first he could not control his muscles at all.

But then it was as though he grew accustomed to his new body. He seized the ball and it seemed to slip from his hands—but what a slip! It arced high into the air and through the center of the hoop.

A wild cheer shook the stands while Leander stared thoughtfully up at the hoop as though wondering what had happened.

Whatever had happened, happened again—and again. As soon as Leander touched the ball, it arced. As soon as it arced it curved into the basket. It would happen so suddenly that no one ever saw Leander aim, or make any effort at all. Interpreting this as sheer expertise, the crowd grew the more hysterical.

But then, of course, the inevitable happened and the game descended into total chaos. Catcalls erupted from the stands; the scarred and broken-nosed alumni who were rooting for Capone Reformatory made violent remarks of a derogatory nature and fistfights blossomed in every corner of the audience.

What I had failed to tell Azazel, you see, thinking it to be self-evident, and what Azazel had failed to realize was that the two baskets on the court were not identical: that one was the home basket and the other the visitors' basket, and that each player aimed for the appropriate basket. The basketball, with all the lamentable ignorance of an inanimate object, arced for whichever basket was nearer once Leander seized it. The result was that time and again Leander would manage to put the ball into the wrong basket.

He persisted in doing so despite the kindly remonstrances of Nerdsville coach, Claws ("Pop") McFang, which he shrieked through the foam that covered his lips. Pop McFang bared his teeth in a sigh of sadness at having to eject Leander from the game, and wept openly when they removed his fingers from Leander's throat so that the ejection could be carried through.

My friend, Leander was never the same again. I had thought, naturally, that he would find escape in drink, and become a stern and thoughtful wino. I would have understood that. He sank lower than that, however. He turned to his studies.

Under the contemptuous, and even sometimes pitying, eyes of his schoolmates, he slunk from lecture to lecture, buried his head in books, and receded into the dank depths of scholarship.

Yet through it all, Juniper clung to him. "He needs me," she said, her eyes misting with unshed tears. Sacrificing all, she married him after they graduated. She then clung to him even while he sank to the lowest depths of all, being stigmatized with a Ph.D. in physics.

He and Juniper live now in a small co-op on the upper west side somewhere. He teaches physics and does research in cosmogony, I understand. He earns $60,000 a year and is spoken of in shocked whispers, by those who knew him when he was a respectable jock, as a possible candidate for the Nobel Prize.

Juniper never complains, but remains faithful to her fallen idol. Neither by word nor deed does she ever express any sense of loss, but she cannot fool her old godfather. I know very well that, on occasion, she thinks wistfully of the vine-covered mansion she'll never have, and of the rolling hills and distant horizons of her small dream estate.

"That's the story," said George, as he scooped up the change the waiter had brought, and copied down the total from the credit-card receipt (so that he might take it off as a tax-deduction, I assume). "If I were you," he added. "I would leave a generous tip."

I did so, rather in a daze, as George smiled and walked away. I didn't really mind the loss of the change. It occurred to me that George got only a meal, whereas I had a story I could tell as my own and which would earn me many times the cost of the meal.

In fact, I decided to continue having dinner with him now and then.

One Night of Song

As it happens, I have a friend who hints, sometimes, that he can call up spirits from the vasty deep.

Or at least one spirit—a tiny one, with strictly limited powers. He talks about it sometimes but only after he has reached his fourth scotch and soda. It's a delicate point of equilibrium—three and he knows nothing about spirits (the supernatural kind); five and he falls asleep.

I thought he had reached the right level that evening, so I said, "Do you remember that spirit of yours, George?"

"Eh?" said George, looking at his drink as though he wondered why that should require remembering.

"Not your drink," I said. "The little spirit about two centimeters high, whom you once told me you had managed to call up from some other place of existence. The one with the paranatural powers."

"Ah," said George. "Azazel. Not his name, of course. Couldn't pronounce his real name, I suppose, but that's what I call him. I remember him."

"Do you use him much?"

"No. Dangerous. It's too dangerous. There's always the temptation to play with power. I'm careful myself; deuced careful. As you know, I have a high standard of ethics. That's why I felt called upon to help a friend once. The damage *that* did! Dreadful! Doesn't bear thinking of."

"What happened?"

"I suppose I ought to get it off my chest," said George, thoughtfully. "It tends to fester—"

I was a good deal younger then [said George] and in those days women made up an important part of one's life. It seems silly now, looking back on it, but I distinctly remember thinking, back in those days, that it made much difference which woman.

Actually, you reach in the grab bag and whichever comes out, it's much the same, but in those days—

I had a friend, Mortenson—Andrew Mortenson. I don't think you know him. I haven't seen much of him myself in recent years.

The point is, he was soppy about a woman, a particular woman. She was an angel, he said. He couldn't live without her. She was the only one in the universe and without her the world was crumbled bacon bits dipped in axle grease. You know the way lovers talk.

The trouble was she threw him over finally and apparently did so in a particularly cruel manner and without regard for his self-esteem. She had humiliated him thoroughly, taking up with another right in front of him, snapping her fingers under his nostrils and laughing heartlessly at his tears.

I don't mean that literally. I'm just trying to give the impression he gave me. He sat here drinking with me, here in this very room. My heart bled for him and I said, "I'm sorry, Mortenson, but you mustn't take on so. When you stop to think of it clearly, she's only a woman. If you look out in the street, there are lots of them passing by."

He said, bitterly, "I intend a womanless existence from now on, old man—except for my wife, of course, whom, every now and then, I can't avoid. It's just that I'd like to do something in return to this woman."

"To your wife?" I said.

"No, no, why should I like to do something to my wife? I'm talking about doing something for this woman who threw me over so heartlessly."

"Like what?"

"Damned if I know," said he.

"Maybe I can help," I said, for my heart was still bleeding for him. "I can make use of a spirit with quite extraordinary powers. A small spirit, of course"—I held my finger and thumb up less than an inch apart so that he was sure to get the idea—"who can only do so much."

I told him about Azazel and, of course, he believed me. I've often noticed that I carry conviction when I tell a tale. Now when *you* tell a story, old man, the air of disbelief that descends upon the room is thick enough to cut with a chain saw, but it's not that way with me. There's nothing like a reputation for probity and an air of honest directness.

His eyes glittered as I told him. He said could he arrange to give her something that I would ask for.

"If it's presentable, old man. I hope you have nothing in your mind like making her smell bad or having a toad drop out of her mouth when she talks."

"Of course not," he said, revolted. "What do you take me for? She gave me two happy years, on and off, and I want to make an adequate return. You say your spirit has only limited power?"

"He's a small thing," I said, holding up my thumb and forefinger again.

"Could he give her a perfect voice? For a time, anyway. At least for one performance."

"I'll ask him." Mortenson's suggestion sounded the gentlemanly thing to do. His ex-mistress sang cantatas at the local church, if that's the proper term. In those days I had quite an ear for music and would frequently go to these things (taking care to dodge the collection box, of course). I rather enjoyed hearing her sing and the audience seemed to absorb it politely enough. I thought at the time that her morals didn't quite suit the surroundings, but Mortenson said they made allowances for sopranos.

So I consulted Azazel. He was quite willing to help; none of this nonsense, you know, of demanding my soul in exchange. I remember I once asked Azazel if he wanted my soul and he didn't even know what it was. He asked me what I meant and it turned out I didn't know what it was, either. It's just that he's such a little fellow in his own universe that it gives him a feeling of great success to be able to throw his weight around in our universe. He *likes* to help out.

He said he could manage three hours and Mortenson said that would be perfect when I gave him the news. We picked a night when she was going to be singing Bach or Handel or one of those old piano-bangers, and was going to have a long and impressive solo.

Mortenson went to the church that night and, of course, I went too. I felt responsible for what was going to happen and I thought I had better oversee the situation.

Mortenson said, gloomily, "I attended the rehearsals. She was just singing the same way she always did; you know, as though she had a tail and someone was stepping on it."

That wasn't the way he used to describe her voice. The music of the spheres, he said on a number of occasions, and it was all uphill from there. Of course, though, he had been thrown over, which does warp a man's judgment.

I fixed him with a censorious eye. "That's no way to talk of a woman you're trying to bestow a great gift upon."

"That's just it. I want her voice to be perfect. Really *perfect.* And I now see—now that the mists of love have cleared from my eyes—that she has a long way to go. Do you think your spirit can handle it?"

"The change isn't timed to start till 8:15 P.M." A stab of suspicion went through me. "You hadn't been hoping to use up the perfection on the rehearsal and then disappoint the audience?"

"You have it all wrong," he said.

They got started a little early and when she got up in her white dress to sing it was 8:14 by my old pocket watch which is never off by more than two seconds. She wasn't one of your peewee sopranos; she was built on a generous scale, leaving lots of room for the kind of resonance you need when you reach for that high note and drown out the orchestra. Whenever she drew in a few gallons of breath with which to manipulate it all, I could see what Mortenson saw in her, allowing for several layers of textile material.

She started at her usual level and then at 8:15 precisely, it was as though another voice had been added. I saw her give a little jump as though she didn't believe what she heard, and one hand, which was held to her diaphragm, seemed to vibrate.

Her voice soared. It was as though she had become an organ in perfect pitch. Each note was perfect, a note invented freshly at that moment, besides which all other notes of the same pitch and quality were imperfect copies.

Each note hit squarely with just the proper vibrato, if that's the word, swelling or diminishing with enormous power and control.

And she got better with each note. The organist wasn't looking at the music, he was looking at her, and—I can't swear to it —but I think he stopped playing. If he were playing, I wouldn't have heard him anyway. There was no way in which you could hear *anything* while she was singing. Anything else but her.

The look of surprise had vanished from her face, and there was a look of exaltation there instead. She had put down the music she had been holding; she didn't need it. Her voice was singing by itself and she didn't need to control or direct it. The conductor was rigid and everyone else in the chorus seemed dumbfounded.

The solo ended at last and the chorus sounded in what was a whisper, as though they were all ashamed of their voices and distressed to turn them loose in the same church on the same night.

For the rest of the program it was all her. When she sang, it was all that was heard even if every other voice was sounding. When she didn't sing, it was as though we were sitting in the dark, and we couldn't bear the absence of light.

And when it was over—well, you don't applaud in church, but they did then. Everyone in that church stood up as though they had been yanked to their feet by a single marionette string, and they applauded and applauded, and it was clear they would applaud all night unless she sang again.

She did sing again; her voice alone, with the organ whispering hesitantly in the background; with the spotlight on her; with no one else in the chorus visible.

Effortless. You have no idea how effortless it was. I wrenched my ears away from the sound to try to watch her breathing, to catch her taking in breath, to wonder how long a note could be held at full volume with only one pair of lungs to supply the air.

But it had to end and it was over. Even the applause was over. It was only then that I became aware that, next to me, Mortenson had been sitting with his eyes glittering, with his whole being absorbed in her singing. It was only then that I began to gather what had happened.

I am, after all, as straight as a Euclidean line and have no deviousness in me, so I couldn't be expected to see what he was after. You, on the other hand, who are so crooked you can run up a spiral staircase without making any turns, can see at a glance what he was after.

She had sung perfectly—but she would never sing perfectly again.

It was as though she were blind from birth, and for just three hours could see—see all there was to see, all the colors and shapes and wonders that surround us all and that we pay no attention to because we're so used to it. Suppose you could see it all in its full glory for just three hours—and then be blind again!

You could stand your blindness if you knew nothing else. But to know something else briefly and then return to blindness? No one could stand that.

That woman has never sung again, of course. But that's only

part of it. The real tragedy was to us, to the members of the audience.

We had perfect music for three hours, *perfect* music. Do you think we could ever again bear to listen to anything less than that?

I've been as good as tone-deaf ever since. Recently, I went to one of those rock festivals that are so popular these days, just to test myself out. You won't believe me, but I couldn't make out one tune. It was all noise to me.

My only consolation is that Mortenson, who listened most eagerly and with the most concentration, is worse off than anyone in that audience. He wears earplugs at all times. He can't stand *any* sound above a whisper.

Serves him right!

The Smile That Loses

I said to my friend George over a beer recently (*his* beer; I was having a ginger ale), "How's your implet these days?"

George claims he has a two-centimeter-tall demon at his beck and call. I can never get him to admit he's lying. Neither can anyone else.

He glared at me balefully, then said, "Oh, yes, you're the one who knows about it! I hope you haven't told anyone else!"

"Not a word," I said. "It's quite sufficient that I think you're crazy. I don't need anyone thinking the same of me." (Besides, he had told at least half a dozen people about the demon, to my personal knowledge, so there's no necessity of *my* being indiscreet.)

George said, "I wouldn't have your unlovely inability to believe anything you don't understand—and you don't understand so much—for the worth of a pound of plutonium. And what would be left of you, if my demon ever found out you called him an implet, wouldn't be worth an atom of plutonium."

"Have you figured out his real name?" I asked, unperturbed by this dire warning.

"Can't! It's unpronounceable by any earthly pair of lips. The translation is, I am given to understand, something like: 'I am the King of Kings; look upon my works, ye mighty, and despair.' —It's a lie, of course," said George, staring moodily at his beer. "He's small potatoes in his world. That's why he's so cooperative here. In *our* world, with our primitive technology, he can show off."

"Has he shown off lately?"

"Yes, as a matter of fact," said George, heaving an enormous sigh and raising his bleak blue eyes to mine. His ragged white mustache settled down only slowly from the typhoon of that forced exhalation of breath.

It started with Rosie O'Donnell [said George], a friend of a niece of mine, and a fetching little thing altogether.

She had blue eyes, almost as brilliant as my own; russet hair, long and lustrous; a delightful little nose, powdered with freckles in the manner approved of by all who write romances; a graceful neck, a slender figure that wasn't opulent in any disproportionate way, but was utterly delightful in its promise of ecstasy.

Of course, all of this was of purely intellectual interest to me, since I reached the age of discretion years ago, and now engage in the consequences of physical affection only when women insist upon it, which, thank the fates, is not oftener than an occasional weekend or so.

Besides which, Rosie had recently married—and, for some reason, adored in the most aggravating manner—a large Irishman who does not attempt to hide the fact that he is a very muscular and, possibly, bad-tempered person. While I had no doubt that I would have been able to handle him in my younger days, the sad fact was that I was no longer in my younger days—by a short margin.

It was therefore with a certain reluctance that I accepted Rosie's tendency to mistake me for some close friend of her own sex and her own time of life, and to make me the object of her girlish confidences.

Not that I blame her, you understand. My natural dignity, and the fact that I inevitably remind people of one or more of the nobler of the Roman emperors in appearance, automatically attracts beautiful young women to me. Nevertheless, I never allowed it to go too far. I always made sure there was plenty of space between Rosie and myself, for I wanted no fables or distortions to reach the undoubtedly large, and possibly bad-tempered, Kevin O'Donnell.

"Oh, George," said Rosie one day, clapping her little hands with glee, "you have no idea what a *darling* my Kevin is, and how happy he makes me. Do you know what he does?"

"I'm not sure," I began, cautiously, naturally expecting indelicate disclosures, "that you ought to—"

She paid no attention. "He has a way of crinkling up his nose and making his eyes twinkle, and smiling brightly, till everything about him looks so happy. It's as though the whole world turns into golden sunshine. Oh, if I only had a photograph of him exactly like that. I've tried to take one, but I never catch him quite right."

I said, "Why not be satisfied with the real thing, my dear?"

"Oh, well!" She hesitated, then said, with the most charming blush, "he's not *always* like that, you know. He's got a *very* difficult job at the airport and sometimes he comes home just worn out and exhausted, and then he becomes just a little touchy, and scowls at me a bit. If I had a photograph of him, as he really is, it would be such a comfort to me. —*Such* a comfort." And her blue eyes misted over with unshed tears.

I must admit that I had the merest trifle of an impulse to tell her of Azazel (that's what I call him, because I'm not going to call him by what he tells me the translation of his real name is) and to explain what he might do for her.

However, I'm unutterably discreet—I haven't the faintest notion how *you* managed to find out about my demon.

Besides, it was easy for me to fight off the impulse for I am a hard-shelled, realistic human being, not given to silly sentiment. I admit I have a semisoft spot in my rugged heart for sweet young women of extraordinary beauty—in a dignified and avuncular manner—mostly. And it occurred to me that, after all, I could oblige her without actually telling her about Azazel. —Not that she would have disbelieved me, of course, for I am a man whose words carry conviction with all but those who, like you, are psychotic.

I referred the matter to Azazel, who was by no means pleased. He said, "You keep asking for abstractions."

I said, "Not at all. I ask for a simple photograph. All you have to do is materialize it."

"Oh, is that all I have to do? If it's that simple, *you* do it. I trust you understand the nature of mass-energy equivalence."

"Just *one* photograph."

"Yes, and with an expression of something you can't even define or describe."

"I've never seen him look at me the way he would look at his wife, naturally. But I have infinite faith in your ability."

I rather expected that a helping of sickening praise would fetch him round. He said, sulkily, "You'll have to take the photograph."

"I couldn't get the proper—"

"You don't have to. I'll take care of that, but it would be much easier if I had a material object on which to focus the abstraction. A photograph, in other words; one of the most inadequate kind, even; the sort I would expect of you. And only *one* copy, of course. I cannot manage more than that and I will not sprain my subjunctival muscle for you or for any other pinheaded being in your world."

Oh, well, he's frequently crotchety. I expect that's simply to establish the importance of his role and impress you with the fact that you must not take him for granted.

I met the O'Donnells the next Sunday, on their way back from Mass. (I lay in wait for them actually.) They were willing to let me snap a picture of them in their Sunday finery. She was delighted and he looked a bit grumpy about it. After that, just as unobtrusively as possible, I took a head shot of Kevin. There was no way I could get him to smile or dimple or crinkle or whatever it was that Rosie found so attractive, but I didn't feel that mattered. I wasn't even sure that the camera was focused correctly. After all, I'm not one of your great photographers.

I then visited a friend of mine who was a photography wiz. He developed both snaps and enlarged the head shot to an eight by eleven.

He did it rather grumpily, muttering something about how busy he was, though I paid no attention to that. After all, what possible value can his foolish activities have in comparison to the important matters that occupied me? I'm always surprised at the number of people who don't understand this.

When he completed the enlargement, however, he changed his attitude entirely. He stared at it and said, in what I can only describe as a completely offensive tone, "Don't tell me you managed to take a photo like this."

"Why not?" I said, and held out my hand for it, but he made no move to give it to me.

"You'll want more copies," he said.

"No, I won't," I said, looking over his shoulder. It was a remarkably clear photograph in brilliant color. Kevin O'Donnell was smiling, though I didn't remember such a smile at the time I snapped it. He seemed good-looking and cheerful, but I was rather indifferent to that. Perhaps a woman might observe more, or a man like my photographer friend—who, as it happened, did not have my firm grasp on masculinity—might do so.

He said, "Just one more—for me."

"No," I said firmly, and took the picture, grasping his wrist to make sure he would not withdraw it. *"And* the negative, please. You can keep the other one—the distance shot."

"I don't want *that,*" he said, petulantly, and was looking quite woebegone as I left.

I framed the picture, put in on my mantelpiece, and stepped back to look at it. There was, indeed, a remarkable glow about it. Azazel had done a good job.

What would Rosie's reaction be, I wondered. I phoned her and asked if I could drop by. It turned out that she was going shopping but if I could be there within the hour—

I could, and I was. I had the photo gift-wrapped, and handed it to her without a word.

"My goodness!" she said, even as she cut the string and tore off the wrapping. "What is this? Is there some celebration, or—"

By then she had it out, and her voice died away. Her eyes widened and her breath became shorter and more rapid. Finally, she whispered, "Oh, my!"

She looked up at me. "Did you take this photograph last Sunday?"

I nodded.

"But you caught him exactly. He's *ador*able. That's *just* the look. Oh, may I *please* keep it?"

"I brought it for you," I said, simply.

She threw her arms about me and kissed me hard on the lips. Unpleasant, of course, for a person like myself who detests sentiment, and I had to wipe my mustache afterward, but I could understand her inability to resist the gesture.

I didn't see Rosie for about a week afterward.

Then I met her outside the butcher shop one afternoon, and it would have been impolite not to offer to carry the shopping bag home for her. Naturally, I wondered whether that would mean another kiss and I decided it would be rude to refuse if the dear little thing insisted. She looked somewhat downcast, however.

"How's the photograph?" I asked, wondering whether, perhaps, it had not worn well.

She cheered up at once. "Perfect! I have it on my record player stand, at an angle such that I can see it when I'm at my chair at the dining room table. His eyes just look at me a little slantwise, so *roguishly* and his nose had *just* the right crinkle. Honestly, you'd swear he was alive. And some of my friends can't keep their eyes off it. I'm thinking I should hide it when they come, or they'll steal it."

"They might steal *him,*" I said, jokingly.

The glumness returned. She shook her head and said, "I don't think so."

I tried another tack. "What does Kevin think of the photo?"

"He hasn't said a word. Not a word. He's not a visual person, you know. I wonder if he sees it at all."

"Why don't you point it out and ask him what he thinks?"

She was silent while I trudged along beside her for half a block, carrying that heavy shopping bag and wondering if she'd expect a kiss in addition.

"Actually," she said, suddenly, "he's having a lot of tension at work so it wouldn't be a good time to ask him. He gets home late and hardly talks to me. Well, you know how men are." She tried to put a tinkle in her laughter, but failed.

We had reached her apartment house and I turned the bag over to her. She said, wistfully, "But thank you once again, and over and over, for the photograph."

Off she went. She didn't ask for a kiss, and I was so lost in thought that I didn't notice that fact till I was halfway home and it seemed silly to return merely to keep her from being disappointed.

About ten more days passed, and then she called me one morning. Could I drop in and have lunch with her? I held back and pointed out that it would be indiscreet. What would the neighbors think?

"Oh, that's silly," she said. "You're so incredibly old— I mean, you're such an incredibly old friend, that they couldn't possibly—Besides, I want your advice." It seemed to me she was suppressing a sob as she said that.

Well, one must be a gentleman, so I was in her sunny little apartment at lunch time. She had prepared ham and cheese sandwiches and slivers of apple pie, and there was the photograph on the record player as she had said.

She shook hands with me and made no attempt to kiss me, which would have relieved me were it not for the fact that I was too disturbed at her appearance to feel any relief. She looked absolutely haggard. I ate half a sandwich waiting for her to speak and when she didn't, I was forced to ask outright for the reason, there was such a heavy atmosphere of gloom about her.

I said, "Is it Kevin?" I was sure it was.

She nodded and burst into tears. I patted her hand and wondered if that was enough. I stroked her shoulder abstractedly and she finally said, "I'm afraid he's going to lose his job."

"Surely not. Why?"

"Well, he's so *savage;* even at work, apparently. He hasn't smiled for ages. He hasn't kissed me, or said a kind word, since I don't remember when. He quarrels with *everyone,* and *all* the time. He won't tell me what's wrong, and he gets furious if I ask. A friend of ours who works at the airport with Kevin called up yesterday. He says that Kevin is acting so sullen and unhappy at the job that the higher-ups are noticing. I'm *sure* he'll lose his job, but what can I *do?"*

I had been expecting something like this ever since our last meeting, actually, and I knew I would simply have to tell her the truth—damn that Azazel. I cleared my throat. "Rosie—the photograph—"

"Yes, I know," she said, snatching it up and hugging it to her breasts. "It's what keeps me going. This is the *real* Kevin, and I'll always have him, *always,* no matter what happens." She began to sob.

I found it very hard to say what had to be said, but there was not way out. I said, "You don't understand, Rosie. It's the photograph that's the problem. I'm sure of it. All that charm and cheerfulness in the photograph had to come from somewhere. It had to be scraped off Kevin himself. Don't you understand?"

Rosie stopped sobbing. "What are you *talking* about? A photograph is just the light being focused, and film, and things like that."

"Ordinarily, yes, but *this* photograph—" I gave up. I knew Azazel's shortcomings. He couldn't create the magic of the photograph out of nothing, but I wasn't sure I could explain the science of it, the law of conservation of merriment, to Rosie.

"Let me put it this way," I said. "As long as that photograph sits there, Kevin will be unhappy, angry and bad-tempered."

"But it certainly *will* sit there," said Rosie, putting it firmly back in its place, "and I can't see why you're saying such crazy things about the one wonderful object— Here, I'll make some coffee." She flounced off to the kitchen and I could see she was in a most offended state of mind.

I did the only thing I could possibly do. After all, I had been the one who had snapped the photograph. I was responsible—through Azazel—for its arcane properties. I snatched up the frame quickly, carefully removed the backing, the the photo itself. I tore the photograph across into two pieces—four—eight—sixteen, and placed the final scraps of paper in my pocket.

The telephone rang just as I finished, and Rosie bustled into the living room to answer. I restored the backing and set the frame back in place. It sat there, blankly empty.

I heard Rosie's voice squealing with excitement and happiness. "Oh, Kevin," I heard her say, "how wonderful! Oh, I'm so glad! But why didn't you tell me? Don't you *ever* do that again!"

She came back, pretty face glowing. "Do you know what that terrible Kevin did? He's had a kidney stone for nearly three weeks now—seeing a doctor and all—and in terrible, nagging pain, and facing possible surgery—and he wouldn't tell me for fear it would cause me worry. The idiot! No wonder he was so miserable, and it never once occurred to him that his misery made me far more unhappy than knowing about it would have. Honestly! A man shouldn't be allowed out without a keeper."

"But why are you so happy now?"

"Because he passed the stone. He just passed it a little while ago and the first thing he did was to call me, which was very thoughtful of him—and about time. He sounded *so* happy and cheerful. It was just as though my old Kevin had come back to me. It was as though he had become exactly like the photograph that—"

Then, in half a shriek, *"Where's the photograph?"*

I was on my feet, preparing to leave. I was walking rather briskly toward the door, saying, "I destroyed it. That's why he passed the stone. Otherwise—"

"You *destroyed* it? You—"

I was outside the door. I didn't expect gratitude, of course, but what I *was* expecting was murder. I didn't wait for the elevator but hastened down the stairs as quickly as I reasonably could, the sound of her long wail penetrating the door and reaching my ears for a full two flights.

I burned the scraps of the photograph when I got home.

I have never seen her since. From what I have been told, Kevin has been a delightful and loving husband and they are most happy together, but the one letter I received from her— seven pages of small writing, and nearly incoherent—made it plain that she was of the opinion that the kidney stone was the full explanation of Kevin's ill humor, and that its arrival and departure in exact synchronization with the photograph was sheer coincidence.

She made some rather injudicious threats against my life and, quite anticlimactically, against certain portions of my body, making use of words and phrases I would have sworn she had never heard, much less employed.

And I suppose she will never kiss me again, something I find, for some odd reason, disappointing.

To the Victor

I don't often see my friend George, but when I do I make it a practice to ask after this small demon he claims he can call up.

"A bald and aged science fiction writer," he would say to me, "has stated that any technology sufficiently advanced beyond the customary would seem like magic. And yet, my small friend Azazel is no extraterrestrial oddity, but a bona fide demon. He may only be two centimeters high, but he can do amazing things. —How did you find out about him?"

"By listening to you."

George drew his face into vertical disapproving lines and said sepulchrally, "I never discuss Azazel."

"Except when you're talking," I said. "What's he been doing lately?"

George fetched a sigh from the region of his toes and expelled it, fairly beer-laden, into the unoffending atmosphere. "There," he said, "you touch a bit of sadness within me. My young friend, Theophilus, is a little the worse for our efforts, mine and Azazel's, although we meant well." He lifted his mug of beer to his face and then went on.

My friend Theophilus [said George], whom you have never met for he moves in circles rather higher than the sordid ones you frequent, is a refined young man who is a great admirer of the graceful lines and divine carriage of young women—something to which I am fortunately immune—but who lacked the capacity to inspire reciprocation in them.

He would say to me, "I can't understand it, George. I have a good mind; I am an excellent conversationalist; witty, kind, reasonably good-looking—"

"Yes," I would reply, "you do have eyes, nose, chin, and mouth all in the usual places and in the usual number. I'll go that far."

"—and incredibly skilled in the theory of love, although I haven't actually been given much chance to put it into practice, and yet I seem to be unable to attract attention from these delightful creatures. Observe that they seem to be all about us, and yet not one makes the slightest attempt to scrape up an acquaintance with me, although I sit here with the most genial expression on my face."

My heart bled for him. I had known him as an infant when, as I recall, I had once held him, at the request of his mother, who was breast-feeding him to repletion, while she rearranged her dress. These things form a bond.

I said, "Would you be happier, my dear friend, if you *did* attract attention?"

"It would be paradise," he said, simply.

Could I deny him paradise? I put the matter to Azazel, who as usual was sulky about it. "Couldn't you ask me for a diamond?" he said. "I can manage you a good half-carat stone of the first water by rearranging the atoms in a small piece of coal—but irresistibility to women? How do I do that?"

"Couldn't you rearrange some atoms in him?" said I, trying to be helpful. "I want to do *something* for him, if only out of regard for his mother's awesome nutritional equipment."

"Well, let me think. Human beings," said Azazel, "secrete pheromones. Of course, with your modern penchant for bathing at every opportunity and for drenching yourselves in artificial scent, you are scarcely aware of the natural way of inspiring sentiment. I can, perhaps, so rearrange your friend's biochemical

makeup as to cause the production of unusual quantities of an
unusually effective pheromone when the sight of one of the un-
gainly females of your repellent species impinges upon his ret-
ina."

"You mean he'll stink?"

"Not at all. It will scarcely surface as a conscious odor but it
will have its effect on the female of the species in the form of a
dim and atavistic desire to come closer and to smile. She will
probably be stimulated to form answering pheromones of her
own and I presume that everything that follows will be auto-
matic."

"The very thing, then," I said, "for I am certain that young
Theophilus will give a good account of himself. He is an up-
standing fellow with drive and ambition."

That Azazel's treatment was effective I discovered when I
next stumbled upon Theophilus. It was at a sidewalk café.

It took me a moment to see him, for what initially attracted
my attention was a group of young women distributed in circular symmetry. I am, fortunately, unperturbed by young women
since I have reached the age of discretion, but it was summer
and they were, one and all, dressed in a calculated insufficiency
of clothing which I—as is suitable in a man of discretion—dis-
creetly studied.

It was only after several minutes during which, I remember, I
noted the strain and tension placed upon a button that kept a
particular blouse closed, and speculated whether— But that is
neither here nor there. It was only after several minutes that I
noted that it was none other than Theophilus who was at the
center of the circular arrangement and who seemed to be the
cynosure of these summery women. No doubt the gathering
warmth of the afternoon accentuated his pheromonic potency.

I made my way into the ring of femininity and, with fatherly
smiles and winks and an occasional avuncular pat of the shoulder, sat down at a chair next to Theophilus, one which a winsome lass had vacated for me with a petulant pout. "Theophilus,

my young friend," I said, "this is a charming and inspiring sight."

It was then I noticed that there was a small frown of appalling sadness upon his face. I said with concern, "What is wrong?"

He spoke through motionless lips in a whisper so low I scarcely heard him. "For God's sake, get me out of here."

I am, of course, as you know, a man of infinite resource. It was the work of a moment for me to rise and say, "Ladies, my young friend here, as the result of a fundamental biologic urge, must visit the men's room. If you will all sit here, he will be right back."

We entered the small restaurant and left by the rear door. One of the young ladies, who had biceps that bulged in a most unlovely manner, and who had an equally unlovely streak of suspicion in her, had made her way around to the rear of the restaurant, but we saw her in time and managed to make it to a taxi. She pursued us, with appalling fleetness, for two blocks.

Secure in Theophilus's room, I said, "Clearly, Theophilus, you have discovered the secret of attracting young women. Is not this the paradise you longed for?"

"Not quite," said Theophilus, as he slowly relaxed in the air-conditioning. "They protect each other. I don't know how it happened but I suddenly discovered, some time ago, that strange young women would approach me and ask if we had not met in Atlantic City. I have never," he added with indignation, "been in Atlantic City in my life.

"No sooner had I denied the fact, when another would approach and claim that I had just dropped my handkerchief and that she would like to return it, and then a third would come up and say, 'How would you like to get into the movies, kid?' "

I said, "All you have to do is pick out one of them. I would take the one who offered to get you into the movies. It's a soft life, and you'd be surrounded by soft starlets."

"But I can't pick out *any* of them. They watch each other like hawks. As soon as I seem to be attracted to any one of them, all the rest turn on her and start pulling her hair and pushing her out. I am as womanless as ever I was, and in the old days I at least didn't have to stare at them as they heaved their bosoms at me."

I sighed in sympathy and said, "Why not set up an elimination tournament? When surrounded by ladies, as you were just now, say to them, 'Dear ones, I am profoundly attracted to each and every one of you. Therefore I will ask you to line up in alphabetical order so that each one of you may kiss me in turn. The one who does so with the most refined abandon will be my guest for the night.' The worst that can happen will be that you will get a lot of eager kissing."

"Hmm," said Theophilus. "Why not? To the victor belong the spoils, and I would love being spoiled by the appropriate victor." He licked his lips and then pursed them and made practice kisses in the air. "I think I could manage. Do you think it would be less wearing if I insisted on hands-behind-the-back while kissing?"

I said, "On the whole I think not, Theophilus my friend. You should be willing to exert some effort in this cause. I suspect that no-holds-barred would be the better rule."

"Perhaps you are right," said Theophilus, never one to cling to his view in the face of advice from one who could recall copious experience in such matters.

It was about this time that I had to venture out of town on business and it was not until a month had passed that I met Theophilus again. It was in a supermarket and there he was pushing a cart that was moderately filled with groceries. The look on his face smote me. It was a hunted one, as he looked this way and that.

I came up to him and he ducked, with a strangled cry. Then he recognized me and said, "Thank God—I was afraid you were a woman."

I shook my head. "Still that problem? You did not hold the elimination tournament, then?"

"I tried. That was the problem."

"What happened?"

"Well—" He looked this way and that, then moved to one side to peer down an aisle. Satisfied that the coast was clear, he spoke to me in a soft and hurried tone, like one who knew that discretion was necessary and that time was limited.

"I arranged it," he said. "I had them fill out applications, complete with age, brand of mouthwash used, references—all the usual—and then I set the date. I had arranged to hold the tournament in the Grand Ballroom of the Waldorf-Astoria, with an ample supply of lip salve, and with the services of a professional masseur plus a tank of oxygen to keep me in shape. The day before the tournament, however, a man came to my apartment.

"I say a man, but to my dazzled eyes, he seemed more like an animated heap of bricks. He was seven feet tall and five feet broad with fists the size of steamshovels. He smiled, revealing fangs, and said, 'Sir, my sister is one of those who will compete in the tournament tomorrow.'

" 'How pleased I am to hear that,' I said, eager to keep the discussion on a friendly plane.

" 'My *little* sister,' he said, 'a delicate flower on the rough ancestral tree. She is the apple of the eye of my three brothers and myself, and not one of us could bear the thought of her being disappointed.'

" 'Do your brothers resemble you, sir?' I asked.

" 'Not at all,' he said, sorrowfully. 'As a result of childhood illness, I have been stunted and wizen all my life. My brothers, however, are fine figures of men who stand this high.' He lifted his hand to a point about eight and a half feet above the ground.

" 'I am sure,' I said fervently, 'your charming sister will have an excellent chance.'

" 'I am delighted to hear that. Actually, I am gifted with second sight in compensation, I think, for my unfortunate puniness of physique, and somehow I am certain that my little sister will win the competition. For some strange reason,' he went on, 'my little sister has taken a girlish liking to you, and my brothers and myself would feel lower than hound dogs if she were disappointed. And if we were—'

"He grinned even more fangily than before and slowly cracked the knuckles of his right hand, one by one, making a sound like that of thigh bones breaking. I had never heard a thigh bone break but a sudden surge of second sight told me that was what the sound was like.

"I said, 'I have a feeling, sir, that you may be right. Do you have a photograph of the damsel for reference?' "

" 'Oddly enough,' he said, 'I have.' He produced one in a frame and for a moment I must admit my heart sank. I didn't see how she could possibly win the competition.

"And yet there must be something to second sight, for despite the odds against her the young lady won a clear victory. There was a near approach to a riot when that fact was announced, but the winner herself cleared the room with marvelous celerity and ever since we have been, unfortunately—or, rather, *fortunately* —inseparable. In fact, there she is, hovering over the meat counter. She is a great eater of meat—sometimes cooked."

I saw the maiden in question and at once recognized her as the one who had chased our taxi for two blocks. Clearly a determined young woman. I admired her rippling biceps, her sturdy gastrocnemii, and her strong eyebrow ridges.

I said, "You know, Theophilus, it may be possible to decrease your attraction to women to its former insignificant level."

Theophilus sighed. "I wouldn't feel safe. My fiancée and her amply designed brothers might misinterpret her loss of interest. Besides, there are compensations. I can, for instance, walk any street in the city at any hour of the night, no matter how intrinsically dangerous that might be, and feel totally secure if she is with me. The most unreasonable traffic policeman is sweetness itself if she chances to frown upon him. And she is both outgoing and innovative in her demonstrations of affection. No, George, I accept my fate. On the fifteenth of next month, we will marry and she will carry me over the threshold of the new home which her brothers have supplied us. They have amassed a fortune in the car-compacting business, you see, because of their low over-head; they use their hands. It's just that sometimes I long—"

His eyes had wandered, involuntarily, to the fragile form of a fair young woman who was strolling down the aisle toward him. She happened to look at him even as he looked at her, and a tremor seemed to course over her being.

"Pardon me," she said shyly, her voice a musical lilt, "but didn't you and I meet in a Turkish bath recently?"

Even as she said that there was the sound of firm footsteps from behind us and we were interrupted by a wrathful baritone. "Theophilus, my sweet," it said, "are you being annoyed by this —floozy?"

Theophilus's light-of-love, her forehead tightened into a mag-nificent frown, bore down upon the young lady, who shrank in upon herself in obvious terror.

I quickly interposed myself between the two women—at con-siderable risk to myself, of course, but I am well known to be as brave as a lion. I said, "This sweet child is my niece, madam. Having spied me from a distance, she had hastened in this direc-tion to imprint a chaste kiss upon my forehead. That this also carried her in the direction of your dear Theophilus was a com-plete, but inevitable, coincidence."

It distressed me that the ugly streak of suspicion I had noted in Theophilus's lovely lady on our first meeting now evidenced itself again. "Oh, yeah?" she said, in a tone utterly lacking in that bonhomie I would have liked to find. "In that case, let me see you leave. Both of you. Right now."

On the whole, I felt it wise to do so. I linked arms with the young lady and we walked away, leaving Theophilus to his fate.

"Oh, sir," said the young lady, "that was terribly brave and quick-witted of you. Had you not come to my rescue I must surely have suffered assorted scratches and contusions."

"Which would have been a shame," I said gallantly, "for a body such as yours was surely not made for scratches. Or for contusions, either. Come, you mentioned a Turkish bath. Let us seek one together. In my apartment, as it happens, I have one— or at least an American bath, which is virtually the same thing."

After all, to the victor—

The Dim Rumble

I try hard not to believe what my friend George tells me. How can I possibly believe a man who tells me he has access to a two-centimeter-tall demon he calls Azazel; a demon who is really an extraterrestrial personage of extraordinary, but strictly limited, powers?

And yet George does have this ability to gaze at me unblinkingly out of his blue eyes and make me believe him temporarily —while he's talking. It's the Ancient Mariner effect, I suppose.

I once told him that I thought his little demon had given him the gift of verbal hypnosis, but George sighed and said, "Not at all! If he has given me anything, it is a curse for attracting confidences—except that that has been my bane since long before I ever encountered Azazel. The most extraordinary people insist on burdening me with their tales of woe. And sometimes—"

He shook his head in deep dejection. "Sometimes," he said, "the load I must bear as a result is more than human flesh and blood should be called upon to endure. Once, for instance, I met a man named Hannibal West . . ."

I noticed him first [said George] in the lounge of a hotel at which I was staying. I noticed him chiefly because he encumbered my view of a statucsque waitress who was most becomingly and insufficiently dressed. I presume he thought I was looking at him, something I would certainly not willingly have done, and he took it as an overture of friendship.

He came to my table, bringing his drink with him, and seated himself without a by-your-leave. I am, by nature, a courteous man and so I greeted him with a friendly grunt and glare, which he accepted in a calm way. He had sandy hair plastered down across his scalp, pale eyes and an equally pale face, together with the concentrated gaze of a fanatic, though I admit I didn't notice that until later on.

"My name," he said, "is Hannibal West, and I am a professor of geology. My particular field of interest is speleology. You wouldn't, by any chance, be a speleologist yourself?"

I knew at once he was under the impression he had recognized a kindred soul. My gorge rose at the possibility, but I remained courteous. "I am interested in all strange words," I said. "What is speleology?"

"Caves," he said. "The study and exploration of caves. That is my hobby, sir. I have explored caves on every continent except Antarctica. I know more about caves than anyone in the world."

"Very pleasant," I said, "and impressive." Feeling that I had in this way concluded a most unsatisfactory encounter, I signaled for the waitress to renew my drink and watched, in scientific absorption, her undulating progress across the room.

Hannibal West did not recognize the conclusion, however. "Yes," he said, nodding vigorously, "you do well to say it is impressive. I have explored caves that are unknown to the world. I have entered underground grottoes that have never felt the footsteps of a human being. I am one of the few people alive today who has gone where no man, or woman, for that matter, has ever gone before. I have breathed air undisturbed, till then, by the lungs of a human being, and have seen sights and heard sounds no one else has ever seen or heard—and lived." He shuddered.

My drink had arrived and I took it gratefully, admiring the grace with which the waitress bent low to place it on the table before me. I said, my mind not really on what I was saying, "You are a fortunate man."

"That I am not," said West. "I am a miserable sinner called upon by the Lord to avenge the sins of humanity."

Now at last I looked at him sharply, and noted a glare of fanaticism that nearly pinned me to the wall. "In caves?" I asked.

"In caves," he said, solemnly. "Believe me. As a professor of geology, I know what I am talking about."

I had met numerous professors in my lifetime who had known no such thing, but I forbore mentioning the fact.

Perhaps West read my opinion in my expressive eyes, for he fished a newspaper clipping out of a briefcase at his feet and passed it over to me. "Here!" he said, "Just look at that!"

I cannot say that it much rewarded close study. It was a three-paragraph item from some local newspaper. The headline read "A Dim Rumble" and the dateline was East Fishkill, New York. It was an account to the effect that local residents had complained to the police department of a dim rumble that left them uneasy and caused much disturbance among the cat and dog population of the town. The police had dismissed it as the sound of a distant thunderstorm, though the weather department heatedly denied having produced any that day anywhere in the region.

"What do you think of *that?*" asked West.

"Might it have been a mass epidemic of indigestion?"

He sneered as though the suggestion were beneath contempt, though no one who has ever experienced indigestion would consider it that. Beneath the diaphragm, perhaps.

He said, "I have similar news items from papers in Liverpool, England; Bogotá, Colombia; Milan, Italy; Rangoon, Burma; and perhaps half a hundred other places the world over. I collected them. All speak of a pervasive dim rumble that created fear and uneasiness and drove animals frantic, and all were reported within a two-day period."

"A single worldwide event," I said.

"Exactly! Indigestion, indeed." He frowned at me, sipped at his drink, then tapped his chest. "The Lord has placed a weapon in my hand, and I must learn to use it."

"What weapon is this?" I asked.

He didn't answer directly. "I found the cave quite by accident," he said, "something I welcome, for any cave whose opening advertises itself too openly is common property and has been host to thousands. Show me an opening narrow and hidden, one that is overgrown with vegetation, obscured by fallen rocks, veiled by a waterfall, precariously placed in an all but inaccessible spot, and I will show you a virgin cave worthy of inspection. You say you know nothing of speleology?"

"I have been in caves, of course," I said. "The Luray Caverns in Virginia—"

"Commercial!" said West, screwing up his face and looking about for a convenient spot on the floor upon which to spit. Fortunately, he didn't find one.

"Since you know nothing about the divine joys of spelunking," he went on, "I will not bore you with any account of where I found it, and how I explored it. It is, of course, not always safe to explore new caves without companions, but I perform solo explorations readily. After all, there is no one who can match me in this sort of expertise, to say nothing of the fact that I am as bold as a lion.

"In this case it was indeed fortunate I was alone, for it would not have done for any other human being to discover what I discovered. I had been exploring for several hours when I entered a large and silent room with stalactites above and stalagmites below in gorgeous profusion. I skirted about the stalagmites, trailing my unwinding twine behind me, since I am not fond of losing my way, and then I came across what must have been a thick stalagmite that had broken off at some natural plane of cleavage. There was a litter of limestone to one side of it. What had caused the break I cannot say—perhaps some large animal, fleeing into the cave under pursuit, had blundered into the stalagmite in the dark, or else a mild earthquake had found this one stalagmite weaker than others.

"In any case, the stump of the stalagmite was now topped by a smooth flatness just moist enough to glisten in my electric light. It was roughly round and strongly resembled a drum. So strongly did it resemble one that I automatically reached out and tapped it with my right forefinger."

He gulped down the rest of his drink and said, "It *was* a drum; or at least it was a structure that set up a vibration when tapped. As soon as I touched it, a dim rumble filled the room; a vague sound just at the threshold of hearing and all but subsonic. Indeed, as I was able to determine later on, the portion of the sound that was high enough in pitch to be heard was a tiny fraction of the whole. Almost all the sound expressed itself in mighty vibrations far too slow to affect the ear, though it shook the body itself. That unheard reverberation gave me the most unpleasantly uneasy feeling you could imagine.

"I had never encountered such a phenomenon before. The energy of my touch had been minute. How could it have been converted into such a mighty vibration? I have never managed to understand that completely. To be sure, there are powerful energy sources underground. There could be a way of tapping the heat of the magma, converting a small portion of it to sound. The initial tap could serve to liberate additional sound energy— a kind of sonic laser, or, if we substitute 'sound' for 'light' in the acronym, we can call it 'saser.' "

I said austerely, "I've never heard of such a thing."

"No," said West with an unpleasant sneer, "I dare say you haven't. It is nothing anyone has heard of. Some combination of geologic arrangements has produced a natural saser. It is something that would not happen, by accident, more often than once in a million years, perhaps, and even then in only one spot on the planet. It may be the most unusual phenomenon on Earth."

"That's a great deal," I said, "to deduce from one tap of a forefinger."

"As a scientist, sir, I assure you I was not satisfied with a single tap of a forefinger. I proceeded to experiment. I tried harder taps and quickly realized that I could be seriously damaged by the reverberations in the enclosure. I set up a system whereby I could drop pebbles of various sizes on the saser by means of a makeshift long-distance apparatus while I was outside the cave. I discovered that the sound could be heard surprising distances outside the cave. Using a simple seismometer, I found that I could get distinct vibrations at distances of several miles. Eventually I dropped a series of pebbles one after the other and the effect was cumulative."

I said, "Was that the day when dim rumbles were heard all over the world?"

"Exactly," he said. "You are by no means as mentally deprived as you appear. The whole planet rang like a bell."

"I've heard particularly strong earthquakes do that."

"Yes, but this saser can produce a vibration more intense than that of any earthquake and can do so at particular wavelengths; at a wavelength, for instance, that can shake apart the contents of cells—the nucleic acids of the chromosomes, for instance."

I considered that, thoughtfully. "That would kill the cell."

"It certainly would. That may be what killed the dinosaurs."

"I've heard it was done by the collision of an asteroid with the Earth."

"Yes, but in order to have that done by ordinary collision, the asteroid postulated must be huge. Ten kilometers across. And one must suppose dust in the stratosphere, a three-year winter, and some way of explaining why some species died out and others didn't in a most illogical fashion. Suppose, instead, that it was a much smaller asteroid that struck a saser and that it disrupted cells with its sound vibration. Perhaps ninety percent of the cells in the world would be destroyed in a matter of minutes with no enormous effect on the planetary environment at all. Some species would manage to survive, some would not. It would be entirely a matter of the intimate details of comparative nucleic acid structure."

"And that," I said, with a most unpleasant feeling that this fanatic was serious, "is the weapon the Lord has placed into your hands?"

"Exactly," he said. "I have worked out the exact wavelengths of sound produced by various manners of tapping the saser and I am trying now to determine which wavelength would specifically disrupt human nucleic acids."

"Why human?" I demanded.

"Why not human?" demanded he, in his turn. "What species is crowding the planet, destroying the environment, eradicating other species, filling the biosphere with chemical pollutants? What species will destroy the Earth and render it totally nonviable in a matter of decades perhaps? Surely not some other than *Homo sapiens?* If I can find the right sonic wavelength, I can strike my saser in the proper manner and with the proper force to bathe the Earth in sonic vibrations that will, in a matter of a day or so, for it takes time for sound to travel, wipe out humanity, while scarcely touching other life forms with nucleic acids of differing intimate structure."

I said, "You are prepared to destroy billions of human beings?"

"The Lord did it by means of the Flood—"

"Surely you don't believe the biblical tale of the—"

West said austerely, "I am a creationist geologist, sir."

I understood everything. "Ah," I said, "and the Lord promised he would never again send a Flood upon the Earth, but he didn't say anything about sound waves."

"Exactly! The billions of dead will fertilize and fructify the Earth, serve as food for other forms of life which have suffered much at the hands of humanity and deserve recompense. What's more, a remnant of humanity shall undoubtedly survive. There are bound to be a few human beings who will have nucleic acids of a type that will not be sensitive to the sonic vibrations. That remnant, blessed by the Lord, can begin anew, and will perhaps have learned a lesson as to the evil of Evil, so to speak."

I said, "Why are you telling me all this?" And, indeed, it had occurred to me that it was strange he was doing so.

He leaned toward me and seized me by the lapel of my jacket —a most unpleasant experience, for his breath was rather overpowering—and said, "I have the inner certainty that you can help me in my work."

"I?" I said. "I assure you that I haven't any knowledge whatsoever concerning wavelengths, nucleic acids, and—" But then, bethinking myself rapidly, I said, "Yet, come to think of it, I may have just the thing for you." And in a more formal voice, with the stately courtesy that is one of my characteristics, I said, "Would you do me the honor, sir, of waiting for me for perhaps fifteen minutes?"

"Certainly, sir," he answered, with equal formality. "I will occupy myself with further abstruse mathematical calculations."

As I hastened out of the lounge I passed a ten-dollar bill to the bartender with a whispered, "See that that gentleman, if I may speak loosely, does not leave until I return. Feed him drinks and put it on my tab, if absolutely necessary."

I never fail to carry with me those simple ingredients I use to call up Azazel, and in a very few minutes he was sitting on the bed lamp in my room, suffused with his usual tiny pink glow.

He said censoriously, in his piping little voice, "You interrupted me when I was in the midst of constructing a pasmaratso with which I fully expected to win the heart of a lovely samini."

"I regret that, Azazel," I said, hoping he would not delay me by describing the nature of the pasmaratso or the charms of the samini, for neither of which I cared the paring of a fingernail, "but I have here a possible emergency of the most extreme sort."

"You always say that," he said discontentedly.

Hastily I outlined the situation, and I must say he grasped it at once. He is very good that way, never requiring long explanations. My own belief is that he peeks at my mind, although he always assures me that he considers my thoughts inviolable. Still, how far can you trust a two-centimeter demon who, by his own admission, is constantly trying to overreach lovely samini, whatever they are, by the most dishonorable ruses? Besides, I'm not sure whether he says he considers my thoughts inviolable or insufferable, but that is neither here nor there.

"Where is this human being you speak of?" he squeaked.

"In the lounge. It is located—"

"Don't bother. I shall follow the aura of moral decay. I think I have it. How do I identify the human being?"

"Sandy hair, pale eyes—"

"No, no. His mind."

"A fanatic."

"Ah, you might have said so at once. I have him—and I see I shall require a thorough steam bath when I return home. He is worse than you are."

"Never mind that. Is he telling the truth?"

"About the saser? —Which, by the way, is a clever conceit."

"Yes."

"Well, that is a difficult question. As I often say to a friend of mine who considers himself a great spiritual leader: What is truth? I'll tell you this; he considers it the truth. He believes it. What a human being believes, however, no matter with what ardor, is not necessarily objective truth. You have probably caught a hint of this in the course of your life."

"I have. But is there no way you can distinguish between belief that stems from objective truth, and belief that does not?"

"In intelligent entities, certainly. In human beings, no. But apparently you consider this man an enormous danger. I can rearrange some of the molecules of his brain and he will then be dead."

"No, no," I said. It may be a silly weakness on my part but I do object to murder. "Couldn't you rearrange molecules in such a way that he will lose all memory of the saser?"

Azazel sighed in a thin, wheezing way. "This is really much more difficult. Those molecules are heavy and they stick together. Really, why not a clean disruption—"

"I insist," I said.

"Oh, very well," said Azazel sullenly, and then he went

through a whole litany of puffing and panting designed to show me how hard he was working. Finally he said, "It's done."

"Good. Wait here, please. I just want to check it out and then I'll be right back."

I rushed down hastily and Hannibal West was still sitting where I had left him. The bartender winked at me as I passed. "No drinks necessary, sir," said that worthy person, and I gave him five dollars more.

West looked up cheerfully. "There you are."

"Yes, indeed," I said. "Very penetrating of you to notice that. I have the solution of the problem of the saser."

"The problem of the what?" he asked, clearly puzzled.

"That object you discovered in the course of your speleological explorations."

"What are speleological explorations?"

"Your investigations of caves."

"Sir," said West, frowning. "I have never been in a cave in my life. Are you mad?"

"No, but I have just remembered an important meeting. Farewell, sir. Probably, we shall never meet again."

I hastened back to the room, panting a little, and found Azazel humming to himself some tune favored by the entities of his world. Really, their taste in what they call music is atrocious.

"His memory is gone," I said, "and, I hope, permanently."

"Of course," said Azazel. "The next step, now, is to consider the saser itself. Its structure must be very neatly and precisely organized if it can actually magnify sound at the expense of Earth's internal heat. No doubt a tiny disruption at some key point—something that may be within my mighty powers—could wipe out all saser activity. Exactly where is it located?"

I stared at him, thunderstruck. "How should I know?" I said.

He stared at me, probably thunderstruck also, but I can never make out the expressions on his tiny face. "Do you mean to say you had me wipe out his memory *before* you obtained that vital piece of information?"

"It never occurred to me," I said.

"But if the saser exists—if his belief was based on objective truth—someone else may stumble upon it, or a large animal might, or a meteorite might strike it, and at any moment, day or night, all life on Earth may be destroyed."

"Good Lord!" I muttered.

Apparently my distress moved him, for he said, "Come, come, my friend, look at the bright side. The worst that might happen is that human beings will all be wiped out. Just human beings. It's not as though they're *people.*"

Having completed his tale, George said despondently, "And there you are. I have to live with the knowledge that the world may come to an end at any moment."

"Nonsense," I said heartily. "Even if you've told me the truth about this Hannibal West which, if you will pardon me, is by no means assured, he may have been having a sick fantasy."

George looked haughtily down his nose at me for a moment, then said, "I would not have your unlovely tendency toward skepticism for all the loveliest samini on Azazel's native world. How do you explain this?"

He withdrew a small clipping from his wallet. It was from yesterday's New York *Times* and was headed "A Dim Rumble." It told of a dim rumble that was perturbing the inhabitants of Grenoble, France.

"One explanation, George," I said, "is that you saw this article and made up the whole story to suit."

For a moment, George looked as though he would explode with indignation, but when I picked up the rather substantial check that the waitress had placed between us, softer feelings overcame him and we shook hands on parting, amiably enough.

And yet, I must admit I haven't slept well since. I keep sitting up at about 2:30 A.M. listening for the dim rumble I could swear had roused me from sleep.

Saving Humanity

My friend George, sighing lugubriously, said to me one evening, "I have a friend who is a klutz."

I nodded wisely. "Birds of a feather," I said.

George gazed at me in astonishment. "What have feathers to do with it? You have the most remarkable ability to skid away from a subject. It is the result, I suppose, of your thoroughly inadequate intellect—which I mention in pity, and not as reproof."

"Well, well," I said, "let that be as it may. When you refer to your friend the klutz, are you speaking of Azazel?"

Azazel was the two-centimeter demon or extraterrestrial being (take your pick) concerning whom George talks constantly, ceasing only in response to a direct question. Freezingly, he said, "Azazel is not a subject for conversation, and I do not understand how you come to have heard of him."

"I happened to be within a mile of you one day," I said. George paid no attention, but said:

I first came across the uneuphonious word "klutz," in fact, through a conversation with my friend Menander Block. You have never met him, I'm afraid, for he is a university man and therefore rather selective in his friendships, for which one, observing you, can scarcely blame him.

The word, klutz, he told me, referred to an awkward, clumsy person. "And that's me," he said. "It comes from a Yiddish word that, taken literally, means a piece of wood, a log, a block; and, of course, my name, as you will note, is Block."

He heaved an enormous sigh. "And yet I am not a klutz in the strict meaning of the word. There is nothing wooden, loggish, or blockish about me. I dance as lightly as a zephyr and as gracefully as a dragonfly; I am sylphlike in every motion; and numerous young women could testify, if I thought it safe to allow them to do so, of my skill as a disciple of the amatory art. It is, rather, that I am a klutz at long distance. Without being myself affected, everything about me becomes klutzish. The very Universe itself seems to trip over its own cosmic feet. I suppose if you want to mix languages and combine Greek with Yiddish, I am a 'teleklutz.' "

"How long has this been going on, Menander?" I asked.

"All my life, but, of course, it was only as an adult that I realized this peculiar quality I possess. While still a youth, I simply assumed that what happened to me was the normal state of affairs."

"Have you discussed this with anyone?"

"Of course not, George, old fellow. I would be considered mad. Can you see a psychoanalyst, for instance, confronting the phenomenon of teleklutzism? He would have me in the funny house halfway through my first session and write a paper on his discovery of a new psychosis and probably become a millionaire as a result. I'm not going to the booby hatch just to enrich some psychomedical leech. I cannot tell *anyone* this."

"Then why are you telling me this, Menander?"

"Because, on the other hand, it seems to me I must tell someone if I am to remain functional. As it happens, you are the least someone I know."

I did not follow his reasoning there, but I could see that I was about to be subjected once again to the unwanted confidences of my friends. It was the price, I well knew, of the fact that I was proverbial for my understanding, sympathy, and, most of all, for my close-mouthed reticence. No secret placed in my keeping would ever reach the ears of anyone else. —I make an exception in your case, of course, since it is well known that you have an attention span of five seconds, and a memory span of rather less.

I signaled for another drink and indicated, by a certain arcane sign that I alone know, that it was to be placed on Menander's tab. A laborer, after all, is worthy of his hire. I said, "Just how does this teleklutzism manifest itself, Menander?"

"In its simplest form, and in the manner that was first brought to my attention, it shows up in the peculiar weather that accompanies my travels. I do not travel very much, and when I do, I go by car, and when I do *that,* it rains. It doesn't matter what the weather forecast is; it doesn't matter how brightly the sun is shining when I start out. The clouds gather, grow darker and it begins to drizzle and then to pour. When my teleklutzism is in particular fettle, the temperature drops and we have an ice storm.

"Of course, I am careful not to be foolish. I refuse to drive into New England until March is safely over. Last spring, I drove to Boston on April 6—which promptly had the first April blizzard in the history of the Boston Weather Bureau. I once drove to Williamsburg, Virginia, on March 28, assuming that I might be allowed a few days of grace considering that I was penetrating Dixie. Hah! Williamsburg had nine inches of snow that day and the natives were trying to rub some of it between their fingers and were asking each other what the white stuff was.

"I have often thought that if we imagined the universe to be under the personal direction of God, we might picture Gabriel rushing into the divine presence to cry out, 'Holy One, two galaxies are about to collide in an unimaginably enormous catastrophe,' and God would answer, 'Don't bother me now, Gabriel; I'm busy making it rain on Menander.' "

I said, "You might make the best of the situation, Menander. Why not sell your services, for fabulous sums, as a drought-breaker?"

"I have thought of that, but the mere thought dries up any rain that might occur during my travels. Besides, if the rain came when it was needed, it would probably produce a flood.

"And it's not only rain, or traffic jams, or the disappearance of landmarks; there are a myriad other things. Expensive objects break spontaneously in my presence, or are dropped by others through no fault attributable to myself. There is an advanced particle accelerator in operation in Batavia, Illinois. One day an enormously important experiment was ruined because of the failure of its vacuum, a completely unexplained failure. Only I knew (the next day, that is, when I read of the incident in the paper) that at the very moment of failure, I happened to be passing the outskirts of Batavia in a bus. It was raining, of course.

"At this very moment, old fellow, some of the fine five-day-old wine in the cellars of this fine establishment, being aged in the plastic, is turning sour. Someone brushing past this table at this moment will, when he arrives home, find that the pipes in his cellar have burst at the precise moment he passed me; except that he won't know that he passed me at that precise moment and that the passage was the cause. And so it will be with scores of accidents—supposed accidents, that is."

I felt sorry for my young friend. And my blood froze at the thought that I was sitting next to him and that at my cozy digs unimaginable catastrophes might be taking place.

I said, "You are, in short, a jinx!"

Menander threw his head back and stared down his nose at me in a most unpleasant way. "Jinx," he said, "is the common term; teleklutz is the scientific one."

"Well, then, jinx or teleklutz, suppose I told you I could perhaps remove this curse from you?"

"Curse is right," Menander said gloomily. "I have often thought that at the time of my birth an ill-natured fairy, irked at not having been invited to the christening— Are you trying to tell me you can cancel curses because you are a good fairy?"

"I am not any kind of fairy," I said severely. "Just suppose I can remove this cur—condition of yours."

"How on earth could you do that?"

"Not exactly on Earth," I said. "But how about it?"

"What do *you* get out of it?" he asked, suspiciously.

"The heartwarming feeling of having helped save a friend from a horrible life."

Menander thought about it and then shook his head firmly. "That's not enough."

"Of course, if you want to offer me some small sum . . ."

"No, no. I wouldn't think of insulting you that way. Offer a sum of money to a *friend?* Place a fiscal value on friendship? How could you think that of me, George? What I meant was that removing my teleklutzism isn't enough. You must do more than that."

"How can one do more?"

"Consider! Through my life I have been responsible for anything from inconvenience to catastrophe to perhaps millions of innocent people. Even if I brought no ill-fortune to a single person from this moment on, the evil I have done thus far—even though none of it was voluntary or in any way to be considered my fault—is more than I can bear. I must have something that will cancel it all out."

"Like what?"

"I must be in a position to save humanity."

"Save humanity?"

"What else can possibly balance the immeasurable damage I have done? George, I insist. If you are going to remove my curse, replace it with the ability to save humanity in some great crisis."

"I'm not sure that I can."

"*Try,* George. Don't shy away at this crisis. If you're going to do a job, do it well, I always say. Think of humanity, old friend."

"Wait a moment," I said, alarmed, "you're putting this whole thing on my shoulders."

"Of course I am, George," Menander said warmly. "Broad

shoulders! Good shoulders! Made to bear burdens! Go home, George, and arrange to remove this curse from me. A grateful humanity will shower you with blessings except, of course, that they will never hear of it, for I will tell no one. Your good deeds are not to be shamed by exposure, and rely on me, I will never expose them."

There is something wonderful about unselfish friendship that can be duplicated by nothing else on earth. I rose at once to get to my task and left so quickly that I neglected to pay my half of the dinner bill. Fortunately, Menander did not notice this till I was safely out of the restaurant.

I had some trouble getting in touch with Azazel, and when I did, he didn't seem good-natured about it at all. His two-centimeter-tall body was wrapped in a pinkish glow, and in his piping voice he said, "Has it occurred to you that I might be showering?"

And indeed there was a very faint smell of ammonia about him.

I said humbly, "This is a rather enormous emergency, oh Mighty-One-for-Whom-Words-Are-Insufficient."

"Well then, tell me, but mind, don't take all day about it."

"Certainly!" I said, and outlined the matter with admirable conciseness.

"Hmm," said Azazel. "For once you have presented me with an interesting problem."

"I have? Do you mean there is indeed such a thing as teleklutzism?"

"Oh, yes. You see, quantum mechanics makes it quite clear that the properties of the universe depend, to a certain extent, on the observer. Just as the universe affects the observer, the observer affects the universe. Some observers affect the universe adversely, or at least adversely with respect to some other observers. Thus, one observer may accelerate the supernovadom of some star, which would irritate other observers who may find themselves uncomfortably close to that star at the time."

"I see. Well, can you help my friend Menander, and remove this quantum-observational effect of his?"

"Oh, of course! Simple! It will take ten seconds and then I can return to my shower and to the rite of laskorati I will undertake with two samini of unimaginable loveliness."

"Wait! Wait! That's not enough."

"Don't be silly. Two samini are *quite* enough. Only a lecher would want three."

"I mean removing the teleklutzism isn't enough. Menander also wants to be in a position to save humanity."

For a minute, I thought Azazel was going to forget our long friendship and all I had done for him in the way of supplying him with interesting problems that probably improved his mind and his magical abilities. I did not understand all he said, for most of the words were in his own language but they sounded very much like saws scraping along rusty nails.

Finally, having cooled down to a dim red heat, he said, "Now how am I going to do that?"

"Is anything too much for the Apostle of Incredibility?"

"You bet! . . . But let's see!" He thought for a while, and burst out, "But who in the universe would *want* to save humanity? Where's the worth in doing that? You stink up this whole section . . . Well, well, I think it can be done."

It didn't take ten seconds. It took half an hour and a very uncomfortable half hour it was, too, with Azazel groaning part of the time and the rest of the time stopping to wonder whether the samini were going to wait for him.

He was done eventually and, of course, it meant I would have to test out the matter on Menander Block.

When I next saw Menander I said, "You're cured."

He stared at me hostilely, "Do you know that you stuck me with the dinner check the other night?"

"Surely a minor point compared with the fact that you're cured."

"I don't feel cured."

"Well, come. Let's take a drive together. You take the wheel."

"It looks cloudy already. Some cure!"

"Drive! What have we to lose?"

He backed the car out of his garage. A man passing by on the other side of the street did not trip over an overloaded garbage can.

Menander drove down the street. The light did not turn red as he approached, and two cars skidding toward each other at the intersection next but one missed each other by a comfortable margin.

By the time he was at the bridge, the clouds had thinned out and a warm sun was shining down upon the car. It was not in his eyes.

When we finally got home he was weeping unashamedly, and I parked the car for him. I scraped it slightly, but it was not *I* that had had my teleklutzism cured. At that, it might have been worse. I might have scraped my own car.

For the next few days he was seeking me out constantly. I was the only one, after all, who could understand the miracle that had taken place.

He would say, "I went to a dance, and not one couple tripped over each other's feet and fell down and broke a collarbone or two. I could dance sylphlike with utter abandon and my partner never got sick to her stomach, even though she had eaten most unwisely."

Or, "At work they were installing a new air-conditioning unit and not once did it fall upon a workman's toes, breaking them permanently."

Or even, "I visited a friend in a hospital, something I once wouldn't have dreamed of doing, and in not one of the rooms that I passed did the intravenous needle pop out of a vein. Nor did a single hypodermic miss its appropriate target."

Sometimes he would ask me brokenly, "Are you sure that I will have a chance to save humanity?"

"Absolutely," I would say. "That's part of the cure."

But then one day he came to me and there was a frown on his face. "Listen," he said. "I just went to the bank to ask a question about my bank balance, which is a little lower than it should be because of the way you manage to get out of restaurants before the bill shows up, and I couldn't get an answer because the computer went down just as I walked in. Everyone was puzzled. Is the cure wearing off?"

"It can't do that," I said. "Maybe it had nothing to do with you. There might be some other teleklutz around who hasn't been cured. Maybe he happened to walk in just as you did."

But that wasn't it. The bank's computer went down on two other occasions when he tried to check his bank balance. (His nervousness over the paltry sums I had neglected to take care of was quite nauseating in a grown man.) Finally, when the computer at his firm went down when he walked past the room in which it was housed, he came to me in what I can only describe as panic.

"It's back, I tell you. It's back!" he screamed. "I can't take it this time. Now that I'm accustomed to normality, I can't go back to my old life. I'll have to kill myself."

"No, no, Menander. That's going too far."

He seemed to check himself at the edge of another scream and thought over my sensible remark. "You're right," he said. "That *is* going too far. Suppose I kill you instead. After all, no one will miss you, and it will make me feel a *little* better."

I saw his point, but only to a slight extent. I said, "Before you do anything at all, let me check this out. Be patient, Menander. After all, so far it's only happened with computers, and who cares about computers?"

I left quickly before he could ask me how he was supposed to get an instantaneous bank balance if computers were always going down at his approach. He was really a monomaniac on the subject.

So was Azazel, on another subject. It seems that this time he was actually involved in whatever he was doing with the two samini, and he was still turning somersaults when he arrived. To this day, I don't know what the somersaults had to do with it.

I don't think he ever actually cooled down, but he did manage to explain to me what happened and then I was faced with having to explain it to Menander.

I insisted on meeting him in the park. I chose a fairly crowded section since I would have to rely on instant rescue if he should lose his head figuratively, and try to make me lose mine literally.

I said, "Menander, your teleklutzism still works, but only for computers. *Only for computers.* You have my word on that. You are cured for everything else *forever.*"

"Well then, cure me for computers."

"As it happens, Menander, that can't be done. You are not cured for computers, and forever." I rather whispered the last word but he heard me.

"Why? What kind of a harebrained, idiotic, malapropistic, omniklutzistic rear end of a diseased Bactrian camel are you?"

"You make it sound as though there are many kinds, Menander, which doesn't make sense. Don't you understand that you wanted to save the world, and that's why it happened?"

"No, I don't understand. Explain it to me and take your time. You have fifteen seconds."

"Be reasonable! Humanity is facing a computer-explosion. Computers are going to become rapidly more versatile, more capable and more intelligent. Human beings are going to be ever more dependent upon them. Eventually a computer will be built that will take over the world and leave humanity with nothing to do. It may then well decide to wipe out humanity as unnecessary. Of course, we tell ourselves smugly that we can always 'pull the plug,' but you know we won't be able to do that. A computer smart enough to do the work of the world without us will be able to defend its own plug and, for that matter, find its own electricity.

"It will be unbeatable, and humanity will be doomed. And that, my friend, is where you come in. You will be brought into its presence or perhaps you will only arrange to pass within a few miles of it and it will instantly break down, and humanity will be saved! *Humanity will be saved!* Think of it! Think of it!"

Menander thought of it. He didn't look happy. He said, "But meanwhile I can't come near computers."

"Well, the computer-klutzism had to be nailed down and made absolutely permanent so we could be sure that when the time came nothing would go wrong, that the computer would not somehow defend itself against you. It's the price you pay for this great gift of salvation that you yourself asked for and for which you will be honored through all future history."

"Yes?" he said. "And when is this salvation to take place?"

I said, "According to Azaz—my sources, it should take place in sixty years or so. But look at it this way. Now you know that you will live to be at least ninety years old."

"And meanwhile," said Menander in a loud voice, oblivious to the way people nearby turned to stare at us, "meanwhile the world will grow more and more computerized and I will be unable to get near more and more places. I'll be unable to do more and more things and will be in a total prison of my own making—"

"But in the end you will save humanity! That's what you wanted!"

Menander shrieked, "To hell with humanity!" rose, and hurled himself at me.

I managed to get away but only because there were people about who seized the poor fellow.

Today, Menander is in deep analysis with a Freudian psychiatrist of the most determined description. It will surely cost him a fortune and will, of course, do him no good whatever.

George, having finished his story, gazed into his pot of beer, for which I knew I would have to pay.

He said, "There's a moral to this story, you know."

"What is it?"

"People just don't have any gratitude!"

A Matter of Principle

George stared somberly into his glass, which contained my drink (in the sense that I would surely be paying for it) and said, "It is only a matter of principle that makes me a poor man today."

He then fetched a huge sigh up from the region of his umbilicus and said, "In mentioning 'principle' I must, of course, apologize for using a term of which you are not cognizant, except perhaps as the title of an official at the grade school from which you nearly graduated. As a matter of fact, I am myself a man of principle."

"Really?" I said. "I presume you have been granted this character trait by Azazel only two minutes ago, for you had never exhibited it, to anyone's knowledge, before then."

George looked at me in an aggrieved manner. Azazel is the two-centimeter demon who possesses stunning magical powers —and only George is able to conjure him up at will. He said, "I cannot imagine where you have heard of Azazel."

"It's a complete mystery to me too," I said agreeably, "or would be if it weren't your sole subject of conversation these days."

"Don't be ridiculous," said George. "I never mention him."

Gottlieb Jones [said George] was a man of principle too. You might think that an utter impossibility, considering that his occupation was that of an advertising copywriter, but he rose superior to his vile calling with an ardor it was most attractive to watch.

Many times he would say to me, over a friendly hamburger and dish of French fries, "George, words cannot describe the horror of the job I have, or the despair that fills me at the thought that I must find persuasive ways of selling products that every instinct tells me human beings are better off without. Only yesterday, I had to help sell a new variety of insect repellent which, by test, has mosquitoes emitting supersonic screams of delight as they flock to it from miles around. 'Don't be mosquito bait,' my slogan reads. 'Use Skeeter-Hate.' "

"Skeeter-Hate?" I repeated, shuddering strongly.

Gottlieb covered his eyes with one hand. I'm sure he would have used both, had he not been shoveling French fries into his mouth with the other. "I live with this shame, George, and sooner or later I must leave the job. It violates my principles of business ethics *and* my writing ideals, and I am a man of principle."

I said courteously, "It does bring you fifty thousand a year, Gottlieb, and you do have a young and beautiful wife plus an infant child to support."

"Money" said Gottlieb violently, "is dross! It is the worthless bribe for which a man sells his soul. I repudiate it, George; I cast it from me with scorn; I will have nothing to do with it."

"But Gottlieb, surely you are doing no such thing. You accept your salary, do you not?" I will admit that for an uncomfortable moment I thought of a penniless Gottlieb and the number of lunches his virtue would make it impossible for him to buy the two of us.

"Well, yes, I do. My dear wife, Marilyn, has a disconcerting way of introducing her household allowance into conversations of an otherwise purely intellectual sort, to say nothing of her idle references to various purchases she foolishly makes at clothing stores and appliance shops. This does have a constraining influence on my plans of action. As for young Gottlieb Junior, who is now nearly six months old, he is not quite ready to understand the utter unimportance of money—though I will do him the justice of admitting that he has never yet actually asked me for any."

He signed, and I sighed with him. I had frequently heard of the uncooperative nature of wives and children where finances are concerned, and it is, of course, the chief reason I have remained uncommitted in this respect through a long lifetime, during which my ineffable charm has caused me to be pursued ardently by a variety of beautiful women.

Gottlieb Jones unwittingly interrupted several pleasant reminiscences in which I was harmlessly indulging myself by saying, "Do you know my secret dream, George?"

And for a moment he had so lubricious a gleam in his eyes that I started in mild alarm, thinking he had somehow read my mind.

He added, however, "It is my dream to be a novelist, to write trenchant exposés of the quivering depths of the human soul, to hold up before a humanity that is at once shuddering and delighted the glorious complexities of the human condition, to write my name in large indelible letters across the face of classic literature, and to march down the generations in the glorious company of men and women such as Aeschylus, Shakespeare, and Ellison."

We had finished our meal, and I waited tensely for the check, judging to a nicety the moment when I would allow my attention to be distracted. The waiter, weighing the matter with the keen perception inseparable from his profession, handed it to Gottlieb.

I relaxed and said, "Consider, my dear Gottlieb, the appalling consequences that might follow. I have read but recently, in a newspaper of the highest reliability which a gentleman near me happened to be holding, that there are thirty-five thousand published novelists in the United States; that of these but seven hundred make a living of their craft, and that fifty—only fifty, my friend—are rich. In comparison with this, your present salary—"

"Bah," said Gottlieb. "It is a matter of little moment to me whether I make money or not, just so I gain immortality and bestow a priceless gift of insight and understanding to all future generations. I could easily bear the discomfort of having Marilyn take a job as waitress or bus driver, or some other undemanding position. I am quite certain she would, or should, consider it a privilege to work by day and care for Gottlieb Junior by night so that my artistry might have full play. Only . . ." He paused.

"Only?" I said encouragingly.

"Well, I don't know why it is, George," he said, a rather petulant note entering his voice, "but there is a trifle that stands in the way. I don't seem to be able quite to do it. My brain teems with ideas of tremendous moment. Scenes, scraps of dialogue, situations of extraordinary vitality tumble through my mind constantly. It is only the very unimportant matter of actually placing it all into appropriate words that seems to elude me. It must be a minor problem, for every incompetent scrivener, such as that friend of yours with the peculiar name, seems to be at no loss for a way of turning out books by the hundred, and yet I cannot quite grasp the trick."

(He surely must have meant you, my dear fellow, since the phrase "incompetent scrivener" seems so apt. I would have defended you, of course, but I felt that that would be a losing proposition.)

"Surely," I said, "you can't have tried hard enough."

"Have I not? I have hundreds of sheets of paper, each containing the first paragraph of a marvelous novel—the first paragraph and no more. Hundreds of different first paragraphs for hundreds of different novels. It is the second paragraph that, in every case, is the stumbling block."

A brilliant idea struck me, but I was not surprised. My mind welters constantly in brilliant ideas.

"Gottlieb," I said, "I can solve this problem for you. I can make you a novelist. I can make you rich."

He looked at me with an unlovely gleam of skepticism. *"You* can?" he said, with a most unflattering emphasis on the pronoun.

We had risen and left the restaurant. I noted that Gottlieb had forgotten to leave a tip, but felt it to be scarcely politic for me to mention the fact as he might have then made the appalling suggestion that I take care of it.

"My friend," I said. "I have the secret of the second paragraph, and therefore can make you rich and famous."

"Hah! What is the secret?"

I said delicately (and here we come to the brilliant idea that had struck me), "Gottlieb, a laborer is worthy of his hire."

Gottlieb laughed shortly. "My confidence in you is such, George, that I have no fear in stating that if you can make me a rich and famous novelist, you can have half my earnings—after business expenses are deducted, of course."

I said, even more delicately, "I know you to be a man of principle, Gottlieb, so that your bare word will hold you to an agreement as though you were bound with hoops of the finest-alloy steel, but just for a laugh—ha, ha—would you be willing to put that statement into written form and have it signed and— just to make the laugh even heartier—ha, ha—notarized? We can each have a copy."

That little transaction took up only half an hour of time, since it involved only a notary public who was also a typist and a friend of mine.

I put my copy of the precious paper carefully into my wallet and said, "I cannot give you the secret immediately, but as soon as I have arranged matters I will let you know. You can then try to write a novel and you will find that you will have no trouble with the second paragraph—or the two thousand and second. Of course, you will not owe me anything until the first advance—a very large one, I'll be bound—comes in."

"You'd better believe it," said Gottlieb nastily.

I went through the ritual that called up Azazel that very evening. He is only two centimeters tall, and is a personage of no account on his own world. That is the only reason he is willing to help me out in various trivial ways. It makes him feel important.

Of course, I can never persuade him to do anything that will serve, in some direct fashion, to make me rich. The little creature insists that this would be an unacceptable commercialization of his art. Nor does he seem convinced by my assurance that anything he will do for me will be used in an utterly selfless way for the good of the world. When I said that, he made a queer sound, the significance of which I did not understand, and which he said he had learned from a native of the Bronx.

It was for that reason that I did not explain the nature of my agreement with Gottlieb Jones. It would not be Azazel who would be making me rich. It would be Gottlieb who would be doing so after Azazel had made *him* rich—but I despaired of making Azazel understand the nice distinction involved.

Azazel was, as usual, irritated by having been called up. His tiny head was decorated with what looked like minute fronds of seaweed and it appeared from his somewhat incoherent account that he had been in the midst of an academic ceremony in which some honor or other was being conferred upon him. Being of no real account on his own world, as I said earlier, he had the tendency to attach far too much importance to such an event, and was bitter in his comments.

I shrugged it off. "You can, after all," I said, "take care of my trifling request and then return to the exact moment at which you left. No one will even know you were gone."

He grumbled a little but had to admit that I was right, so that the air in his immediate vicinity ceased crackling with miniature lightning.

"What do you want, then?" he demanded.

I explained.

Azazel said, "His profession is that of the communication of ideas, is that it? The translation of ideas into words, as in the case of your friend with the peculiar name?"

"That is it, but he wishes to do it with increased efficiency, and to please those he deals with so that he achieves much acclaim—and wealth, too, but he wants that only as tangible evidence of the acclaim, for he despises money in itself."

"I understand. We have wordsmiths on our world, too, and one and all value only the acclaim and would not accept the smallest unit of currency were it not that they must have it as tangible evidence of the acclaim."

I laughed indulgently. "A foible of the profession. You and I are fortunate to be above such things."

"Well," said Azazel. "I can't be here for the rest of the year, can I, or I'll have trouble pinpointing the precise time of my return. Is this friend of yours within mental reach?"

We had trouble finding him, even though I pointed out the location of his advertising firm on a map and gave my usual eloquent and accurate description of the man, but I don't want to bore you with irrelevant detail.

Gottlieb was eventually found, and after a brief study Azazel said, "A peculiar mind of the type universal among your unpleasant species. Gummy, yet fragile. I see the wordsmith circuit and it is knotted and bumpy, which makes it no surprise that he is having trouble. I can remove the obstructing bit but that could endanger the stability of his mind. I think not, if I am skillful enough, but there is always the chance of accident. Do you suppose he would be willing to take the risk?"

"Oh, undoubtedly!" I said. "He is intent on fame and on serving the world with his art. He wouldn't hesitate to take the risk at all."

"Yes, but you are a devoted friend of his, I gather. He may be blinded by his ambition and his desire to do good, but you may see more clearly. Are *you* willing to have him take the chance?"

"My only aim," I said, "is to bring him happiness. Go ahead, and hack away as carefully as you can, and if things go wrong—well, it will have been in a good cause." (And it was, of course,

since if things went right, I would get half of the financial consequences.)

And so the deed was done. Azazel made heavy weather about
it, as he always did, and lay there panting for a while, and muttering something about unreasonable requests, but I told him to
think of the happiness he was bringing millions of people and
urged him to avoid the unendearing quality of self-love. Much
improved by my edifying words, he left in order to see to the
completion of whatever trifling honor had come his way.

It was about a week later that I sought out Gottlieb Jones. I
had made no effort to see him sooner, for I felt it might take him
some small period of time to adjust to his new brain. Besides, I
preferred to wait and inquire about him indirectly just at first to
see if he had been brain-damaged in any way in the process. If he
had, I would have seen no point in the meeting. My loss—and
his, too, I suppose—would make a meeting too poignant.

I heard nothing untoward about him and certainly he seemed
quite normal when I met him coming out of the building that
housed his firm. I noted at once the air of settled melancholy
about him. I paid that little attention, for writers, I have long
noticed, are prone to melancholy. It is something about the profession, I believe. The constant contact with editors, perhaps.

"Ah, George," he said listlessly.

"Gottlieb," I said, "how good to see you. You are looking
more handsome than ever." (Actually, like all writers, he is quite
ugly, but one must be polite.) "Have you tried to write a novel
lately?"

"No, I haven't." Then, as though he had suddenly remembered, he said, "Why? Are you ready to give me that secret of
yours concerning the second paragraph?"

I was delighted that he remembered, for that was another
indication that his brain was as sharp as it had ever been.

I said, "But that's all done, my dear fellow. There was no need
for me to explain anything; I have more subtle methods than
that. You need merely go home and sit down at your typewriter

and you will find yourself writing like an angel. Rest assured that your troubles are over and that novels will tumble smoothly out of your typewriter. Write two chapters and an outline of the rest, and I am absolutely certain that any publisher you show it to will shout with joy and make out a huge check, every cent of which will be half yours."

"Hah!" snorted Gottlieb.

"My assurance," I said, placing my hand upon my heart, which, as you know, is large enough, in a figurative sense, to fill my entire thoracic cavity. "In fact, I feel it to be entirely safe for you to quit this foul job of yours in order that it might in no way contaminate the pure material that will now be emerging from your typewriter. You have but to try, Gottlieb, and you will agree that I have more than earned my half."

"You mean you want me to quit my job?"

"Exactly!"

"I can't do it."

"Certainly you can. Turn your back on this ignoble position. Spurn the stultifying task of commercial puffery."

"I tell you I can't quit. I've just been fired."

"Fired?"

"Yes. And with expressions of lack of admiration which were of a type that I have no intention of ever forgiving."

We turned to walk toward the small and inexpensive place where we usually dined. "What happened?" I asked.

He told me, morosely, over a pastrami sandwich. He said, "I was writing copy for a room-freshener and I was overwhelmed by the enforced gentility of it all. It was all we could do to use the word 'odor.' Suddenly, I just want to speak my mind. If we were going to promote this damned garbage, why not do it right? So I put at the head of my finicky copy *Shrink the Stink,* and at the bottom *Quench the Stench,* and then had it messengered over to the account without bothering to consult anybody.

"After it was messengered, though, I thought, 'Why not?' and sent a memo to my boss, who had a very loud and very instant apoplectic fit. He called me in and told me I was fired along with some very harsh words that I knew he had never learned at his mother's knee—unless she was a very unusual mother. So here I am, out of a job."

He looked up at me with a hostile scowl. "I suppose you'll tell me this is your doing."

I said, "Of course it is. You did what you subconsciously knew was right. You deliberately had yourself fired so you could spend all your time at your true *art*. Gottlieb, my friend, go home now. Write your novel and make sure you get no less than one hundred thousand dollars' advance. Since there will be no business expenses to speak of, except a few pennies for paper, you will not have to deduct anything and can keep fifty thousand."

He said, "You're crazy."

"I am confident," I said, "and to prove it, I will pay for the lunch."

"You *are* crazy," he said, in an awed kind of voice, and actually left me to pay the bill, though he must have known that my offer was merely a rhetorical device.

I phoned him the next night. Ordinarily, I would have waited longer. I would not have wanted to rush him. Still, I now had a financial investment in him. Lunch had cost me eleven dollars, to say nothing of a quarter tip, and I was naturally restless. You can understand that.

"Gottlieb," I said, "how is the novel going?"

"Fine," he said absently. "No problem. I knocked off twenty pages, and very good stuff, too."

Yet he sounded casual, as though it was something else on his mind. I said, "Why aren't you jumping for joy?"

"Over the novel? Don't be silly. Feinberg, Saltzberg and Rosenberg called."

"Your advertising—Your ex-advertising firm?"

"Yes. Not all of them, of course; just Mr. Feinberg himself. He wants me back."

"I trust, Gottlieb, you told him exactly how far up—"

But Gottlieb interrupted me. "Apparently," he said, "the air-freshener account went wild over my copy. They wanted to use it and they wanted to commission a whole group of ads, for TV as well as for the printed media, and they wanted only the writer of that first ad to organize the campaign. They said that what I had done had been bold and hard-hitting and that it perfectly suited the decade of the eighties. They said they wanted to produce advertising that was unprecedentedly forceful and for that they needed me. Naturally, I said I would consider it."

"That's a mistake, Gottlieb."

"I ought to be able to hit them for a raise, a substantial one. I have not forgotten the cruel things Feinberg said when he kicked me out—some in Yiddish."

"Money is dross, Gottlieb."

"Of course, George, but I want to see how *much* dross is involved."

I wasn't very worried. I knew how the task of writing advertising copy grated on Gottlieb's sensitive soul, and I knew how attractive would be the ease with which he could write a novel. It was only necessary to wait and (to coin a phrase) let nature take its course.

But then the air-freshener ads came out and they made an instant hit with the public. "Quench the Stench" became a by-word with the youth of America and each use was, willy-nilly, a plug for the product.

I imagine that you yourself remember that fad—but of course you do, for I understand rejection slips containing the phrase became *de rigueur* among the periodicals for which you try to write, and you must have experienced it many times.

Other ads of the sort came out and were just as successful.

And suddenly I understood. Azazel had arranged to give Gottlieb the mind-set that made it possible for him to please the public with his writing, but, being small and of no account, he had been unable to fine-tune the mind in order to make the gift applicable to novels only. It might well be that Azazel did not even know what a novel was.

Well, did it matter?

I can't say that Gottlieb was exactly pleased when he came home and found me at his doorstep, but he was not so entirely lost to shame as to refuse to invite me in. In fact, it was with some satisfaction that I realized he could not fail to invite me to dinner, though he sought (deliberately, I think) to destroy that pleasure by having me hold Gottlieb Junior for a lengthy period of time. It was a fearful experience.

Afterward, when we were alone in his dining room, I said, "And how much dross are you making, Gottlieb?"

He looked at me reproachfully. "Don't call it dross, George. It's disrespectful. Fifty thousand a year, I admit, is dross, but a hundred thousand a year, plus some very satisfactory perks, is financial status.

"What's more, I will soon establish my own firm and become a multimillionaire, at which level money becomes virtue—or power, which is the same thing, of course. With my power, for instance, I will be able to drive Feinberg out of business. That will teach him to address me in terms that no gentleman should use to another. Do you happen to know what 'shmendrick' means, by the way, George?"

I couldn't help him there. I am conversant with a number of languages, but Urdu is not one of them. I said, "Then you have grown rich."

"And plan to grow far richer."

"In that case, Gottlieb, may I point out that this happened only after I agreed to make you rich, at which time you, in turn, promised to give me half your earnings?"

Gottlieb's eyebrows drew together in a frown. "Did you? Did I?"

"Why, yes. I admit it is the sort of thing that is very easy to forget, but fortunately it was all placed in writing—in return for services rendered—signed—notarized, all that sort of thing. And I happen to have a photocopy of the agreement with me."

"Ah. May I see it, then?"

"Certainly, but may I stress that it is merely a photocopy, so that if you should accidentally happen to tear it into little pieces in your eagerness to examine it closely, I will still have the original in my possession."

"A wise move, George, but do not fear. If all is as you say, not one jot nor tittle—not even a penny—will be withheld from you. I am a man of principle and I honor all agreements to the letter."

I gave him the photocopy and he studied it carefully. "Ah yes," he said, "I do remember. Of course. There's only one little point—"

"What?" I asked.

"Well, here on this paper it refers to my earnings as a novelist. I am not a novelist, George."

"You intended to be, and you can be one any time you sit down at the typewriter."

"But I no longer intend to be, George, and I do not expect to sit down at the typewriter."

"But great novels will mean immortal fame. What can your idiotic slogans bring you?"

"Lots and lots of money, George, plus a huge firm which I will own, and which will employ many miserable copywriters whose very lives I will hold in the hollow of my hand. Did Tolstoy ever have that? Does del Rey?"

I couldn't believe it. "And after what I have done for you, you will refuse to give me one red cent, simply because of a single word in our solemn agreement?"

"Have you ever tried your own hand at writing, George? Because I couldn't have put the situation into words more clearly and succinctly myself. My principles hold me to the letter of the agreement, and I am a man of principle."

From that position he would not budge, and I realized it would do no good to bring up the matter of the eleven dollars I had spent for our last lunch together.

To say nothing of the quarter tip.

George rose and left, and did so in such a state of histrionic despair that I couldn't bring myself to suggest that he first pay his half of the drinks. I called for the bill and noted that it came to twenty-two dollars.

I admired George's careful arithmetic in paying himself back and felt constrained to leave a half-dollar tip.

The Evil Drink Does

"The evil drink does," said George, with a heavily alcoholic sigh, "would be hard to assess."

"Not if you were sober," I said.

He stared at me out of his light blue eyes with a look compounded of reproach and indignation. "When," he said, "was I anything else?"

"Since you were born," I said, and then, realizing I was doing him an injustice, I amended my remark hastily. "Since you were weaned."

"I take it," said George, "that that is one of your ineffectual attempts at humor." And with a fine absence of mind, he lifted my drink to his lips, sipped and put it down again, holding on to it with a grip of iron.

I let it go. Taking a drink from George was much akin to taking a bone from a hungry bulldog.

He said, "In making my remark, I was thinking of a young woman, one in whom I took much interest in an avuncular fashion, by the name of Ishtar Mistik."

"An unusual name," I said.

"But an appropriate one, for Ishtar is the name of the Babylonian goddess of love, and a veritable goddess of love is what Ishtar Mistik was—in potential, at least."

Ishtar Mistik [George said] was what would be called a fine figure of a woman, if one had a congenital tendency to deal in understatement. Her face was beautiful in the classic sense, every feature perfect, and it was crowned by an aureole of golden hair that was so fine and sparkling as to seem a halo. Her body could only be described as Aphrodisian. It was billowing and beautiful, a combination of firmness and yieldingness encased in smooth perfection.

You may wonder, thanks to your foul mind, how I am so aware of the tactile state of her charms, but I assure you it is a long-distance assessment that I can make because of my general experience in such matters, and not because of any direct observation in this particular case.

Fully dressed she would make a better centerfold than any you might find in the more ordinary fashion of display in the magazines devoted to the artistic views of such things. A narrow waist, topped and bottomed by such equi-balanced lushness as you could not well imagine without having seen her; long legs, graceful arms, her every movement designed for rapture.

And although one could scarcely be so coarse-grained as to demand anything more of such physical perfection, Ishtar also had a keen and supple mind, having completed her studies at Columbia University with a *magna cum laude*—though one might fairly suppose that the average college professor, in grading Ishtar Mistik, might feel moved to give her the benefit of the doubt. Since you yourself are a professor, my dear friend (and I say this without meaning to hurt your feelings), I can have only the lowest opinion of the profession generally.

One might have thought that, with all this, Ishtar could have her pick of men, and renew her pick from a fresh batch each day. In fact, it had crossed my mind now and then that if she ever picked me I would endeavor to meet the challenge out of my gentlemanly regard for the fair sex, but I must admit I hesitated to make that fact clear to her.

For if Ishtar did have a slight fault, it was that she was rather a formidable creature. She was not more than an inch above six feet; had a voice which, when she was moved, rather resembled a trumpet call; and had been known to have turned on a fairly large hoodlum who had incautiously tried to take liberties with her, lifting him bodily and tossing him across the road, a rather wide one, and into a lamppost. He spent six months in the hospital.

There was a certain reluctance on the part of the male population to make any advances in her direction, therefore, even of the most respectful kind. The undeniable impulse to do so was always aborted by a long consideration as to whether it was physically safe to make the attempt. Even I myself, brave as a lion though you know me to be, found myself thinking of the possibility of broken bones. Thus, to coin a phrase, conscience doth make cowards of us all.

Ishtar well understood the situation, and complained to me of it bitterly. I remember the occasion very well. It was a gorgeous late spring day and we occupied a bench in Central Park. It was the occasion, I recall, when no fewer than three joggers failed to negotiate a curve while turning to look at Ishtar and ended up nose to bark with a tree.

"I am likely to remain virginal all my life," she said, her deliciously curved lower lip trembling. "No one seems interested in me, no one at all. And I will be twenty-five soon."

"You understand, my—my dear," I said, cautiously reaching toward her to pat her hand, "that young men are in awe of your physical perfection and do not feel worthy of you."

"That is ridiculous," she said forcefully enough for distant passers-by to turn inquiringly in our direction. "What you're trying to say is that they are scared silly of me. There's something about the way in which those silly things look up at me when we're introduced, and rub their knuckles after we shake hands, which just tells me that nothing will happen. They just say, 'Pleased to meet you,' and move away quickly."

"You have to encourage them, Ishtar dear. You must look upon a man as a fragile flower who can bloom properly only under the warm sunshine of your smile. Somehow you must

indicate to him that you are receptive to his advances and refrain
from any attempt to seize him by the collar of his jacket and the
seat of his pants and bash his head against the wall."

"I have never done that," she said indignantly. "Hardly ever.
And how on earth do you expect me to indicate myself to be
receptive? I smile and say, 'How do you do?' don't I, and I
always say, 'What a nice day it is' even when it isn't."

"Not enough, my dear. You must take a man's arm and tuck
it gently under your own. You might tweak a man's cheek,
stroke his hair, nibble daintily at his fingertips. Little things like
that are indicative of a certain interest, a certain willingness on
your part to engage in friendly hugs and kisses."

Ishtar looked horrified. "I couldn't do that. I just couldn't. I
was brought up in the strictest possible way. It is impossible for
me to behave in anything but the most correct manner. It must
be the man who makes the advances and even then I must hold
back as hard as I can. My mother always taught me that."

"But Ishtar, do it when your mother isn't looking."

"I couldn't. I'm just too—too inhibited. Why can't a man just
—just come at me?" She flushed at some thought that must have
passed through her mind at those words, and her large but perfectly shaped hand clutched at her heart. (I wondered idly if she
knew how privileged her hand was at such a time.)

I think it was the word "inhibited" that gave me my idea. I
said, "Ishtar, my child, I have it. You must indulge in alcoholic
beverages. There are a number that are quite pleasant-tasting
and lend one a healthful invigoration. If you were to invite a
young man to share several grasshoppers with you, or mar-
garitas, or any of a dozen other drinks I might mention, you
would find that your inhibitions would quickly decrease and so
would his. He would be emboldened to make suggestions to you
that no gentleman should make to a lady, and you would be
emboldened to giggle when he did so and suggest that you visit a
hotel of your acquaintance where your mother would not find
you."

Ishtar sighed and said, "How wonderful that would be, but it wouldn't work."

"Certainly it would. Almost any man would be glad to join you in a drink. If he hesitates, offer to pick up the check. No man of any worth whatever would refuse a drink when a lady offers to—"

She interrupted. "That's not it. It's *my* problem. I can't drink."

I had never heard of such a thing. "You merely open your mouth, my dear—"

"I know that. I can *drink*—I mean I can swallow the stuff. It's the effect on me. It makes me very woozy."

"But you don't drink *that* much, you—"

"One drink makes me woozy, except when it makes me sick and I throw up. I've tried lots of times, and I just can't have more than one drink, and once I have it, I am really in no mood for—you know. It's a defect in my metabolism, I believe, but my mother says it's a gift from heaven designed to keep me virtuous against the wiles of wicked men who would try to deprive me of my purity."

I must admit that I was left nearly speechless for a moment at the thought of someone who would actually find merit in an inability to indulge in the pleasures of the grape. But the thought of such perversity hardened my resolution, and threw me into such a state of indifference to danger that I actually squeezed the resilience of Ishtar's upper arm and said, "My child, leave it to me. I shall arrange everything."

I knew exactly what I had to do.

I have undoubtedly never mentioned my friend Azazel to you, for on this subject I am totally discreet—I see you are about to protest that you know of him, and considering your well-known record as a despiser of truth (if I may say this without intention of embarrassing you) I am not surprised.

Azazel is a demon possessed of magical powers. A *small* demon. He is, in point of fact, merely two centimeters tall. That, however, is good since it makes him quite anxious to demonstrate his worth and ability to one like myself whom he is pleased to consider an inferior being.

He responded to my call as always, although it is useless of you to expect me to give you the details of the method I use for obtaining his presence. It would be beyond your puny brain (no offense) to control him.

He arrived rather out of humor. Apparently he was watching something in the nature of a sporting event on which he had wagered close to a hundred thousand zakinis and he seemed a little put out at not being able to witness the result. I pointed out that money was dross and that he was put in this universe to help intelligences in need and not to pile up worthless zakinis which he would, in any case, lose upon the next bet even if he won them now, which was doubtful.

These rational and unanswerable points did nothing at first to calm down the miserable creature whose predominant characteristic is a rather disgusting tendency to selfishness, so I offered him a quarter-dollar. Aluminum is, I believe, the medium of exchange in his world and while it is not my intention to encourage him to expect a material return for the trifling assistance he might give me, I gathered the quarter was something in excess of a hundred thousand zakinis to him and, in consequence, he rather handsomely admitted that my concerns were of more importance than his own. As I always say, the force of reason is bound to make itself felt eventually.

I explained Ishtar's problem and Azazel said, "For once, you have set me a reasonable problem."

"Of course," I said. After all, as you know, I am not an unreasonable man. I need only have my own way to be satisfied.

"Yes," said Azazel. "Your miserable species does not metabolize alcohol efficiently, so that intermediate products accumulate in the bloodstream and these produce various unpleasant symptoms associated with intoxication—a word appropriately derived, my studies of your dictionaries assure me, from Greek words meaning 'poison within.' "

I sneered. The modern Greeks, as you know, mix their wine with rosin, and the ancient Greeks mixed it with water. It was no wonder they spoke of "poison within" when they had poisoned the wine before ever drinking it in the first place.

Azazel went on, "It will only be necessary to adjust the enzymes appropriately in order to have her metabolize the alcohol swiftly and unerringly to the stage of the two-carbon fragment which is the metabolic crossroads for fat, carbohydrate, and protein metabolism and there will then be no evidence of intoxication at all. Alcohol will thus become a wholesome food for her."

"We have to have *some* intoxication, Azazel; just enough to produce a healthful indifference to foolish strictures learned at the maternal knee."

He seemed to understand me at once. "Ah, yes. I know about mothers. I remember my third mother telling me, 'Azazel, you must never clap your nictitating membranes together in front of a young malobe,' when how else can you—"

I interrupted him again. "Can you arrange for just a slight bit of accumulation of intermediate in order to produce just a wee bit of exhilaration?"

"Easily," said Azazel, and, in an unlovely display of greed, stroked the quarter I gave him, which, on edge, was taller than he was.

It was not till about a week later that I had a chance to test Ishtar. It was in a midtown hotel bar where she illuminated the place to the point where several patrons put on dark glasses and stared.

She giggled. "What are we doing here? You *know* I can't drink."

"This won't be a drink, dear girl, not a *drink.* It's just a peppermint squash. You'll like it." I had prearranged matters and signaled for a grasshopper.

She sipped at it delicately and said, "Oh, it *is* good," then leaned back and allowed it to pour down her throat with abandon. She passed the tip of her beautiful tongue over her equally beautiful lips and said, "May I have another?"

"Of course," I said genially. "At least, you might have one were it not for the fact that I seem to have foolishly left my wallet—"

"Oh, I'll pay. I have *lots* of money."

A beautiful woman, I've always said, stands never so tall as when she stoops to take a wallet out of the purse between her feet.

Under those circumstances, we drank freely. At least she did. She had another grasshopper, then a vodka, then a double whiskey and soda and a few other things and when it was all down, she showed absolutely no sign of intoxication, though her winsome smile was more intoxicating than anything she had imbibed. She said, "I feel so nice and warm, and so *ready,* if you know what I mean."

I thought I did, but I wished to jump to no conclusions. "I don't think your mother would like it." (Testing, testing.)

She said, "What does my mother know about it? Nothing! And what is she *going* to know about it? Nothing." She looked at me speculatively, and then leaned over and lifted my hand to her perfect lips. "Where can we go?" she said.

Well, my friend, I think you know my feeling about such things. To refuse a young lady who asks with yearning politeness for a simple favor is not something I am likely to do. I've been brought up to be a gentleman at all times. But on *this* occasion, several thoughts occurred to me.

First, though you might scarcely credit this, I am a little—just a touch—past my best days, and a woman as young and strong as Ishtar might take some time to satisfy, if you understand me. Then, afterward, if she should remember what had happened, and should choose to resent it and to feel as though I had taken advantage of her, the consequences might be uncomfortable. She was a creature of impulse and she might produce a handful of broken bones before I had a chance to explain.

So I suggested a walk to my rooms and took the long route.

The fresh evening air cleared her head of its mild warmth and I was safe.

Others were not. More than one young man came to tell me of Ishtar for, as you know, there is something about the benign dignity of my bearing that elicits confidences. It was never in a bar, unfortunately, for the men in question seemed to avoid bars, for a time, at least. They had usually tried to match Ishtar drink for drink—for just a while—with unhappy results.

"I'm absolutely positive," one of them said, "that she had a hidden pipe that led from the corner of her mouth down to a hogshead under the table, but I couldn't spot it. But if you think *that* was something, you should have been there later."

The poor fellow was gaunt with the horror of the experience. He tried to tell me, but he was almost incoherent. "The *demands,*" he kept saying over and over again. "Insatiable! Insatiable!"

I was glad I had had the good sense to avoid something that men in their prime had barely survived.

I did not see much of Ishtar at that time, you understand. She was very busy—yet I could see she was consuming the supply of nubile men at a fearful rate. Soon or later she would have to extend her range. It was sooner.

She met me one morning as she was about to leave for the airport. She was more *zaftig* than ever, more pneumatic, more startling in all possible measurements. Nothing of what she had gone through seemed to have affected her, except for the more and better.

She pulled a bottle out of her purse. "Rum," she said. "They drink that down in the Caribbean and it's a very mild and very pleasant beverage."

"Are you going to the Caribbean, dear?"

"Oh, yes, and elsewhere. The men at home seem to be of poor endurance and weak spirit. I am very disappointed in them, although there have been moments of high adventure. I am very grateful to you, George, for making it possible. It seems to have begun when you first introduced me to that peppermint squash. It seems a shame that you and I haven't—"

"Nonsense, dear girl. I work for humanity, you know. I never think of myself at all."

She placed a kiss upon my cheek that burned like sulfuric acid and she was gone. I mopped my brow in considerable relief, but I did flatter myself that for once, my application to Azazel had brought about something that had ended happily, for Ishtar who, through inheritance, was independently wealthy, could now indulge indefinitely and without harm in her artless enthusiasms for alcoholic and masculinic pleasures.

Or so I thought.

It was not until more than a year had passed that I heard from her again. She was back in town and she phoned me. It was a while before I realized who it was. She was hysterical.

"My life is over," she screamed at me. "Even my mother no longer loves me. I can't understand how it happened but I'm sure it's your fault. If you had not introduced me to that peppermint squash, I just know that nothing like this would ever have happened."

"But what has happened, my dear?" I asked, trembling. An Ishtar who was furious with me would not be an Ishtar it would be safe to approach.

"You come here. I'll show you."

My curiosity will someday be the end of me. On that occasion, it nearly was. I couldn't resist going to her mansion on the outskirts of town. Wisely, I left the front door open behind me. When she approached with a butcher knife, I turned and fled with a speed that I would have been proud of in my younger days. Fortunately, she was in no position to follow, considering her condition.

She left again, shortly afterward, and, as far as I know, has not returned since. I live in dread that someday she will. The Ishtar Mistiks of this world do not forget.

George seemed to think he had come to the end of the story. "But what had happened?" I asked.

"You don't see? Her body chemistry had been adjusted to convert alcohol very efficiently to the two-carbon fragment that was the crossroads of carbohydrate, fat, and protein metabolism. Alcohol was to her a healthful food. And she drank like a six-foot sponge—incredibly. And all of it slid down the metabolic chain to the two-carbon fragment and, from that, up the metabolic chain to fat. She had, in a word, become stout; in two words, grossly obese. All that gorgeous beauty had expanded and exploded into layer upon layer of lard."

George shook his head in mingled horror and regret and said, "The evil drink does would be hard to assess."

Writing Time

George said, "I once knew someone a little like you."

We had a window seat at the small restaurant where we were having lunch, and George was looking out pensively.

I said, "That's astonishing. I should have thought I was unique."

"You are," said George. "The man I am referring to was only a *little* like you. For the ability to scribble, scribble, scribble while keeping the brain totally detached, you stand alone."

"Actually," I said, "I use a word processor."

"I use the word 'scribble,' " said George loftily, "in what a real writer would understand as the metaphorical sense." Then he paused over his chocolate mousse to sigh dramatically.

I knew the sign. "You're going to tell me one of your flights of fancy concerning Azazel, aren't you, George?"

He looked at me scornfully, "You've been flying your own fancy so long and so limply, you don't know the ring of truth when you hear it. But never mind. It is too sad a tale to tell you."

"Except that you're going to anyway, aren't you?"

George sighed again.

It's that bus stop out there [said George] that reminds me of Mordecai Sims, who made a moderate living for himself by turning out endless reams of variegated trash. Not as much as you do, of course, and not as trashy, which is why he is only a little like you. To do him justice, I occasionally read some of his material and found them quite so-so. Without meaning to hurt your feelings, you've never reached that mark—at least according to reports, for I have never been quite low enough in my mind to read you myself.

Mordecai was different from you in another respect; he was terribly impatient. Observe yourself in the mirror over there, assuming you have no objection to being reminded of what you look like, and see how you sit here carelessly, one arm thrown over the back of the chair and the rest of you slumped into casual shapelessness. One would never think, to look at you, that you had any concern as to whether your daily quota of randomly typed paper would be turned out or not.

Mordecai was not like that. He was always conscious of his deadlines—behind which he was in perpetual danger of falling.

I lunched with him regularly every Tuesday in those days and he tended to make the experience a hideous one with his chatter. "I've got to have that piece in the mail by tomorrow morning at the latest," he would say, "and I've got to do a bit of revision on another piece first, and I just don't have the time. Where the devil is that check? Why doesn't the waiter show up? What do they do with themselves in the kitchen? Have swimming contests in the gravy?"

He was always particularly impatient with respect to the check, and I would fear that he might bolt, leaving it behind for me to evade, somehow. To do him justice that never happened, but the feeling that it might tended to spoil the meal.

Or look at that bus stop out there. I have been observing it for fifteen minutes. You'll notice that no bus has come and that it is a windy day with a late fall nip to the air. What we see are collars turned up, hands thrust into pockets, noses turning red or blue, feet being shuffled for warmth. What we don't see is any rebellion in the ranks, any fists waved angrily to heaven. All those waiting there are broken into passivity by the injustice of life.

Not Mordecai Sims. If he were in that bus line, he would be dashing out into the road to survey the distant horizon for any sign of a vehicle; he would be growling and snarling and waving his arms; he would be urging a mass march on City Hall. He would, in short, be depleting his adrenal glands.

Many's the time he turned to me with his complaints, attracted, as so many are, by my cool air of competence and understanding.

"I am a busy man, George," he would say rapidly. He always talked rapidly. "It's a shame, a scandal, and a crime the way the world conspires against me. I had to drop in at a hospital for some routine tests—God knows why except that my doctor foolishly thinks he has to make a living—and I was told at arrive at 9:40 A.M. at such and such a desk.

"I got there at 9:40 A.M. precisely, of course, and on the desk in question was a sign saying: 'Open for business at 9:30 A.M.' That is what it said George—in English without a letter out of place. Behind the desk, however, there was no one.

"I checked my watch and said to someone who looked hang-dog enough to be a hospital attendant. 'Where,' I said, 'is the nameless villain who should be behind that desk?'

" 'Not here yet,' said the lowborn knave.

" 'It says this place is open for business at 9:30 A.M.'

" 'Someone will be here sooner or later, I guess,' he answered with a vicious indifference.

"It was, after all, a hospital. I might be dying. Did anyone care? No! I had a deadline looming for an important item I had expended half my guts on, something that would earn me enough money to pay my doctor's bill (assuming I had nothing better to spend it on, which wasn't likely). Did anyone care? No! It was not till 10:04 that someone showed up, and when I rushed to the desk, that belated devil stared at me haughtily and said, 'You'll have to wait your turn.' "

Mordecai was full of stories like that; of banks of elevators in which every single one was moving slowly upward while he waited in the lobby; of people who lunched from twelve to three-thirty and began their four-day weekends on Wednesday whenever he needed to consult them.

"I don't see why anyone bothered to invent time, George," he would say. "It's just a device to make possible the formation of novel methods of wastage. Do you realize that if I could convert the hours I must spend waiting on the convenience of assorted malapert varlets into writing time for myself, I could increase my output by anywhere from ten to twenty percent. Do you further realize that, despite the criminal parsimony of publishers, that would mean a corresponding increase in my income? —Where is that miserable check?"

I could not help but think it would be a kindly deed to help him increase his income, since he had the good taste to spend some of it on me. What's more, he had a way of selecting first-class places at which to dine, and that warmed my heart. —No, not like this one, old fellow. Your taste falls far short of what it ought to be, as, I am told, one can tell from your writing.

I therefore began to stir my powerful mind for ways to help him.

I did not immediately think of Azazel. In those days, I had not yet grown accustomed to him; after all, a two-centimeter-tall demon *is* a little out of the ordinary.

Eventually, though, it occurred to me to wonder whether Azazel could do anything about building up someone's writing time. It didn't seem likely and I might be just wasting his time, but what's time to an otherworldly creature?

I went through the necessary routine of ancient spells and incantations to call him forth from wherever it is he comes, and he arrived asleep. His tiny eyes were closed and there was a high-pitched hum coming from him that rose and fell in an irregular and unpleasant fashion. It may have been the equivalent of a human snore.

I wasn't sure how one went about waking him, and finally I decided to allow a drop of water to fall on his stomach. He had a perfectly spherical abdomen, you know, as though he had swallowed a ball bearing. I haven't the slightest idea of whether that is the norm on his world, but once when I mentioned it he demanded to know what a ball bearing was and then, when I explained, he threatened to zapulniclate me. I didn't know what that meant, but from the tone of his voice I gathered it was something unpleasant.

The drop of water did wake him, and he was absurdly annoyed, too. He kept talking about having been half drowned and went into tedious detail as to the proper method of waking one up on his world. It was something about dancing and flower petals and soft, musical instruments and the touch of the fingers of gorgeous dancing maidens. I told him that on our world we just played garden hoses on each other and he made some remark about ignorant barbarians and eventually cooled down sufficiently to allow me to talk sense to him.

I explained the situation and I rather thought that, without more ado, he would say a few words of gibberish and that would be that.

He did no such thing. Instead he looked grave and said, "See here, you are asking me to interfere with the laws of probability."

I was pleased that he had grasped the situation. "Exactly," I said.

"But that's not easy," he said.

"Of course not," I said. "Would I ask you to do it if it were easy? If it were easy I'd do it myself. It's only when it's not easy that I have to call on someone as magnificently superior as yourself."

Nauseating, of course, but essential when you deal with a demon who is as sensitive about his height as about his ball-bearing belly.

He looked gratified at my logic and said, "Well, I don't say it's *impossible.*"

"Good."

"It would require an adjustment of the Jinwhipper continuum of your world."

"Exactly. You took the words out of my mouth."

"What I will have to do is introduce a few nodes in the interconnection of the continuum with your friend, the one with the deadlines. What are deadlines, by the way?"

I tried to explain and he said, with a windy little suspiration, "Ah, yes, we have such things in our more ethereal demonstrations of affection. Allow a deadline to pass and the dear little creatures never let you hear the end of it. I remember once—"

But I will spare you the sordid details of his insignificant sex life.

"The only thing is," he said finally, "that once I introduce the nodes, I won't be able to undo them."

"Why not?"

Azazel said, with elaborate casualness. "Theoretically impossible, I'm afraid."

I didn't believe that at all. It was just that the miserable little incompetent didn't know how. Still, since he was quite competent enough to make life impossible for me, I did not let him know I had seen through his charade, but simply said, "You won't have to undo it. Mordecai is after additional writing time and once he has it he will be satisfied for life."

"In that case I shall do it."

For a long time, he made passes. It looked like something a magician would do, except that his hands seemed to flicker and turn invisible now and then for shorter or longer intervals. They were so small, to be sure, it was hard to tell whether they were visible or not even under normal circumstances.

"What are you doing?" I asked, but Azazel shook his head, and his lips moved as though he were counting.

Then, apparently finished, he lay back on the table and panted.

I said, "Is it done?"

He nodded and said, "I hope you realize I had to lower his entropy quotient more or less permanently."

"What does that mean?"

"It means that things will be a little more orderly in his neighborhood than one should suspect."

"Nothing wrong with being orderly," I said. (You might not think it, old fellow, but I have always believed in being orderly. I keep an accurate list of every cent I owe you. The details are on innumerable scraps of paper that are here and there in my apartment. You can have them any time you want them.)

Azazel said, "Of course there's nothing wrong with being orderly. It's just that you can't really defy the second law of thermodynamics. It means that things will be a little *less* orderly elsewhere in order to restore the balance."

"In what way?" I said, checking my zipper. (One can never be too careful.)

"In various ways, mostly unnoticeable. I've spread the effect through the solar system, so that there will be a few more asteroid collisions than would ordinarily take place, a few more eruptions on Io, and so on. Mostly, it's the sun that will be affected."

"How?"

"I estimate it will get hot enough to make life on Earth impossible about two and a half million years sooner than it would have before I noded the continuum."

I shrugged. What are a few million years when it's a question of having someone pick up my dinner checks with that cheerful disposition one likes to see?

It was about a week afterward that I once again dined with Mordecai. He seemed rather excited as he checked his coat, and when he arrived at the table where I was waiting patiently with my drink, he smiled brilliantly.

"George," he said, "what an unusual week I have had." He held his hand up without looking and did not seem at all surprised when a menu was placed in it. Mind you, this was a restaurant at which the waiters, a haughty and imperious lot, gave out no menus without an application in triplicate that had been countersigned by the manager.

Mordecai said, "George, everything has been going like clockwork."

I suppressed a smile. "Indeed?"

"When I walk into the bank, there's an empty window and a smiling cashier. When I walk into the post office, there's an empty window and—well, I guess you wouldn't actually expect a post office employee to smile, but at least he registered a letter of mine with scarcely any snarl at all. The buses drive up as I arrive, and I barely had my hand up in yesterday's rush hour when a taxi swerved and stopped for me. A checker cab, too. When I asked to be taken to Fifth and Forty-ninth, he took me there, showing every sign he knew the layout of the streets of the city. He even spoke English. —What would you like to have, George?"

A glance at the menu was sufficient. Apparently it was arranged that even I should not delay him. Mordecai then tossed his menu to one side and proceeded to give the order for both of us rapidly. I noticed that he did not look up to see whether a waiter was actually at his side. He had already grown accustomed to assume one would be.

And one was.

The waiter rubbed his hands together, bowed, and proceeded to serve the meal with celerity, grace, and efficiency.

I said, "You do seem to be having the most amazing streak of luck, Mordecai, my friend. How do you account for it?" (I must admit that I had a passing thought that I might make him believe I was responsible. After all, if he knew that, would he not surely shower me with gold, or, in these debased times, with paper?)

"Simple," he said, tucking his napkin into his shirt collar and seizing his knife and fork in a death grip, for Mordecai, with all his virtues, was not one of your dainty feeders. "It's not luck at all. It's the inevitable result of the workings of chance."

"Of *chance?*" I said indignantly.

Mordecai said, "Certainly. I have spent my whole life enduring the most miserable series of fortuitous delays that the world has ever seen. The laws of chance make it necessary that such an unbroken fund of misfortune be made up for, and that's what's happening now, and should continue to be happening for the rest of my life. I expect it to. I have confidence. Everything is balancing out." He leaned toward me and tapped me on the chest in a most unpleasant way. "Depend upon it. You can't defy the laws of probability."

He spend the entire meal lecturing me on the laws of probability, concerning which, I am sure, he actually knew as little as you do.

I finally said, "Surely all this gives you more writing time?"

"Obviously," he said. "I estimate that my writing time has increased by twenty percent."

"And your output has gone up correspondingly, I imagine."

"Well," he said a little uncomfortably, "not just yet, I'm afraid. Naturally, I have to adjust. I'm not quite used to getting things done so quickly. It took me by surprise."

Frankly, he didn't look surprised to me. He lifted his hand and, without looking, plucked the bill from the fingers of the waiter who was just approaching with it. He glanced at it cursorily and handed it back, with a credit card, to the waiter who had actually waited for it and who then left on the double.

The entire dinner had taken a little over thirty minutes. I will not hide from you the fact that I would have preferred a civilized two and a half hours, with champagne preceding, brandy succeeding, a fine wine or two separating the courses, and cultured conversation filling all the interstices. However, on the bright side was the fact that Mordecai had saved two hours which he could spend money-grubbing for himself and, to an extent, for me.

As it happened, I didn't see Mordecai for three weeks or so after that dinner. I don't remember why that was, but I rather suspect it was one of those occasions in which we took turns being out of town.

At any rate, I was just emerging one morning from a coffee

shop at which I sometimes partake of a roll and scrambled eggs, when I saw Mordecai standing at the corner about half a block away.

It was a miserable day of wet snow—the kind of day on which empty taxis approach you only in order to send a spray of dark gray slush over your pants legs as they shoot past you and turn on their off-duty signs.

Mordecai had his back to me and was just raising his hand when an empty taxi rolled cautiously toward him. To my astonishment, Mordecai looked away. The taxi lingered, then crawled off, disappointment written across the face of its windshield.

Mordecai raised his hand a second time and, from nowhere at all, a second taxi appeared and stopped for him. He got in but, as I could clearly hear even from a distance of forty yards, he did so with a ringing set of expletives not fit to be heard by anyone of tender upbringing, assuming that any such remain in the city.

I phoned him later than morning and arranged to have cocktails with him at a friendly bar we knew that featured one "Happy Hour" after another the whole day long. I could hardly wait, for I simply had to have an explanation from him.

What I wanted to know was the meaning of the expletives he used. —No, old fellow, I don't mean the dictionary meaning of the words, assuming they can be found in the dictionary. I meant why he should have used them at all. By all rights, he should have been ecstatically happy.

When he entered the bar, he was not looking noticeably happy. In fact, he looked distinctly haggard.

He said, "Signal for the waitress, will you, George?"

It was one of those bars where the waitresses were dressed without any undue regard for warmth, which, of course, helped keep *me* warm. I signaled for one gladly, even though I knew she would interpret my gestures as merely signifying a desire to place an order for a drink.

In actual fact, she didn't interpret it at all, for she ignored me by keeping her very bare back firmly to me.

I said, "Really, Mordecai, if you want service, you'll have to signal yourself. The laws of probability have not yet bestirred themselves on my behalf; which is a shame, for it is long past time for my rich uncle to die and to disinherit his son in my favor."

"You have a rich uncle?" asked Mordecai, with a flicker of interest.

"No! And that only makes the whole thing even more unjust. Signal for a drink, will you, Mordecai?"

"The hell with it," said Mordecai grumpily. "Let them wait."

It was not *them* waiting that bothered me, of course, but my curiosity overcame my thirst.

"Mordecai," I said, "you seem unhappy. In fact, although you didn't see me this A.M., I saw you. You actually ignored an empty taxi on a day when they were worth their weight in gold and then swore somewhat when you took a second."

Mordecai said, "Is that so? Well, I'm tired of those bastards. Taxis *haunt* me. They follow me around in long lines. I can't as much as look toward the oncoming traffic without one of them stopping. I'm hovered over by crowds of waiters. Shopkeepers open closed stores at my approach. Every elevator flings itself wide as soon as I enter a building and waits for me stolidly at whatever floor I'm at. At every conceivable business office I am instantly waved through the reception area by grinning hordes of receptionists. Minor functionaries at every level of government exist only to—"

By then I had caught my breath. "But Mordecai," I said, "this is splendid good fortune. The laws of probability—"

What he suggested I do to the laws of probability was entirely impossible, of course, since they are abstractions without corporeal parts.

"But Mordecai," I expostulated, "all this goes to increase your writing time."

"It does *not,*" said Mordecai forcefully. "I can't write at all."

"Why not, for heaven's sake?"

"Because I have lost *thinking* time."

"You have lost *what?*" I asked faintly.

"All this waiting I have had to do—on lines, on street corners, in outer offices—was when I *thought,* when I figured out what I was going to write. It was my all-important preparation time."

"I didn't know that."

"I didn't either, but I know it *now.*"

I said, "I thought you spent all such waiting time fuming and swearing and eating your heart out."

"Part of the time was spent that way. The rest of the time I spent thinking. And even the time that I spent railing at the injustice of the universe was useful, for it revved me up and set all my hormones frothing through my bloodstream so that when I *did* reach my typewriter I let all my frustrations boil off in one great and forceful banging at its keys. My thinking supplied my intellectual motivation and my anger supplied my emotional motivation. Together they resulted in huge blocks of excellent writing pouring out of the dark and infernal fires of my soul. *Now* what have I got? Watch!"

He clicked thumb and middle finger softly and at once a gorgeously unapparelled damsel was within hand reach, saying, "May I serve you, sir?"

Of course she could, but Mordecai merely ordered disconsolate drinks for the two of us.

"I thought," he said, "it was merely a matter of getting adjusted to the new situation, but I know now that no adjustment is possible."

"You can refuse to take advantage of the situation as it is offered to you."

"Can I? You saw me this morning. If I refuse a taxi, it just means another comes. I can refuse fifty times and there'll be one waiting on the fifty-first occasion. They wear me out."

"Well, then, why can't you simply reserve an hour or two every day for thinking time in the comfort of your office?"

"Exactly! In the comfort of my office! I can only think well when I am shifting from foot to foot on a street corner, or sitting on a granite chair in a drafty waiting room, or hungering in an unserviced dining room. I need the impetus of outrage."

"But are you not outraged now?"

"It's not the same thing. One can be outraged at injustice, but how can one be outraged at everyone's being too kind and thoughtful to you—the insensitive louts? I am *not* outraged now; I am merely sad, and I can't write at all when I am sad."

We sat through the most unhappy Happy Hour I have ever encountered.

"I swear to you, George," said Mordecai, "I think I have been cursed. I think that some fairy godmother, furious at having not been invited to my christening, has finally found the one thing worse than being forced into unwanted delay at every turn. She has found the curse of total subservience to one's wishes."

At the sight of his misery, a not-unmanly tear rose to my eye at the thought that I was myself none other than the fairy godmother he referred to, and that somehow he might find this out. After all, if he did, he might in his despair kill himself, or, far worse, me.

Then came the ultimate horror. Having called for the bill and, of course, receiving it at once, he studied it with lackluster eye, tossed it to me and said, with a hollow, hacking laugh, "Here, you pay for it. I'm going home."

I paid. What choice had I? But it left a wound I still feel on damp days. After all, is it right that I had shortened the lifetime of the sun by two and a half million years just so that I would have to pay for drinks? Is that justice?

I never saw Mordecai again. I heard, eventually, that he had left the country and had become a beachcomber somewhere in the South Seas.

I don't know exactly what a beachcomber does, but I suspect they don't get wealthy at it. However, I am quite sure that if he is on the beach and should want a wave, a wave would come at once.

By now, our bill have been brought by a sneering flunky and it lay between us while George ignored it with the flare he usually brings to such a performance.

I said, "You're not thinking of having Azazel do anything for me, George, are you?"

"Not really," said George. "Unfortunately, old fellow, you are not the kind of person whom one thinks of in connection with good deeds."

"Then you'll do nothing for me?"

"Not a thing."

"Good," I said. "Then I'll pay the check."

"It's the least you can do," said George.

Dashing Through the Snow

George and I were sitting at the window of La Bohème, a French restaurant he patronized now and then at my expense, and I said, "It will probably snow."

That was not a great contribution to the world's store of knowledge. It had been dark and lowering all day, the temperature was in the teens, and the weatherman had predicted snow. Still, it hurt my feelings to have George ignore the remark entirely.

He said, "Now consider my friend Septimus Johnson."

"Why?" I said. "What has he to do with the fact that it will probably snow?"

"A natural progression of ideas," said George severely. "That is a process you must have heard others mention, even if you have never experienced it yourself."

My friend Septimus [said George] was a ferocious young man, with a face permanently creased into a scowl and biceps permanently swollen into bulges. He was the seventh child in his family, hence his name. He had a younger brother named Octavius and a younger sister named Nina.

I don't know how far the progression went, but I believe it was the crowded condition of his youthful days that made him strangely enamored of silence and solitude in his later years.

Once he matured, and achieved a certain success with his novels (like you, old fellow, except that the critics say rather flattering things about *his* work on occasion), he found himself with enough money to pamper his perversion. In short, he bought an isolated house on a forgotten piece of territory in upstate New York and retired there for longer or shorter periods in order to write further novels. It was not terribly far from civilization, but as far as the eye could see, at least, it seemed untamed wilderness.

I think I was the only person he ever voluntarily invited to stay with him at his country place. I assume he found himself attracted by the calm dignity of my demeanor and the fascination and variety of my conversation. At least he never explained the source of attraction in so many words, but it can scarcely have been anything else.

One had to be careful with him, of course. Anyone who has ever felt the friendly clap on the back that is Septimus Johnson's favorite mode of greeting knows what it is to have a cracked vertebra. Still, his casual exertion of force came in handy at our first meeting.

I had been beset by a dozen or two hoodlums, who were misled by my upper-class carriage and appearance into assuming I carried untold wealth in cash and jewels on my person. I defended myself furiously for, as it happened, I did not have a penny on me that day, and I knew that the hoodlums, once they found this out, would, in their way natural disappointment, use me with the utmost barbarity.

It was at this point that Septimus appeared, lost in thought over something he was writing. The horde of wretches were in his way and, since he was too wrapped in thought to consider walking in anything but a straight line, he tossed them absently to one side or the other in twos and threes. He happened to come upon me at the bottom of the pile just as light dawned and he saw a way out of his literary dilemma, whatever it was. Feeling me to be a good-luck charm, he invited me to dinner. Feeling dinner at another's expense to be an even better luck charm, I accepted.

By the time dinner was over, I had established the kind of ascendancy over him that led to my being invited to his country place. Such invitations were repeated frequently. As he said at one time, being with me was as close to being alone as possible, and considering how he loved solitude, that was quite obviously a great compliment.

At first I expected a hovel, but I was quite wrong. Septimus had clearly done well with his novels and he had spared no expense. (I know it is rather unkind to speak of successful novels in your presence, old man, but I am, as always, wedded to the facts.)

The house, in fact, although isolated to the point of keeping me in a permanent state of horripilation, was thoroughly electrified, with an oil-fired generator in the basement and solar panels on the roof. We ate well and he had a magnificent wine cellar. We lived in total luxury, something to which I have always been able to adapt myself with astonishing ease, considering my lack of practice.

To be sure, it was impossible to avoid looking out the windows altogether, and the total lack of scenery was remarkably depressing. There were, if you can credit it, hills and fields and a small lake, and incredible quantities of vegetation of a bilious green, but not a sign of human habitation, of highways, or of anything else worth looking at—not as much as a line of telephone poles.

Once, after a good meal and good wine, Septimus said expansively, "George, I find it pleasant to have you here. After listening to you, I find it such a relief to turn to my word processer that my writing has improved substantially. Do feel free to come here at any time. Here," he waved his hand about, "you can escape from all your cares and all the annoyances that may be hounding you. And when I am at work at my word processor, you have free access to my books, to the television set, to the refrigerator and—I believe you know the location of the wine cellar."

As it happened, I did. I had even drawn a little map of guidance for myself, with a large X at the site of the wine cellar and several alternative routes carefully plotted out.

"The only thing is," said Septimus, "this refuge from worldly woe is closed from 1 December to 31 March. I cannot offer you my hospitality then. I must remain in my town house."

I was rather dashed at this. Snow time was woe time for me. After all, my dear fellow, it is in winter that my creditors are most pressing. These grasping people who, as everyone knows, are wealthy enough to be able to ignore the few paltry pennies I may owe them, seem to gain a kind of special delight at the thought that I might be thrown out into the snow. It inspires them to new feats of wolfish greed so that it was then above all I would have welcomed refuge.

I said, "Why not use it in winter, Septimus? With a roaring fire in this magnificent fireplace ably abetting your equally magnificent central heating system, you could laugh at the cold of Antarctica."

"So I could," said Septimus, "but it seems that each winter howling devils of blizzards converge here and dump snow on this demi-paradise of mine. This house, lost in the solitude I adore, is then cut off from the outside world."

"The world is well lost," I pointed out.

"You are perfectly right," said Septimus. "And yet my supplies come from the outside world—food, drink, fuel, laundry. It is humiliating but true that I cannot actually survive without the outside world—at least I couldn't live the kind of sybaritic life that any decent human being would want to live."

I said, "You know, Septimus, it may be that I can think of a way out of this."

"Think away," he said, "but you won't succeed. Still, this home is yours eight months of the year, or at least whenever I am here during those eight months."

It was true, but how could a reasonable man settle for eight months when twelve months existed? That evening I called up Azazel.

I don't think you know about Azazel. He is a demon, a magical imp about two centimeters high who possesses extraordinary power which he is glad to exhibit, because back in his own world, wherever that may be, he is not very highly thought of. Consequently—

Oh, you *have* heard of him? Well really, old fellow, how can I tell you this story in reasoned manner if you feel called upon to insert your own views continually? You don't seem to realize that the art of the true conversationalist consists of being completely attentive, and refraining from interruption on such specious excuses as that of having heard it all before. At any rate—

Azazel was, as always, furious at being called up. Apparently he was engaged in what he called a solemn religious observance. I held my own temper with difficulty. He is always involved in something he imagines to be important and never seems to stop to consider that when I call him up, I am invariably involved in something that *is* important.

I waited calmly till his twittering sputters died out and then I explained the situation.

He listened with a scowl on his tiny face and said at last, "What is snow?"

I sighed and explained.

"You mean solidified water falls from the sky here? Chunks of solidified water? And life survives?"

I didn't bother to mention hail, but said, "It falls as soft, downy flakes, Mighty One." (It always soothed him, you see, to call him foolish names.) "It is inconvenient, however, when it falls to excess."

Azazel said, "If you are going to ask me to rearrange the weather pattern in this world, then I refuse with considerable fervor. That would come under the heading of planet-tampering, which is against the ethics of my highly ethical people. I would not dream of being unethical, especially since if I were caught at it, I would be fed to the dread Lamell Bird, a most filthy creature with dreadful table manners. I would hate to tell you what he'd mix me with."

"I wouldn't dream of having you planet-tamper, Sublime One. I would like to ask something much simpler. —You see, snow, when it falls, is so soft and downy, that it will not support the weight of a human being."

"It is your fault for being so massive," said Azazel scornfully.

"No doubt," I said, "but this mass makes the going difficult. I would like to make my friend less heavy when he is on snow."

It was hard for me to hold Azazel's attention. He kept saying, in a revolted manner, "Solidified water—all over—burying the land." He shook his head as though unable to grasp the concept.

"Can you make my friend less heavy?" I asked, pounding away at what was, after all, a very simple point.

"Of course," said Azazel indignantly. "All it requires is the application of the antigravity principle, activated by the water molecule under appropriate conditions. It isn't easy, but it can be done."

"Wait," I said uneasily, thinking of the dangers of inflexibility. "It would be wise to place the antigravitational intensity under my friend's control. He might find it convenient to flounder on occasion."

"Fit it to your crude autonomic system? Really! You know no limits to your effrontery."

"I only ask," I said, "because it's you. I would know better than to ask this of any other of your species."

This diplomatic untruth had its expected effect. Azazel expanded his chest by two full millimeters and, in a lordly, counter-tenor squeak, said, "It shall be done."

I supposed Septimus gained the ability at that moment, but I couldn't be sure. It was August at the time and there was no snow cover with which to experiment—nor was I in the mood for a quick trip to Antarctica, Patagonia, or even Greenland in a search for experimental material.

Nor was there are point in explaining the situation to Septimus without snow for demonstration. He would not have believed me. He might even have come to the ridiculous conclusion that I—*I*—had been drinking.

But the Fates were kind. I was at Septimus's country home in late November, in what he called his farewell stay for the season, and there was a copious fall of snow—unusually heavy for the month.

Septimus chafed loudly and proclaimed war on the universe for not having spared him this vile insult.

But it was heaven to me—and to him, did he but know. I said, "Fear not, Septimus. Now is the time for you to find out that snow has no terrors for you." And I explained the situation in ample detail.

I suppose it was to be expected that his first reaction would be one of ribald disbelief, but he made certain totally unnecessary animadversions on the state on my mental health.

However, I had had months to work out my strategy. I said, "You may have wondered, Septimus, how I earn my living. You will not be surprised at my reticence when I tell you that I am the key figure in a government research program on antigravity. I can say no more except that you are an invaluable experiment and will greatly advance the program. This has important national security implications."

He stared at me in wide-eyed amazement as I softly hummed a few bars of "The Star-Spangled Banner."

"Are you serious?" he asked.

"Would I palter with the truth?" I asked in my turn. Then, risking the natural rejoinder, I said, "Would the CIA?"

He swallowed it, overcome by the aura of simple veracity that pervades all my statements.

He said, "What am I supposed to do?"

I said, "There's only six inches of snow on the ground. Imagine yourself to be weighing nothing and step out on it."

"I just have to *imagine* it?"

"That's the way it works."

"I'll get my feet wet."

I said sarcastically, "Put on your hip boots, then."

He hesitated and then actually got out his hip boots and struggled into them. This open show of lack of faith in my statements hurt me deeply. In addition, he put on a furry overcoat and an even furrier hat.

"If you're ready——" I said coldly.

"I'm not," he said.

I opened the door and he stepped out. There was no snow on the covered veranda, but as soon as he placed his feet on the steps, they seemed to slide out from under him. He grabbed the balustrade with a desperate grip.

He had somehow reached the bottom of the short flight of steps, and he tried to push himself upright. It didn't work, at least not in the way he intended. He went sliding along for a few feet, arms flailing, and then his feet went up in the air. He came down on his back and continued to slide until he passed a young tree and wrapped an arm around the trunk. He slid around it three or four times and came to a halt.

"What kind of slippery snow do we have here?" he shouted in a voice that trembled with indignation.

I must admit that despite my faith in Azazel, I found myself staring in surprise. He had left no footprints and his sliding body had made no furrow in the snow.

I said, "You don't weigh anything on the snow."

"Lunatic," he said.

I said, "Look at the snow. You've left no marks."

He stared, then make a few cursory remarks of the type that in past years used to be referred to as unprintable.

"And," I went on, "Friction depends in part on the pressure between a sliding body and what it slides upon. The lower the pressure, the less the friction. You weigh nothing, so your pressure on the snow is zero, the friction is zero, and you therefore slide on snow as though it were the smoothest ice."

"What am I suppose to do then? I can't have my feet slide out on me like that!"

"It doesn't hurt, does it? If you don't weigh anything, and you land on your back, it doesn't hurt."

"Even so. Not being hurt is insufficient excuse for spending my life on my back in the snow."

"Come, Septimus, think yourself heavy again and then get up."

He scowled in his usual fashion and said, "Just think myself heavy, eh?" But he did, and got clumsily to his feet.

He stood inches deep in it now and when he tried, cautiously, to walk, he had no more trouble than one usually does in snow.

"How do you do it, George?" he said, with much more respect in his voice than I usually managed to elicit. "I wouldn't have thought you were such a scientist."

"The CIA forces me to mask my keen scientific know-how," I explained. "Now imagine yourself lighter little by little, and walk as you do it. You'll leave shallower and shallower tracks and the snow will grow more and more slippery. Stop when you feel it becoming dangerously slippery."

He did as he was told, for we scientists have a strong intellectual grip over lesser mortals. "Now," I said, "try sliding around. When you want to stop, just make yourself heavier—and do it gradually or you'll go over on your nose."

He caught the knack immediately, being the athletic type. He told me once he could do anything in the way of sport but swim. His father, when he was a boy of three, had tossed him into the water in a kindly attempt to get him to swim without the tedious necessity of instruction, and the young Septimus had required ten minutes of mouth-to-mouth resuscitation as a result. He said it had left him with a lifetime fear of water and an aversion to snow as well. "Snow is just solid water," he said, exactly as Azazel would have.

The aversion to snow failed to make itself evident under the new conditions, however. He began sliding about with an ear-splitting "Whee!" and would, from time to time, make himself heavier as he turned, casting up a thick spray of snow and coming to a halt.

He said, "Wait!" dashed into the house and emerged—if you will believe it—with ice skates affixed to boots.

"I learned how to skate on my lake," he explained as he began to put them on, "but I never enjoyed it. I was always afraid the ice would break. Now I can skate on land without danger."

"But remember," I said anxiously, "it only works above the H_2O molecule. If you come to a bare patch of earth, or exposed pavement, your lightness will vanish instantly. You'll hurt yourself."

"Don't worry," he said, getting to his feet and taking off. I watched him speed along for at least half a mile over the frozen wastes of his acreage and to my ears there came the distant bellow of: "Dashing through the snow/ in a one-horse open sleigh—"

Septimus, you must understand, guesses at the pitch of each note, and always guesses wrong. I put my hands over my ears.

There followed what I truly believe was the happiest winter of my life. All winter long I was snug and warm in the house, eating and drinking like a king, reading improving books in which I tried to outguess the author and identify the murderer, and speculating with grim delight on the frustrations of my creditors back in the city.

Through the window, I could watch Septimus in his endless skating over the snow. He said it made him feel like a bird and gave him a three-dimensional delight he had never known. Well, to each his own.

I did warn him he must not let himself be seen. "It would endanger me," I said, "for the CIA would not approve this private experimentation—but I don't care about my personal danger for, to a person like myself, science comes above all. However, if you were ever seen skimming over snow as you do, you would become an object of curiosity and dozens of newspapermen would swarm over you. The CIA would hear of it and you would have to undergo experimentation with hundreds of scientists and military men poking at you. You would never be alone for a minute. You would become a national celebrity and you would be at all times within reach of thousands of people concerned over you."

Septimus shuddered strongly at the prospect as I knew an isolation-lover would have to. Then he said, "But how will I get supplies when I am snowed in? That was the whole purpose of this experiment."

I said, "I'm sure the trucks will almost always be able to make their way up the roads and you can store up enough to tide you over those times when they can't. If you *do* need something on an emergency basis when you are truly snowed in, you can skim as close to town as you dare, making sure no one sees you—there'll be very few people in the open at such times anyway, possibly no one—then restore your weight, tramp the last few hundred feet, and look worn out. Pick up what you need, tramp away a few hundred feet, and take off again. See?"

Actually, it was never necessary to do that even once during that winter; I knew all along that he had exaggerated the snow danger. And no one ever saw him during his skimming, either.

Septimus couldn't get enough. You should have seen his face when snow held off for more than a week or the temperature rose above freezing. You can't imagine how he feared for the safety of the snow cover.

What a marvelous winter! What a tragedy that it was the only one!

What happened? I'll tell you what happened. You remember what Romeo said just before he slipped the knife into Juliet? You probably don't, so I'll tell you. He said, "Let a woman in your life and your serenity is through."

The following fall, Septimus met a woman—Mercedes Gumm. He had met women before; he was no anchorite, but they had never meant much to him. A short period of socialization, romance, ardor, and then he forgot them, and they him. No harm in it. After all, I myself have been ferociously pursued by many young women and I never found harm in it at all, even though they frequently cornered me and forced me to—but I drift away from the story.

Septimus came to me in a very cast-down mood. "I love her, George," he said. "I am driven to distraction by her. She is the very lodestone of my existence."

"Very pretty," I said. "You have my permission to carry on with her for a while."

"Thanks, George," said Septimus gloomily. "Now what I need is *her* approval. I don't know why it should be, but she doesn't seem to take to me much."

"Odd," I said. "You are usually quite successful with women. You are after all, rich, muscular, and not uglier than most."

"I think it's the muscular part," said Septimus. "She thinks I'm an oaf."

I had to admire Miss Gumm's perception. Septimus, to put it as kindly as possible, *was* an oaf. I thought it best, however, as I imagined his biceps writhing under his jacket sleeves, not to mention my estimate of the situation.

He said, "She says she doesn't admire the physical in men. She wants someone thoughtful, intellectual, deeply rational, philosophical and a whole bucketful of adjectives like those. She says I'm not any of these things."

"Have you told her you're a novelist?"

"Of course I've told her that. And she's read a couple of novels of mine, too. But you know, George, they tend to be about football players and she says she found that revolting."

"I take it she's not the athletic type."

"Certainly not. She swims," and he made a face, probably remembering being mouth-to-mouth resuscitated at the tender age of three, "but that doesn't help."

"In that case," I said consolingly, "forget her, Septimus. Women are easy to come by. As one leaves, another arrives. There are many fish in the sea and birds in the air. They are all alike in the dark. One woman or another, it makes no difference."

I would have continued indefinitely, but he seemed to grow

oddly restless as he listened, and one doesn't care to make an oaf restless.

Septimus said, "George, you offend me deeply with those sentiments. Mercedes is the only girl in the world for me. I couldn't live without her. She is inseparably bonded to the core of my being. She is the very breath of my lungs, the beat of my heart, the vision of my eyes. She—"

He *did* continue indefinitely, and it didn't seem to bother him in the least that he was offending *me* deeply with those sentiments.

He said, "So I see no way out but of insisting on marriage."

The words were the knell of doom. I knew exactly what the result would be. As soon as they were married, that would mean the end of my paradise. I don't know why it is, but if there is one thing that new wives insist upon, it is that bachelor friends must go. I would never be invited to Septimus's country place again.

"You can't do that," I said in alarm.

"Oh, I admit it seems hard, but I think I can do it. I have worked out a plan. Mercedes may think I'm an oaf, but I'm not entirely unintellectual. I will invite her to my country place at the beginning of winter. There, in the quiet and peace of my Eden, she will feel her being expand and she will come to realize the true beauty of my soul."

That, I thought, was expecting far too much even of Eden, but what I said was, "You're not planning to show her how you can skim over the snow, are you?"

"No, no," he said. "Not until we're married."

"Even then—"

"Nonsense, George," said Septimus censoriously. "A wife is a husband's second self. A wife can be trusted with the dearest secrets of one's soul. A wife—"

Again, he went on indefinitely, and all I could do was say weakly, "The CIA won't like it."

His brief comment on the CIA was one with which the Soviets would heartily have agreed. Cuba and Nicaragua as well.

"Somehow I'll persuade her to come with me at the beginning

of December," he said. "I trust you will understand, George, if
we two plan to be alone. I know you wouldn't dream of interfering with the romantic possibilities that would arise between
Mercedes and myself in the peaceful solitude of nature. We
would surely be drawn together by the magnetism of silence and
slow time."

I recognized the quotation, of course. It was what Macbeth
said just before he slipped the knife into Duncan, but I merely
stared at Septimus in a cold and dignified way. A month later,
then, Miss Gumm *did* go to Septimus's country place and I did
not.

What happened at the country place, I did not witness. I
know it only through the spoken testimony of Septimus so I
cannot vouch for all the details.

Miss Gumm *was* a swimmer, but Septimus, feeling an uncon-
querable aversion to that particular hobby, asked no questions
about it. Nor did Miss Gumm apparently feel it necessary to
force detail on an unquestioning oaf. For that reason, Septimus
never found out that Miss Gumm was one of those madwomen
who enjoyed donning a bathing suit in the depth of winter,
breaking the ice in the lake and dropping into the freezing water
for a healthful, invigorating swim.

It followed that one bright and frosty morning, while Septimus was snoring in oafish slumber, Miss Gumm arose, put on
her bathing suit, terry-cloth cloak, and sneakers, and went along
the snow-covered path to the lake. The rim was lightly iced up
but the interior was still free of cover and, removing the cloak
and sneakers, she plunged into the frigid water with what must
have been every evidence of enjoyment.

It was not long after that that Septimus awoke and, with a
lover's fine instinct, instantly realized that his beloved Mercedes
was not in the house. He went through it calling her name.
Finding her clothes and other belongings in her room, he realized she had not secretly left for the city, as had been his first
fearful thought. She must then be outside.

Hastily, he put boots on his bare feet and slipped his heaviest overcoat over his pajamas. He dashed outside, calling her name.

Miss Gumm heard him, of course, and waved her arms madly in his direction, shouting "Right here, Sep. Right here."

What followed next I'll tell you in Septimus's own words. He said, "To me it sounded like 'Here, help, help!' I reached the natural conclusion that my love had ventured out onto the ice in a moment of madness and had fallen in. How could it ever occur to me that she would willingly throw herself into freezing water?

"Such was my great love for her, George, that I instantly determined to dare the water which ordinarily I cravenly feared —especially ice-cold water—and to rush to her rescue. Well, perhaps not *instantly*, but honestly, it was after not more than two minutes of thought, or three at the outside.

"Then I shouted, 'I'm coming, my own, my loved one. Keep your head above water.' and I started out. I wasn't going to *walk* there through the snow. I felt there wasn't enough time. I decreased my weight as I ran, and then took off on a magnificent slide, right across the shallow snow-cover, right across the ice that rimmed the lake, and right into the water with a horrendous splash.

"As you know I can't swim and am, indeed, deadly afraid of water. My boots and overcoat dragged me down, too, and I would certainly have drowned if Mercedes had not rescued me.

"You would think that the romance of rescuing me would have drawn us closer together, welded us into one, but—"

Septimus shook his head, and there were tears in his eyes, "It didn't work that way. She was furious. 'You oaf,' she shrieked. 'Imagine plunging into the water in your overcoat and boots and not even being able to swim. What on earth did you think you were doing? Do you know what a struggle it was to get you out of the lake? And you were in such a panic you clipped me on the jaw. You nearly knocked me out and had us *both* drown. And it still hurts.'

"She packed and left in a complete huff, and I had to remain behind with something that quickly developed into a very nasty cold, one I still haven't quite gotten over yet. I haven't seen her since then—she won't answer my letters; she won't return my phone calls. My life is over, George."

I said, "Just out of curiosity, Septimus, why *did* you throw yourself into the water? Why didn't you stand on the lakeshore, or as far out on the ice as you dared, and reach a long stick out to her or throw her a rope if you could get one?"

Septimus looked aggrieved. "I didn't intend to throw myself into the water. I intended to slide along the top."

"Slide along the top? Didn't I tell you your weightlessness would only work on ice?"

Septimus's look became one of ferocity. "I *thought* that was it. You said it only worked on H_2O. That includes water, doesn't it?"

He was right. H_2O sounded more scientific and I had to maintain my air of scientific genius. I said, "But I meant *solid* H_2O."

"But you didn't *say* solid H_2O," he said, as he slowly rose with what I felt to be the clear intention of dismembering me.

I didn't remain to check on the accuracy of my feeling. I have never seen him since. Nor have I ever again been to his country paradise. I believe he lives on a South Sea island now, largely, I think, because he never wants to see ice or snow again.

It's as I say, "Let a woman in your life—" though, come to think of it, it may have been Hamlet who said that just before he slipped his knife into Ophelia.

George let a large, vinous sigh bubble forth from the depths of what he considers his soul and said, "But they're closing the place and we had better leave. Have you paid the bill?"

Unfortunately, I had.

"And can you lend me a fiver, old man, to get me home?"

Even more unfortunately, I could.

Logic Is Logic

George was not one of those craven souls who felt that the fact that he was not paying for a meal deprived him of the right to criticize it. He expressed his disappointment to me, therefore, with as much delicacy as he could—or as much as he thought I deserved, which is not quite the same thing, of course.

"This smorgasbord," he said, "is distinctly inferior. The meat balls are not hot enough, the herring is not salty enough, the shrimp are not crisp enough, the cheese is not sharp enough, the deviled eggs are not peppery enough, the—"

I said, "George, that's the third heaping plate you've devoured. One more bite and you will have to undergo surgery to release the gastric pressure. Why are you eating so much of this inferior material?"

George said haughtily, "Is it for me to humiliate my host by refusing to eat his food?"

"It's not my food; it's the restaurant's."

"The owner of this miserable hovel is he to whom I am referring. Tell me, old man, why don't you belong to some good club?"

"I? Pay enormous sums for dubious returns?"

"I mean a *good* club, which I can then grace as your guest in return for a sumptuous meal. But no," he added querulously, "that is a mad dream. What good club would compromise its position by allowing you to be a member?"

"Any club that would allow you as a guest would certainly allow me—" I began, but George was already lost in reminiscence.

"I remember," he said, eyes glistening, "when I dined at least once a month at a club that featured the most lavish and the most intricate buffet that ever graced any groaning board since the days of Lucullus."

"I presume you freeloaded as someone's guest."

"I don't know that that is a necessary presumption, but by sheer chance you happen to be correct. It was Alistair Tobago Crump, VI, who was actually the member and, which is more important, my occasional host."

"George," I said, "is this going to be another story in which you and Azazel combine to hurl some poor soul down a declivity of misery and despair in your misguided efforts to help him?"

"I don't know what you mean. We granted him his heart's desire out of sheer kindness and the abstract love of humanity— and my somewhat more concrete love of the buffet. But let me tell you the story from the beginning."

Alistair Tobago Crump, VI, had been a member of the Eden from birth, for his father, Alistair Tobago Crump, V, entered his son's name on the rolls as soon as a personal inspection assured him that the doctor's initial estimate of the infant's sex had been correct. Alistair Tobago Crump, V, had similarly been entered by his father, and so on back to the days when Bill Crump, while sleeping off a drunken stupor, had been pressed into the British Navy just in time to find himself an indignant member of the crew of one of the ships of the fleet that captured New Amsterdam from the Dutch in 1664.

The Eden, as it happens, is the most exclusive club on the North American continent. So haughty is it that its very existence is known only to its members and a very few guests. Even I do not know its location, for I was always taken there blindfolded, in a hansom cab with opaque windows. I can only tell you that for a period of time during the final approach, the horse's hooves passed over a stretch of cobbled road.

No one could belong to the Eden whose ancestry did not extend into the colonial period on both sides of the family. Nor is it ancestry alone that counts. There must be no smudge on the escutcheon. George Washington was blackballed by unanimous vote since he had undeniably rebelled against his sovereign lord.

This same requirement was maintained for any guests, but that did not exclude me, of course. Unlike you, I am not a first-generation immigrant from Dobrudja, or Herzegovina, or some equally unlikely place. My ancestry is impeccable, since all my forebears have infested the territory of this nation since the seventeenth century, and since they, one and all, avoided the sins of rebellion, disloyalty, and un-Americanism during the Revolutionary and Civil wars by cheering both sides impartially as their armies marched past.

My friend Alistair was inordinately proud of his own membership. Many a time and oft did he say to me (for he was one of your classic bores and frequently repeated himself), "George, the Eden is the bone and sinew of my being, the core of my existence. If I had all that wealth and power could bring me, and had not Eden, I would be as naught."

Of course, Alistair *did* have all that wealth and power could bring him, for another requirement for membership at the Eden was great wealth. The annual dues, if nothing else, made that imperative. And again that, in itself, was not enough. The wealth had to be inherited, it could not be earned. Any trace of actually working in return for payment made one clearly ineligible for membership. It was only because my father had thoughtlessly forgotten to leave me several millions of dollars that kept me out of the club, even though I had never undergone the disgrace of working for—

Don't say "I know that," old man. There's no way you could know that.

Naturally, there was no objection to a member's augmenting

his income by interesting methods that did not involve labor for pay. There were always such things as stock manipulation, tax evasion, influence peddling, and other clever devices that come as second nature to the rich.

This was all taken seriously by members of Eden. There had been cases of Edenites who, having lost their money through unaccountable attacks of momentary honesty, preferred to starve slowly to death rather than go to work and lose their membership. Their names are still mentioned in hushed tones and plaques in their honor are to be found in the clubhouse.

No, they couldn't borrow money from fellow members, old man. It's so like you to suggest that. Every member of Eden knows you don't borrow from a rich man when there are uncounted numbers of poor people waiting anxiously in line for the chance to be defrauded. The Bible reminds us that "ye have the poor with you always," and the members of Eden are nothing if not pious.

And yet Alistair was not entirely happy, for it is an unfortunate fact that the membership of the Eden tended to avoid him. I have told you he was a bore. He had no fund of conversation, no cleverness, no opinion of note. In fact, even in the midst of a membership whose total fund of wit and originality was on a fourth-grade grammar-school level, he stood out as remarkably dull.

You can imagine his frustration as he sat there night after night at the Eden alone amidst the crowd. The ocean of conversation, such as it was, washed over him but left him dry. Yet he never missed a night at the club. He even had himself carried there during a violent attach of dysentery in order not to break his record as "Iron Man Crump." This was abstractly admired by the membership, but, for some reason, not widely appreciated.

To be sure, he had the occasional privilege of having me as his guest at the Eden. My ancestry was impeccable, my aristocratic record as a confirmed non-earner was the admiration of all, and in return for the finest of food and the most cobwebby of ambience, all at Crump's expense, I went to the trouble of talking to him and laughing at his perfectly terrible jokes. I found myself pitying the poor fellow from the very bottom of my capacious heart.

Somehow there ought to be some way of making him the life of the party, the toast of Eden, the man with whom ever member longed to be. I pictured aged and respectable Edenites engaged in spavined fisticuffs for the honor of sitting next to him at the evening meal.

After all, Alistair was the very picture of respectability, and all that an Edenite should be. He was tall, he was slim, his face had the look of a ruminative horse, he had lank blond hair, pale blue eyes, and the dull look of formal conservative orthodoxy of a man whose ancestors had all thought sufficiently well of themselves to marry within the clan. All he lacked was any trace of anything in the least interesting to say or do.

But that could surely be fixed. It was a case for Azazel.

For once, Azazel was not annoyed with me for calling him forth from his mystical world. He had been at a banquet of sorts, it seemed, and it had been his turn to pick up the check and I had pulled him away five minutes before that check was due to arrive. He chuckled in a falsetto ululation for, as you know, he is only two centimeters high.

He said, "I will return fifteen minutes later, and by that time someone else will have committed himself to pay that check."

I said, "How will you account for your absence?"

He drew himself up to his full micro-height, twitching his tail. "I will tell them the truth: that I was called away to a conference with an extragalactic monster of extraordinary stupidity, who was in dire need of my intelligence. What do you want this time?"

I told him, and to my amazement he burst into tears. At least he sprayed tiny red spicules from his eyes. I *suppose* they were tears. One got into my mouth and tasted terrible—rather like cheap red wine, or like cheap red wine would taste if I ever allowed myself to taste it.

"How sad," he said. "I know the case of a worthy entity who is constantly snubbed by others who are far his inferiors. I find there is nothing more tragic."

"Who would that be? The entity snubbed, that is."

"I?" he said, thumping his tiny chest till it squeaked.

"I can't imagine that," I said. "You?"

"I can't either," he said, "but it's true just the same. What does this friend of yours do that shows any promise?"

"Well, he does tell jokes. Or he tries to. They're awful. He drones them out, circles the point aimlessly, then forgets it. I have frequently seen a joke of his make a strong man weep."

Azazel shook his head. "Bad. Very bad. Now I happen to be an excellent joke-spinner. Did I ever tell you about the time a plocks and a jinniram were engaged in mutual andesantoree and one of them said—"

"Yes, you did," I said, lying strenuously, "but let us get on to the case of Crump."

Azazel said, "Is there any simple technique that can improve the telling of a joke?"

"A certain glibness, of course," I said.

"Of course," said Azazel. "A mere divalination of the vocal cords could take care of that—assuming you barbarians have such things."

"We do. And then, of course, the ability to handle an accent."

"An accent?"

"Substandard English. Foreigners who have not learned the language as infants but who pick it up in later life invariably mispronounce the vowels, miss out on word order, break up the grammar, and so on."

A look of sheer horror crossed Azazel's tiny face. "But that's a capital offense," he said.

"Not on this world," I said. "It should be, but it isn't."

Azazel shook his head sadly. "Has this friend of yours ever heard these atrocities you call accents?"

"Certainly. Anyone living in New York hears accents of all types at all times. It is correct English such as my own that one hardly ever hears."

"Ah," said Azazel, "it is then only a matter of scapulating the memory."

"What the memory?"

" 'Scapulate,' a form of sharpening, from the word 'scapos' referring to the teeth of a zum-eating dirigin."

"And that will make it possible for him to tell jokes with an accent?"

"Only with those accents he has happened to hear in the course of his life. My powers, after all, are not unlimited."

"Then scapulate away."

A week later I met Alistair Tobago Crump, VI, on Fifth Avenue and Fifty-third Street, and searched his face in vain for any signs of recent triumph.

"Alistair," I said, "have you been telling any jokes lately?"

"George," he said, "no one will listen. There are times when I think I don't tell jokes any better than the average man."

"Well, then, I tell you what. You come with me to a small establishment I know. I will give you a humorous introduction and then you stand up and say anything that's in your mind."

I assure you, old man, it was not easy to persuade him to do this. I had to make use of the full force of my magnetic personality. In the end, though, I won out.

I took him to a rather crummy dive I happened to know. I can describe it best by saying it is rather reminiscent of the places you take me to dinner.

I also happened to know the manager of the dive, which was its great advantage, and I persuaded him to allow me to experiment.

At 11 P.M., when revelry was at its height, I rose to my feet and cowed the audience with my air of dignity. There were only eleven people present, but I felt that was enough with which to experiment.

"Ladies and gentlemen," I said, "we have in our presence a gentleman of great intellect, a master of our language, whom I'm sure you would all love to meet. He is Alistair Tobago Crump, VI, and he is Emersonian Professor of English at Columbia College, and author of 'How To Speak Perfect English.' Professor Crump, will you arise and say a few words to the assembled intellectuals, please."

Crump arose, looking rather confused, and said, "Leesten, denk you ull var' moch."

Well, old man, I've heard you tell jokes in what purports to be a Yiddish accent, but you could pass for a Harvard graduate in comparison to Crump. The thing is that Crump *looked* exactly as you would expect an Emersonian Professor of English to look. And to stare at that woebegone inbred face and suddenly hear a phrase in pure Yinglish knocked the breath out of every person there simultaneously. Such an aroma of alcoholic onions filled the air as you would not believe. And that was followed by a roar of laughter that built up into hysterics.

A look of mild surprise crossed Crump's face. He said to me, in a beautiful Swedish singsong which I won't try to reproduce, "I don't usually get quite *this* strong a reaction."

"Never mind," I said, "keep on talking."

It meant waiting for the laughter to stop which took a while, and then he began telling jokes in Irish brogues, in Scottish burrs, in Cockney, Mitteleuropean, Spanish, Greek. His specialty was clearly Brooklynese, however—your own noble, nearly native tongue, old man.

After that I let him spend some hours at Eden every evening and after dinner I would take him to the establishment. Word of mouth spread the tale. That first night, as I said, the audience had been a sparse one, but in no time at all we had people outside clamoring to get in—and in vain.

Crump took it calmly. In fact, he seemed downcast. He said, "Look, there's no point in wasting all this excellent material of mine on ordinary yokels. I want to show my skill to my fellow members of Eden. They wouldn't listen to my jokes because it had never occurred to me to tell them in dialect. In fact, I didn't realize I could, which just shows the unbelievable self-underestimation into which a quietly humorous and witty fellow such as myself can fall. Just because I am not raucous and do not push myself forward—"

He was speaking in his best Brooklynese, which grates unpleasantly on any delicate ear, if you don't mind my saying so, old man, and so I hastened to assure him that I would take care of everything.

I told the manager of the establishment of the wealth of the members of Eden, neglecting to mention that they were as parsimonious as they were rich. The manager, drooling slightly, sent out complimentary tickets to lure them in. This was on my advice, for I well knew that no true Edenite could resist a free show, especially as I carefully initiated a rumor that stag films would be shown.

The membership showed up in force, and Crump expanded at the sight. "Now I can do it," he said, "I've got a Korean accent that will kill them."

He also had a Southern drawl and a Maine twang that had to be heard to be believed.

The men of Eden, for a few minutes, sat in stony silence, and I had the terrible notion that they didn't understand Crump's subtle humor. But they were only paralyzed with astonishment, and as the astonishment wore off they began to laugh.

Portly bellies shook, pince-nez fell off, white muttonchops waved in the breeze. Every possible disgusting sound—from the dry falsetto cackles of some to the oleaginous base mumblings of others—that could serve to make life hideous proceeded to do so.

Crump expanded at this proper appreciation and the manager, feeling certain that he was at the entrance gate to countless wealth, rushed up to Crump at the intermission and said, "My boy, my boy, I know you asked only for the opportunity to display your art and that you are, and remain above, the filth that people call money, but I can't allow that any longer. Call me foolish. Call me mad. But here, here, my boy, take this check. You have earned it, every penny of it. Lavish it as you will." And with the generosity of the typical entrepreneur who expects millions in return, he pushed into Crump's hand a check for twenty-five dollars.

Well, as I see it, that was the beginning. Crump went on into fame and satisfaction, the idol of the nightclub circuit, the admired of all beholders. Money poured in on him and since he was wealthy beyond the dreams of Croesus due to the industrious orphan-defrauding of his ancestors, he needed none of it, and passed it all on to his business manager—in short, me. Within a year I was a millionaire, and so there goes your characteristically idiotic theory that Azazel and I bring only ill fortune.

I stared at George sardonically. "Since you are several million dollars short of being a millionaire, George, I presume you are now going to tell me it was all a dream."

"Not at all," said George haughtily. "The story is perfectly true, as is every word I utter. And the ending I have just outlined is precisely what would have happened if Alistair Tobago Crump, VI, had not been a fool."

"A fool, was he?"

"Certainly. I leave it to you. Overcome by pride in the munificent twenty-five-dollar check he had received, he framed it, brought it to the Eden and fatuously displayed it to all. What choice did the members have? He had earned money. He had been paid for his labors. They were forced to expel him. And Crump, deprived of his club, went to the injudicious length of having a fatal heart attack in consequence. Surely none of that was the fault of Azazel or myself."

"But if he framed the check, he wasn't really taking any money."

George raised a magisterial right hand as he shoved the bill for the evening meal in my direction with his left. "It is the principle of the thing. I told you the Edenites were strong on religion. When Adam was expelled from Eden, God told him that from then on he would have to work in order to make a living. I think the exact words were 'In the sweat of thy face shalt thou eat bread.' It follows then that, in reverse, if you work to make a living you have to be expelled from Eden. Logic is logic."

He Travels the Fastest

I had just returned from a trip to Williamsburg, Virginia, and my relief at getting back to my beloved typewriter and word processor was mingled with a residue of faint resentment at my having had to go in the first place.

George did not consider the fact that he had just ravened his way through the offerings of a fine restaurant at my hard-earned expense, an adequate reason for offering me sympathy.

He said, after he had dislodged a fiber of steak from between two teeth, "I do not really understand, old fellow, why you should find fault over the fact that otherwise respectable organizations seem to be willing to pay you thousands of dollars to listen to you talk for an hour. Having heard you speak now and then, I would think it far more likely that you speak without charge and refuse to stop unless they pay you thousands of dollars. Surely, the latter is the more likely way of squeezing money out of people—though I have no wish to hurt your feelings, assuming you have any."

"When did you ever hear me speak?" I asked. "The interstices in your own maunderings allow no one more than two dozen words at a time." (Naturally I was careful to make my point in just twenty-four words.)

George ignored me, as I was sure he would. "It shows a particularly unlovely side of your soul," he said, "that in your mad lust for the dross called 'money' you should so freely and frequently consent to undergo the pains of the travel you claim to hate. It reminds me a bit of the tale of Sophocles Moskowitz who had a similar lazy disinclination to stir from his armchair except when the further swelling of his already gross bank account was in view. This disinclination he also euphemized by calling it 'an aversion to travel.' It took my friend Azazel to change *that.*"

"Don't you get your two-centimeter disaster-demon after me," I said in alarm, an alarm that was just as real as it would have been if I had actual cause to think that that figment of George's diseased imagination really existed.

George again ignored me.

It was actually [George said] one of the first times I ever called upon Azazel for help. It was almost thirty years ago, you see. I had only recently learned how to draw the little creature from his own plane, and I had not yet learned to understand his powers.

He boasted of them, to be sure, but where is the living creature, other than myself, who does not consistently overstate his or her own powers and abilities?

I was much more familiar at that time with a magnificent young woman named Fifi who had, a year earlier, decided that Sophocles Moskowitz would not, in person, sufficiently detract from the kind of husband his large fortune would make for her.

Even after they married, she remained a surreptitious, though inexplicably virtuous, friend of mine. Despite her virtue, I was always glad to see her, however, something you will understand when I tell you that her figure was one thing that could *not* be overstated. In her presence I always remembered, with austere satisfaction, certain amiable indelicacies in which we had participated in the past.

"Boom-Boom," I said, for I had never gotten out of the habit of using her stage name, given her by the common consent of the

awed observers of her interesting act, "you are looking well."
This I had no hesitation in saying, for so was I.

"Oh yeah?" she said, in the insouciant manner that always
recalled the streets of New York in all their brassy splendor.
"Well, I ain't feeling good."

I could not believe that for a moment, for if my memory could
be trusted, she must have felt very good indeed from early ado-
lescence, but I said, "What is the trouble, my resilient dear?"

"It's Sophocles, that creep."

"Surely you're not annoyed with your husband, Boom-Boom.
It is impossible for so wealthy a man to be annoying."

"That's all *you* know. What a four-flusher! Listen, you remember you told me Sophocles was as rich as some guy named
Croesus, which is a guy I never heard of? Well, how come you
never told me this guy named Croesus must have been a champion tightwad."

"Sophocles is a tightwad?"

"Champion! Can you beat it? What's the use of marrying a
rich guy who's a tightwad?"

"Surely, Boom-Boom, you can manage to wheedle a little
money out of him by the elusive promise of nocturnal Elysium."

Fifi's forehead crinkled a bit. "I'm not sure what that means,
but I know you, so don't talk dirty. Besides, I promised him he
wouldn't get it, whatever it was you said, if he didn't loosen up,
but he would rather squeeze his wallet than me and, if you think
of it, that's pretty darned insulting." The poor thing whimpered
softly.

I patted her hand in as unbrotherly a fashion as I could manage on short notice.

She burst out passionately, "When I married that bum, I
thought, 'Well, Fifi, here's where you get to go to Paris and the
Riveera and Bonus Airs and Casablanca and like that.' —Huh!
Not a chance!"

"Don't tell me that hound won't take you to Paris."

"He won't go *nowhere*. He says he don't want to leave Man-
hattan. He says he don't like it out there. He says he don't like

plants and trees and animals and grass and dirt and foreigners and any buildings except New York buildings. I say, 'How about some nice shopping mall?' but he don't like that neither."

"Why don't you go without him, Boom-Boom?"

"That would be more fun than with him, you can bet. But with what? That guy's got his pants pockets sewed up with all his credit cards inside. I've got to do all my shopping at Macy's." Her voice rose to a near shriek. "I didn't marry that bozo to shop at Macy's."

I gazed speculatively at various portions of the damsel and regretted that I could not afford them. Before she married, she was occasionally willing to make a contribution to the cause in an art-for-art's sake manner, but I had a feeling that her nobler status as a married woman had hardened her professional view of the matter. In those days, you must understand, I was even more vigorous than I am now in my present prime of life, but I was as unacquainted with the coin of the realm then as now.

I said, "Suppose I could talk him into liking to travel?"

"Oh, boy, I sure wish someone could."

"Suppose *I* could. I suppose you would be grateful."

Her eye rested on me reminiscently. "George," she said, "the day he tells me he's taking me to Paris, you and I do an Asbury Park number. Remember Asbury Park?"

Did I remember that New Jersey coastal resort? Could I forget my aching muscles? Every part of me, almost, was stiff for two days afterward.

I discussed the matter with Azazel over some beer, a stein for me and a drop for him. He found the hops delightfully stimulating. Cautiously I said to him, "Azazel, can those magical powers of yours really do things that would amaze me?"

He looked at me with a soused expression. "Just tell me what you want. Just tell me what you want. I'll show you whether I'm 'old fumble-hands' or not. I'll show them all."

Once, in a moment of stupefaction over some lemon-scented furniture polish (he found the peel extract mind-expanding, he said) he told me that he had once been insulted in that fashion on his own world.

I let him have another drop of beer, and said carelessly, "I have a friend who does not like to travel. I suppose it would be as nothing for a person as skilled and advanced as yourself to change that dislike into an absolute fever to travel."

I must admit some of his eagerness vanished at once. "What I meant," he said, in his whistling voice and odd accent, "was for you to ask something sensible—like making that ugly picture on the wall hang straight by the power of my mind alone." The picture moved as he spoke, and hung crookedly in the other direction.

"Yes, but why should I want my pictures straightened?" I said. "I go to great trouble to get them to hang at a precisely correct nonrectilinear angle. What I do want is to have you imbue Sophocles Moskowitz with a travel mania, one that would lead him to travel, if necessary, even without his wife." I added that because it occurred to me that there might be advantages to having Fifi in town, on occasion, with Sophocles out of town.

Azazel said, "That is not easy. An ingrained dislike for travel may well depend on various brain-deforming childhood experiences. It would require mental engineering of the most advanced sort to make up for that. I don't say it can't be done, since the crude minds of your people are not easily damaged, but I would have to have the person pointed out to me, so that I could identify his mind and study it."

That was easy enough. I had Fifi invite me to dinner as an old college classmate. (She had spent some time on a college campus a few years back, though I don't think she attended classes. She was very extracurricular.)

I brought Azazel with me in my jacket pocket and could occasionally hear him squeaking elaborate mathematical formulas under his breath. I assumed he was analyzing Sophocles Moskowitz's mind, and if so that was an impressive feat, for it did not take much conversation for me to appreciate the fact that his mind was not large enough to allow much scope for analysis.

Once home, I said to Azazel, "Well?"

With an airy wave of his scaly little arm he said, "I can do it. Do you have a multiphase, mento-dynamic synaptometer handy?"

"Not handy," I said. "I lent mine out yesterday to a friend of mine who was leaving for Australia."

"That was stupid of you," grumbled Azazel. "That means I'll have to work by tablecloth calculations."

He remained querulous, too, even after he had finished (as he maintained) successfully.

"It was almost impossible," he said. "Only a person of my own magnificent attainments could have done it and I had to pin down his mind into its present adjusted form with huge spikes."

I took it he was speaking metaphorically, and said so.

To which Azazel replied, "Well, it might as well be huge spikes. No one will be able to budge his mind after this. He's just going to want to travel with such overwhelming firmness that he could almost shake the universe if that was what would be required to make the travel possible. *That* will show those—"

He burst out into a long string of strident syllables in his native language. I didn't understand what he said, of course, but it was quite clear from the fact that the ice cubes in the refrigerator in the next room had all melted that what he said was uncomplimentary. I suspected he was casting some animadversions on those on his native world who had accused him of lack of deftness.

It was not more than three days later that Fifi phoned me. She is not as effective on the phone as in person for reasons that are quite obvious, although, perhaps, not to you with your congenital inability to take note of the finer things of life. One is more aware of the slight hardness in her voice, you see, when one is not able to be directly reminded of a counterbalancing softness elsewhere.

"George," she cackled, "you must be magic. I don't know what you did at that dinner but it worked. Sophocles is going to take me to Paris. It's his own idea and he's awful excited about it. Ain't that great?"

"It's more than great," I said with natural enthusiasm. "It is earth-shaking. We can now indulge in that little promise you made. We can do a repeat of Asbury Park and shake the earth."

Women, however, as even you may have noticed from time to time, lack the feeling that a bargain is sacred. They are quite different from men in this respect. They seem to have no conception of the importance of keeping their word, no feeling for honor.

She said, "We're leaving tomorrow, George, so I ain't got time right now. I'll call you when I get back."

She hung up and that was that. The woman had twenty-four hours to spare and I would scarcely have used half of them—but off she went.

I *did* hear from her when she returned, but that was six months later.

She phoned me again, and at first I didn't recognize her voice. There was something haggard and worn-out about it.

"To whom am I speaking?" I asked with my usual dignity.

She said wearily, "This is Fifi Laverne Moskowitz."

"Boom-Boom," I cried. "You're back! Marvelous! Come on over right now, and let's—"

She said, "George, drop dead! If it's your magic, you're a miserable phony and I wouldn't Asbury Park with you if you could hang by your toes twice as long."

I was astonished. "Didn't Sophocles take you to Paris?"

"Yes, he did. Now ask me did I get my shopping done."

I was willing. "Did you get your shopping done?"

"Like fun! I didn't even get it begun. Sophocles never stopped!" Her voice shed its weariness and, under the stress of emotion, rose to a shriek.

"We reached Paris and kept right on going. He kept pointing out things as we passed at top speed. 'That's the Eiffel Tower,' he said, pointing to some stupid building under construction.

'That's Notre Dame,' he said. He didn't even know what he was talking about. Two football players once smuggled me into Notre Dame and it ain't in Paris. It's in South Bend, Indiana.

"But who cares? We went on to Frankfurt and Bern and Vienna, which them stupid foreigners call Veen. Is there someplace called Treest?"

"Trieste," I said. "Yes, there is."

"Then we went there, too. And we never stopped off at hotels. We stopped at old farmhouses. Sophocles said that was the way to travel. He said you saw the people and nature. Who wants to see people and nature? What we didn't see was showers. And plumbing. After a while you get so, you smell. And I got *things* in my hair. I just now took five showers and I'm *still* not clean."

"Take five more showers in my place," I urged in the most reasonable possible way, "and we can Asbury Park it."

She didn't seem to hear me. It's amazing how deaf women are to simple reason. She said, "He's getting started again next week. He said he wants to cross the Pacific and go to Hong Kong. He's going on an oil freighter. He says that's the way to see the ocean. I said, 'Listen, you screwball creep, you ain't going to get me on no slow boat to China so I can be all to yourself alone.'"

"Very poetic," I said.

"And you know what he said? He said, 'Very well, my dear. I'll go without you.' Then he said something real weird because it made no sense. He said, 'Down to Gehenna or up to the Throne, he travels the fastest who travels alone.' What does that mean? What's Gehenna? How did a throne get into it? Does he think he's Queen of England?"

"It's Kipling," I said.

"Don't be crazy. I never kippled so don't tell me he did. He can hardly do it missionary. I told him I'd divorce him and take him to the cleaners. And he said, 'Suit yourself, my submoronic dear, but you have no grounds and will get nothing. All that is important to me is travel.' Can you beat that? And that submoronic bit. Still trying to sweet-talk me."

You've got to understand, old fellow, that this was one of Azazel's first jobs for me and he hadn't learned control. And I *had* asked him to have Sophocles travel without his wife on occasion.

There was still the advantage to such a situation that I had foreseen from the start. "Boom-Boom," I said, "let's talk over the divorce together between Asbury—"

"And you, you miserable wimp. Whatever magic, or whatever you did, I don't care. Just stay out of my life because I know a guy who will squash you into pancakes as soon as I give him the word. And he kipples, too, because he does everything else."

Boom-Boom, I'm afraid, had gone Bust-Bust, though not in a way I would have wanted her to or, knowing her measurements and style, expected her to.

I called on Azazel but, though he tried, there was no way he could undo what he had done. And he flatly refused to try anything toward making Boom-Boom more reasonable toward me. He said that would be too much for anyone. I don't know why.

He kept track of Sophocles for me, however. The man's mania grew. He crossed the Continental Divide on his hands. He went up the Nile on water skis, all the way to Lake Victoria. He crossed Antarctica on a hang glider.

When President Kennedy announced in 1961 that we would reach the moon by the end of the decade, Azazel said, "That's my adjustment doing its work again."

I said, "You mean that whatever you did to his brain gives him the power to influence the President and the space program?"

"He doesn't do it on purpose," said Azazel, "but I told you the adjustment was strong enough to shake the universe."

And he did go on to the moon, old chap. Remember *Apollo 13*, that was supposedly wrecked in space on the way to the moon in 1970, with the crew just barely getting back to Earth? Actually, Sophocles had stowed away on it and had taken a portion of it to the moon, leaving the actual crew to get back to Earth as best they could with the rest.

He's been on the moon ever since, traveling all over its surface. He has no air, no food, no water, but his adjustment to continual travel must somehow take care of that. In fact, something may have worked out by now to take him to Mars—and elsewhere.

George shook his head sadly. "So ironic. So ironic."

"What's ironic?" I asked.

"Don't you see? Poor Sophocles Moskowitz! He is a new and improved version of the Wandering Jew, and the irony is that he isn't even Orthodox."

George put his left hand to his eyes and fumbled for his napkin with his right hand. In doing so, he accidentally picked up the ten-dollar-bill I had placed at the side of the table as a tip for the waiter. He mopped his eyes with his napkin but I didn't see what happened to the ten-dollar-bill. He left the restaurant sobbing, and the table bare.

I sighed and put out another ten-dollar-bill.

The Eye of the Beholder

George and I were sitting on a bench at the boardwalk and contemplating the broad expanse of the beach and the sparkling sea in the distance. I was immersed in the innocent pleasure of watching the young ladies in their bikinis and wondering what they could get out of the beauties of life that was half as much as they contributed.

Knowing George as I did, I rather suspected his own thoughts to be considerably less nobly aesthetic than mine. I was certain that they would deal with the more useful aspects of those same young ladies.

It was with considerable surprise, then, that I heard him say, "Old man, here we sit drinking in the beauties of nature in the shape of the female form divine—to coin a phrase—and yet surely true beauty is not, and cannot be, so evident. True beauty, after all, is so precious that it must be hidden from the eyes of trivial observers. Have you ever thought that?"

"No," I said, "I've never thought that and, now that you mention it, I still don't. What's more, I don't think that you have ever thought that."

George sighed. "Talking with you, old chap, is like swimming in molasses—very little return for very great effort. I have watched you observing that tall goddess there, the one whose wisps of fine textile do nothing to conceal the few square inches

they purport to cover. Surely you understand that those are
mere superficialities that she displays."

"I have never asked for much out of life," I said in my humble
way. "I'll be satisfied with superficialities of that sort."

"Think how much more beautiful a young woman would be,
even a woman quite unprepossessing to the untutored eyes of
one such as you, if she possessed the eternal glories of goodness,
unselfishness, cheerfulness, uncomplaining industry, and concern for others—all the virtues, in short, that shed gold and
grace on a woman."

"What I'm thinking, George," I said, "is that you must be
drunk. What on earth can you possibly know about virtues such
as those?"

"I am totally familiar with them," said George haughtily, "because I practice them assiduously, and to the full."

"Undoubtedly," I said, "only in the privacy of your own room
and in the dark."

Disregarding your crude remark [George said], I must explain
that even if I did not have personal knowledge of these virtues, I
would have learned of them through my acquaintance with a
young woman named Melisande Ott, née Melisande Renn, and
known to her loving husband Octavius Ott as Maggie. She was
known to me as Maggie also, for she was the daughter of a dear
friend of mine, now, alas, deceased, and she always considered
me her Uncle George.

I must admit that there is a bit of me that, like you, appreci-
ates the subtle qualities of what you call 'superficialities.'—Yes,
old boy, I know I used the term first but we will not get anywhere if you are going to interrupt me constantly over triviali-
ties.

Because of this small weakness in myself, I must also admit
that when, in an access of joy at seeing me, she would squeal and
throw her arms about me, my delight at the event was not quite
as great as it would have been had she been more generously
proportioned. She was quite thin and her bones were painfully

prominent. Her nose was large, her chin weak, her hair rather lank and straight and pure mouse in color, and her eyes an undefinable gray-green. Her cheekbones were broad, so that she rather resembled a chipmunk that had just completed a fine collection of nuts and seeds. In short, she was not the type of young woman whose arrival on the scene would cause any young man present to begin breathing rapidly and striving to get closer.

But she had a good heart. She bore up, with a wistful smile, at the visible winces that shook the average young man who met her for the first time without warning. She served as bridesmaid for all her friends in turn with a fresh group of wistful smiles. She served as godmother to innumerable children, and as baby-sitter to others, and was as deft a bottle feeder as you could see in a long month of Sundays.

She brought hot soup to the deserving poor, and to the undeserving as well, though there were some who said that it was the undeserving who more nearly deserved the visitation. She performed various duties at the local church, several times over—once for herself and once each for those of her friends who preferred the guilty splendors of the movie palaces to selfless service. She taught classes at Sunday school, keeping the children cheerful by making (as they thought) funny faces at them. She also frequently led them all in a reading of the nine commandments. (She left out the one about adultery, for experience had taught her that this invariably led to inconvenient questions.) She also served as a volunteer at the local branch of the public library.

Naturally, she lost all hope of getting married somewhere about the age of four. Even the chance of having a casual date with a member of the opposite sex seemed to her to be a rather impossible dream by the time she had reached the age of ten.

Many a time she would say to me, "I am not unhappy, Uncle George. The world of men is sealed to me, yes, always excepting your dear self and the memory of poor Papa, but there is far more true happiness in doing good."

She would then visit the prisoners in the county jail in order to plead for repentance, and for conversion to good works. It was only one or two of the crasser sort who volunteered for solitary confinement on those days on which she was due to arrive.

But then she met Octavius Ott, a newcomer to the neighborhood, a young electrical engineer with a responsible position at the power company. He was a worthy young man—grave, industrious, persevering, courageous, honest, and reverent—but he was not what you or I would call handsome. In fact, not to put too fine a point on it, he was not what anyone in recorded history would have called handsome.

He had a receding hairline—or, more accurately, a receded one—a bulbous forehead, a snub nose, thin lips, ears that stood well away from his head, and a prominent Adam's apple that was never entirely still. What there was of his hair was rather rust-colored, and he had an irregular sprinkling of freckles on his face and arms.

I happened to be with Maggie when she and Octavius met in the street for the first time. Both were equally unprepared and both started like a pair of skittish horses suddenly confronted by a dozen clowns in a dozen fright wigs who were blowing a dozen whistles. For a moment, I expected both Maggie and Octavius to rear and whinny.

The moment passed, however, and each successfully weathered the flash of panic they had experienced. She did nothing more than place her hand on her heart as though to keep it from leaping out of the rib cage in search of a more secure hiding place, while he wiped his brow as though to erase a horrid memory.

I had met Octavius some days before and so I was able to introduce them to each other. Each held out a tentative hand as though not anxious to add the sense of touch to that of vision.

Later that afternoon, Maggie broke a long silence and said to me, "What an odd young man that Mr. Ott seems to be."

I said, with that originality of metaphor which my friends all enjoy, "You mustn't judge a book by its cover, my dear."

"But the cover exists, Uncle George," she said earnestly, "and we must take that into account. I dare say that the average young woman, frivolous and unfeeling, would have little do with Mr. Ott. It would be a deed of kindness, therefore, to show him that not all young women are totally heedless, but that one at least does not turn against a young man for nothing more than his unfortunate resemblance to—to—" she paused as no comparable member of the animal kingdom occurred to her, so that she had to end lamely, but warmly, with, "whatever it is that he resembles. I must be kind to him."

I do not know whether Octavius had a confidant to whom he could unburden himself in similar fashion. Probably not, for few of us, if any, are blessed with Uncle Georges. Nevertheless I'm quite certain, judging from later events, that precisely the same thoughts occurred to him—in reverse, of course.

In any case, each labored to be kind to the other, tentatively and hesitantly at first, then warmly, and at last passionately. What began as casual encounters at the library became visits to the zoo, then an evening at the movies, then dances, until what finally took place could only be described—if you'll excuse my language—as trysts.

People began to expect to see one whenever they saw the other, for they had become an indissoluble pair. Some of those in the neighborhood complained bitterly that to get a double dose of Octavius and Maggie was more than the human eye could be expected to endure, and more than one supercilious elitist invested in sunglasses.

I will not say that I was totally lacking in sympathy for these extreme views, but others—more tolerant and, perhaps, more reasonable—pointed out that the features on one were, by some peculiar chance, quite opposite to the corresponding features of the other. Seeing the two together tended to introduce a canceling effect, so that both together were more endurable than either separately. Or at least that was what some claimed.

Finally there came a day when Maggie burst in on me and said, "Uncle George, Octavius is the light and life of my existence. He is staunch, strong, steady, sturdy, and stable. He is a lovely man."

"Internally, my dear," I said, "I'm sure he is all of these things. His outward appearance, however, is—"

"Adorable," she said staunchly, strongly, steadily, sturdily, and stably. "Uncle George, he feels about me as I feel about him, and we are going to be married."

"You and Otto?" I said faintly. An involuntary image of the likely issue of such a marriage swam before my eyes and I turned rather faint.

"Yes," she said. "He has told me that I am the sun of his delight and the moon of his joy. Then he added that I was all the stars of his happiness. He is a very poetic man."

"So it seems," I said dubiously. "When are you going to be married?"

"As soon as possible," she said.

There was nothing to do but grit my teeth. The announcement was made, the preparations were carried through, the marriage was performed with myself giving away the bride. Everyone in the neighborhood attended out of disbelief. Even the minister allowed a reverent look of astonishment to cross his face.

Nor did anyone seem to gaze gladly at the young couple. All through the ceremony, the audience stared at its various knees. Except the minister. He kept his eyes firmly fixed on the rose window over the front door.

I left the neighborhood some time after, took up lodgings in another part of the city, and rather lost touch with Maggie. Eleven years later, however, I had occasion to return over a matter of an investment in a friend's learned studies of the racing qualities of horses. I seized the opportunity of visiting Maggie, who was, among her other well-hidden beauties, a marvelous cook.

I arrived at lunch time. Octavius was away at work, but that didn't matter. I am not a selfish man and I gladly ate his portion in addition to mine.

I could not help but notice, however, that there was a shade of grief on Maggie's face. I said, over the coffee, "Are you unhappy, Maggie? Is your marriage not going well?"

"Oh, no, Uncle George," she said vehemently; "our marriage was made in heaven. Although we remain childless, we are so wrapped up in each other that we are barely aware of the loss. We live in a sea of perpetual bliss and have nothing more to ask of the universe."

"I see," I said, my teeth rather on edge. "Then why this shade of grief I seem to detect in you?"

She hesitated, and then burst out, "Oh, Uncle George, you are such a sensitive man. There *is* one thing that does interpose a bit of grit in the wheels of delight."

"And that is?"

"My appearance."

"Your appearance? What is wrong—" I swallowed and found myself unable to finish the sentence.

"I am not beautiful," said Maggie, with the air of one imparting a well-hidden secret.

"Ah!" I said.

"And I wish I were—for Octavius's sake. I want to be lovely just for him."

"Does he complain about your appearance?" I asked cautiously.

"Octavius? Certainly not. He bears his suffering in noble silence."

"Then how do you know he is suffering?"

"My woman's heart tells me so."

"But Maggie, Octavius is himself—well—not beautiful."

"How can you say that?" said Maggie indignantly. "He's gorgeous."

"But perhaps he thinks *you're* gorgeous."

"Oh, no," said Maggie, "how could he think that?"

"Well, is he interested in other women?"

"Uncle George!" said Maggie, shocked. "What a base thought. I'm surprised at you. Octavius has no eyes for anyone but me."

"Then what does it matter if you are beautiful or not?"

"It's for *him,*" she said. "Oh, Uncle George, I want to be beautiful for *him.*"

And, leaping into my lap in a most unexpected and unpleasant way, she moistened the lapel of my jacket with her tears. In fact, it was wringing wet before she was quite through.

I had by then, of course, met Azazel, the two-centimeter demon I may have mentioned to you on occa— Now, old man, there is no need for you to mutter "ad nauseam" in that supercilious manner. Anyone who writes as you do should be embarrassed at bringing up the thought of nausea in any connection whatever.

In any case, I called up Azazel.

Azazel was asleep when he arrived. He had a bag of some green material covering his tiny head and only the muffled sound of quick soprano squeaking from within gave evidence that he was alive. That, and the fact that every once in a while his little sinewy tail stiffened and vibrated with a tinny hum.

I waited several minutes for him to wake up naturally, and when that did not happen I gently removed his head-bag with a pair of tweezers. His eyes opened slowly and focused on me, whereupon he gave an exaggerated start.

He said, "For a moment I thought I was merely having a nightmare. I didn't count on *you!*"

I ignored his childish petulance and said, "I have a task for you to do for me."

"Naturally," said Azazel sourly. "You don't suppose I am expecting you to offer to do a task for me."

"I would in a moment," I said suavely, "if my inferior abilities were sufficient to do anything a personage of your stature and power would find of significant use."

"True, true," said Azazel, mollified.

It is truly disgusting, I might add, the susceptibility of some minds to flattery. I've seen you, for instance, go out of your mind with fatuous joy when someone asks you for an autograph. But back to my tale—

"What is involved?" asked Azazel.

"I wish you to make a young woman beautiful."

Azazel shuddered. "I'm not sure I could bring myself to do that. The standards of beauty among your bloated and miserable species of life are atrocious."

"But they are ours. I will tell you what to do."

"*You* will tell *me* what to do!" he shrieked, vibrating with outrage. "*You* will tell *me* how to stimulate and modify hair follicles, how to strengthen muscles, how to grow or dissolve bone? Indeed! *You* will tell *me* all this?"

"Not at all," I said humbly. "The details of the mechanism that such a deed would require are only to be handled by a being of your magnificent attainments. Allow me, however, to tell you the superficial effects to be achieved."

Azazel was once again mollified, and we went over the matter in detail.

"Remember," I said, "the effects are to be brought to fruition over a period of at least sixty days. A too-sudden change might excite remark."

"Do you mean," said Azazel, "I'm to spend sixty of your days supervising and adjusting and correcting? Is my time worth nothing in your opinion?"

"Ah, but you could then write this up for one of your world's biological journals. It is not a task that many on your world would have the ability or patience to undertake. You will be greatly admired as a result."

Azazel nodded thoughtfully. "I scorn cheap adulation, of course," he said, "but I suppose I have a duty to hold myself up as a role model for inferior members of my species." He sighed with a shrill, whistling sound. "It is troublesome and embarrassing, but it is my duty."

I had a duty as well. I felt I ought to remain in the neighborhood during the interval of change. My horse-racing friend put me up in return for my expertise and advice on the results of various experimental runnings, with the result that he lost very little money.

Each day I sought an excuse to see Maggie and the results slowly began to show. Her hair grew fuller-bodied, and developed a graceful wave. Red-gold glints began to appear, lending it a welcome richness.

Little by little, her jawbone grew more prominent, her cheekbones more delicate and higher. Her eyes developed a definite blue that deepened from day to day to what was almost violet. The eyelids developed just the tiniest oriental slant. Her ears grew more shapely and lobes appeared. Her figure rounded and grew almost opulent, bit by bit, and her waist narrowed.

People were puzzled. I heard them myself. "Maggie," they would say, "what have you done to yourself? Your hair looks simply marvelous. You look ten years younger."

"I haven't done *anything,*" Maggie would say. She was as puzzled as all the others were. Except me, of course.

She said to me, "Do you notice any change in me, Uncle George?"

I said, "You look delightful, but you have always looked delightful to me, Maggie."

"Maybe so," she said, "but I have never looked delightful to me until recently. I don't understand it. Yesterday a bold young man turned to look at me. They always used to hurry by, shading their eyes. This one *winked* at me, however. It caught me so by surprise, I actually smiled at him."

A few weeks later I met her husband, Octavius, at a restaurant, where I was studying the menu in the window. Since he was about to enter it to order a meal, it was the work of a moment for him to invite me to join him and the work of half another moment for me to accept.

"You look unhappy, Octavius," I said.

"I *am* unhappy," he said, "I don't know what's got into Maggie lately. She seems so distracted that she doesn't notice me half the time. She wants to be constantly socializing. And yesterday . . ." A look of such woebegone misery suffused his face that almost anyone would have been ashamed of laughing at it.

"Yesterday?" I said. "What of yesterday?"

"Yesterday she asked me to call her—Melisande. I can't call Maggie a ridiculous name like Melisande."

"Why not? It's her baptismal name."

"But she's my Maggie. Melisande is some stranger."

"Well, she has changed a bit," I said. "Haven't you noticed that she looks more beautiful these days?"

"Yes," said Octavius, biting off the word.

"Isn't that a good thing?"

"No," he said, more sharply still. "I want my plain, funny-looking Maggie. This new Melisande is always fixing her hair, and putting on different shades of eye shadow, and trying on new clothes and bigger bras, and hardly ever talking to me."

The lunch ended in a dejected silence on his part.

I thought I had better see Maggie and have a good talk with her.

"Maggie," I said.

"Please call me Melisande," she said.

"Melisande," I said, "it seems to me that Octavius is unhappy."

"Well, so am I," she said tartly. "Octavius is getting to be such a bore. He won't go out. He won't have fun. He objects to my clothes, my makeup. Who on earth does he think he is?"

"You used to think he was a king among men."

"The more fool I. He's just an ugly little fellow I'm embarrassed to be seen with."

"You wanted to be beautiful just for him."

"What do you mean *wanted* to be beautiful? I *am* beautiful. I was always beautiful. It was just a matter of developing a good hairstyle and knowing how to fix my makeup just right. I can't let Octavius stand in my way."

And she didn't. Half a year later, she and Octavius were divorced and in another half year Maggie—or Melisande—was married again to a man of superficial good looks and unworthy character. I once dined with him and he hesitated so long at picking up the check, I was afraid I might have to pick it up myself.

I saw Octavius about a year after his divorce. He, of course, had not remarried, for he was as odd-looking as ever and milk still curdled in his presence. We were sitting in his apartment which was filled with photos of Maggie, the old Maggie, each one more atrocious than the next.

"You must still be missing her, Octavius," I said.

"Dreadfully!" he replied. "I can only hope she is happy."

"I understand she isn't," I said. "She may come back to you."

Sadly, he shook his head. "Maggie can never come back to me. A woman named Melisande may wish to come back but I couldn't accept her if she did. She isn't Maggie—my lovely Maggie."

"Melisande," I said, "is more beautiful than Maggie."

He stared at me for a long time. "In whose eyes?" he said. "Certainly, not in mine."

It was the last time I saw either of them.

I sat for a moment in silence, then I said, "You amaze me, George. I was actually touched."

It was a poor choice of words. George said, "That reminds me, old fellow—Could I touch you for five dollars for about a week? Ten days tops."

I reached for a five-dollar bill, hesitated, then said, "Here! The story is worth it. It's a gift. It's yours." (Why not? All loans to George are gifts *de facto.*)

George took the bill without comment and put it in his well-worn wallet. (It must have been well-worn when he bought it, for he never uses it.) He said, "To get back to the subject. Could I touch you for five dollars for about a week? Ten days tops."

I said, "But you *have* five dollars."

"That is *my* money," said George, "and no business of yours.

Do I comment on the state of your finances when you borrow money from me?"

"But I have never—" I began, then sighed and handed over five dollars more.

More Things in Heaven and Earth

George had been unusually quiet during dinner and had not even bothered to stop me when I took the trouble to tell him a few of the many bons mots I had committed in the course of the last few days. A light sneer at my best mot was all I got out of him.

Then, over dessert (hot blueberry pie à la mode) he heaved a sigh from the bottom of his abdomen, giving me a not entirely welcome reprise of the shrimps scampi he had eaten earlier in the meal.

"What is it, George?" I asked. "Something seems to be on your mind."

"You amaze me," said George, "by showing this unwonted sensitivity. Usually you are far too wrapped up in your own miserable writing chores to note another's sufferings."

"Yes, but as long as I've noted it," I said, "let's not waste the effort it has cost me."

"I was merely thinking of an old friend of mine. Poor fellow. Vissarion Johnson, his name was. I suppose you never heard of him."

"As it happens," I said, "I never did."

"Well, such is fame, although I suppose it is no disgrace to remain unknown to a person of your limited vision. As it happens, Vissarion was a great economist."

"Surely you jest," I said. "How did you become acquainted with an economist? It sounds like an unusual degree of slumming even for you."

"Slumming? Vissarion Johnson was a man of great learning."

"I don't doubt that for a moment," I said. "It's the integrity of the entire profession I wonder about. There is the story about President Reagan who had grown worried about the federal budget and, in trying to work it out, said to a physicist, 'What is two and two?' The physicist replied at once, 'Four, Mr. President.'

"Reagan considered this a moment, making use of his fingers, and found himself dissatisfied. He therefore asked a statistician, 'What is two and two?' The statistician replied, after some thought, 'The latest poll among fourth-graders, Mr. President, reveals a set of answers that averages fairly close to four.'

"But it was the budget that was under question, so Reagan felt he should carry the question to the top. He asked an economist, therefore, 'What is two and two?' The economist pulled down the shades, looked quickly from side to side, then whispered, 'What would you like the answer to be, Mr. President?' "

George did not by word or facial expression indicate any amusement at this. He said, "You clearly know nothing at all about economics, old fellow."

"Neither do economists, George," I said.

"So let me tell you the sad tale of my good friend the economist Vissarion Johnson. It happened some years ago."

Vissarion Johnson, as I told you [said George], was an economist who was at or near the top of his profession. He had studied at Massachusetts Institute of Technology where he had learned how to write equations of the most abstruse kind, without as much as a tremble of the chalk.

Upon graduation, he entered into practice at once and, thanks to the funds made available to him by a number of clients, learned a great deal about the importance of chance vicissitudes on the daily drift of the stock market. Such was his skill that a few of his clients scarcely lost anything at all.

On a number of occasions he was daring enough to predict that on the morrow the stock market would go either up or down depending on whether the atmosphere was favorable or unfavorable, respectively, and in each case the market did exactly as he had predicted.

Naturally, triumphs such as these made him famous as the Jackal of Wall Street and his advice was sought after by many of the most famous practitioners of the art of making a fast buck.

But he had his eyes fixed on something greater than the stock market, something greater than business machinations, something greater even than the ability to foretell the future. What he wanted was nothing less than the rank of Chief Economist of the United States, or as this functionary is more familiarly known, "economic adviser to the President."

You, with your limited interests, can scarcely be expected to know the extremely delicate position of Chief Economist. The President of the United States must make the decisions that determine governmental regulations of trade and of business. He must control the money supply and the banks. He must suggest or veto measures that will affect agriculture, commerce, and industry. He must decide the divisions of the tax dollar, determining how much of it goes for the military, and whether anything is accidentally left over for anything else. And in all these things he turns, first and foremost, to the Chief Economist for advice.

And when the President turns to him, the Chief Economist must be able to decide instantly and exactly what it is the President wants to hear, and must give it to him together with the necessary meaningless catchphrases which the President can then, in turn, present to the American public. When you told me the tale of the President, the physicist, the statistician, and the economist, old fellow, I thought for a moment that you understood the delicate nature of the economist's task, but your entirely inappropriate cackle of laughter afterward showed me plainly that you had missed the point altogether.

By the time Vissarion was forty, he had achieved all the qualifications needed for any post, however high. It was widely bruited through the halls of the Institute of Governmental Economics that Vissarion Johnson had not once in the last seven years told anyone anything he or she did not want to hear. What's more, he had been voted into the small circle of the CDR by acclamation.

You, in your inexperience of anything beyond your typewriter, have probably never heard of the CDR, which is the acronym for the Club of Diminishing Returns. In fact, very few people have. Even many among the lower ranks of economists do not know of it. It is the small and exclusive band of economists who have thoroughly mastered the intricate realm of thaumaturgical economics—or as one politician once called it, in his quaintly rustic way, "voodoo economics."

It was well known that no one outside the CDR could make his mark in the federal government but that anyone inside it might. Thus, when the chairman of the CDR died rather unexpectedly and a committee of the organization met with Vissarion to offer him the post, Vissarion's heart bounded. As chairman he would certainly be appointed Chief Economist at the next available opportunity, and he would be at the very fount and source of power, moving the President's own hand in exactly the direction in which the President wanted it to go.

One point, however, worried Vissarion, and left him in a terrible quandary. He felt he needed the help of someone with a level head and a keen intelligence and he turned to me at once, as anyone in that situation naturally would.

"George," he said, "to become the chairman of the CDR fulfills my greatest hopes and my wildest dreams. It is the open gateway to a glorious future of economic sycophancy, in which I may even outstrip that second purveyor of confirmation of all presidential guesses—the chief scientist of the United States."

"You mean the scientific adviser to the President."

"If you want to be informal, yes. It needs only for me to become chairman of the CDR and, within two years, I shall certainly be Chief Economist. Except—"

"Except?" I said.

Vissarion seemed to take a firm grip on himself. "I must go back to the beginning. The Club of Diminishing Returns was founded sixty-two years ago, and the name was chosen because the Law of Diminishing Returns is the one economic law that all economists, however well trained, have heard of. Its first president, a much beloved figure who predicted in November 1929 that the stock market was due for a serious downturn, was re-elected year after year and remained president for thirty-two years, dying at the patriarchal age of ninety-six."

"Very commendable of him," I said. "So many people give up far too soon when it only takes grit and determination to hang on till ninety-six or even beyond."

"Our second chairman did almost as well, holding the post for sixteen years. He was the only one who did not become Chief Economist. He deserved it and was appointed to the post by Thomas E. Dewey, the day before election day, but somehow— Our third chairman died after holding the post for eight years, and our fourth died after being chairman for four years. Our late chairman, who just died last month, was the fifth in line, and he held the post for two years. Do you see something peculiar about all this, George?"

"Peculiar? Did they all die natural deaths?"

"Of course."

"Well, considering the post they held, that *is* peculiar."

"Nonsense," said Vissarion with some asperity. "I call your attention to the lengths of time in office for successive chairmen: thirty-two, sixteen, eight, four and two."

I thought for a while. "The numbers seem to grow smaller."

"They don't just grow smaller. Each is exactly half of the previous number.—Believe me, I had it checked by a physicist."

"You know, I think you're right. Has anyone else seen this?"

"Certainly," said Vissarion. "I have shown these figures to my fellow clubmen and they all claim that it is not statistically significant unless the President issues an executive proclamation stating that it is. But don't you see the significance of this? If I accept the post as chairman, I will die after one year. That is certain. And if I do, it will be extremely difficult for the President to appoint me to the post of Chief Economist thereafter."

I said, "Yes, Vissarion, you are in a dilemma. I have known many governmental functionaries who showed no signs of life behind the forehead, but not one who showed no signs of life *at all*. Give me a day to think of this, will you, Vissarion?"

We made arrangements to meet the next day; same time, same place. It was an excellent restaurant, after all, and, unlike you, old man, Vissarion did not begrudge me a crust of bread.

—All right, then, he didn't begrudge me shrimp scampi, either.

It was obviously a case for Azazel and I felt thoroughly justified in putting my small two-centimeter demon to work at this, with his otherworldly powers.

After all, not only was Vissarion a kindly man with a good taste in restaurants, but I honestly felt he could do our nation great service in confirming the President's notions against the objections of people with better judgment. After all, who had elected *them?*

Not that Azazel was glad to be called up. He no sooner saw me than he threw down the contents of his little hands. They were too small for me to make out very clearly but they seemed to be little pasteboard rectangles of curious design.

"There!" he said, his tiny face contorted and turning a rich yellow with rage. His small tail lashed wildly and the miniature horns on his forehead fairly vibrated in the grip of his strong emotion.

"Do you realize, you vile huge mass of inferiority," he shrilled, "that I finally held in my hand a zotchil; and not only a zotchil, but a zotchil with cumin high and pair of reils to boot. They were all bidding me up and I couldn't lose. I would have cleaned up every half-bletchke on the table."

I said severely, "I don't know what you're talking about, but it does sound as though you have been gambling. Is that a refined and civilized thing to do? What would your poor mother say if she knew you were spending your time gambling with a group of bums?"

Azazel seemed taken aback. Then he mumbled, "You are right. My mothers would be broken-hearted. All three of them. Especially my poor middle mother, who sacrificed so much for me." And he broke into soprano howls that were quite dreadful to hear.

"There, there," I said soothingly. I ached to stick my fingers in my ears, but that would have offended him. "You can make it all well by helping a worthy being of this world."

I told him the story of Vissarion Johnson.

"Hmm," said Azazel.

"What does that mean?" I asked anxiously.

"It means 'hmm,' " snapped Azazel. "What else do you think it could possibly mean?"

"Yes, but don't you think that all this is merely coincidence and that Vissarion ought to disregard it?"

"Possibly—were it not that all this can't be coincidence and that Vissarion dare not disregard it. It has to be the working-out of a law of nature."

"How can it be a law of nature?"

"Do you think you know all the laws of nature?"

"Well, no!"

"Of course not. Our great poet, Cheefpreest, wrote a delicate couplet on that once, which I will, with my own great poetic acumen, translate into your barbarous language."

Azazel cleared his throat, thought a moment, then said:

> *"All nature is but art, unknown to thee;*
> *"All chance, direction, which thou canst not see."*

I asked suspiciously, "What does that mean?"

"It means that a law of nature is involved, and we must figure out what it is and how it might be taken advantage of to modify events to our liking. That's what it means. Do you think a great poet of my people would lie?"

"Well, can you do anything about it?"

"Possibly. There are a great many laws of nature, you know."

"Are there?"

"Oh, yes. There's quite a cute little law of nature—devilishly attractive equation when put into Weinbaumian tensors—that governs the heat of soup in relation to the hurry you are in to finish it. It's possible, if this odd diminution of duration of Chairmanly term is governed by the law I think it is governed by, that I can so alter the nature of your friend's being as to ensure him against damage from anything on Earth. He won't be immune to the processes of physiological decay, of course. The workings of what I have in mind won't make him immortal, but it will at least make certain he won't die of infection or of accident, which I imagine he would find satisfactory."

"Entirely so. But when will this come to pass?"

"I'm not completely sure. I'm rather busy these days with a young female of my species who seems uncannily smitten with me, poor soul." He yawned, his small, forked tongue curling into a helix and straightening again. "I seem to be short on sleep, but in two or three days it should be done."

"Yes, but how can I tell when and if all is well?"

"That's easy," said Azazel. "Just wait a few days and then shove your friend under a speeding truck. If he gets up unharmed, the modifications I have introduced will be working. —And now if you don't mind, I just want to play out this one hand and then I will think of my poor mid-mother and leave the game. With my winnings, of course."

Don't think I didn't have plenty of trouble persuading Vissarion that he was perfectly safe.

"Nothing on Earth can harm me?" he kept saying. "How do you know nothing on Earth can harm me?"

"I know. See here, Vissarion, I don't question your specialized knowledge. When you tell me that interest rates are going to fall, I don't quibble and ask you how you know."

"Well, that's all very well, but if I say interest rates are going to fall and then they proceed to rise—and they don't do that more than half the time—merely your feelings are hurt. If, however, I act on the assumption that nothing on Earth can hurt me, and then something on Earth hurts me, I am a lot more than hurt. I am *hurt.*"

There's no arguing with logic, but I kept arguing anyway. I persuaded him at least to attempt no flat refusal of the post but to try to delay them for a few days.

"They'll never accept a delay," he said, but out of nowhere it turned out that that very day was the anniversary of Black Friday and the CDR went into the usual three-day period of mourning and prayers for the dead. The delay therefore came automatically and that alone rather shook Vissarion into thinking that perhaps he did lead a charmed life.

Then, at the end of the mourning period, when he ventured into public again, I was crossing a busy street with him and—I don't really remember how it happened—I suddenly bent to tie a shoelace and somehow I lost my balance and fell against him, and *he* lost his balance and fell into the line of traffic and suddenly there was a devil of a shrieking of brakes and skidding of tires and three cars were totaled.

Vissarion didn't come out of it entirely untouched. His hair was rather mussed, his eyeglasses were slightly askew, and there was a spot of oil on the right knee of his trousers.

He disregarded that, however. He said in awe as he gazed at the carnage, "They never touched me. My goodness, they never touched me."

And the very next day he was caught in the rain without rubbers, umbrella, or raincoat—a nasty, cold rain—and did not catch cold on the spot. He called up, without even bothering to towel his hair, and accepted the post as chairman.

He had a very nice tenure, I must say. He quintupled his fees at once without any of this nonsense of achieving a better batting average as his prognostications were concerned. After all, a client can't expect to have everything. If he gets unparalleled prestige in the professional man he consults, can he reasonably demand better advice *also?*

Furthermore, he enjoyed life. No colds. Nothing communicable at all. He crossed streets with impunity, disregarding the lights when he was in a hurry, and yet only rarely caused accidents to others. He had no hesitation about entering the park at night, and once when a street hooligan placed a knife to his chest and suggested a transfer of funds, Vissarion simply kicked the young financier in the groin and walked on. The hooligan in question was so preoccupied with the kick that he entirely neglected to renew his application.

It was on the anniversary of his succession to the chairmanship when I met him at the parkside. He was on his way to the testimonial luncheon for the occasion. It was a beautiful Indian summer day and, as we took our seats on the park bench, side by side, we felt completely happy and at ease.

"George," he said, "I have had a happy year."

"I'm delighted," I said.

"My reputation is higher than that of any economist who ever lived. Only last month, when I warned that Amalgamated Suds would have to merge with Consolidated Soap and they were forced to consolidate with Merged Soap, everyone marveled at how close I came."

"I remember," I said.

"And now, I want you to be the first to know—"

"Yes, Vissarion?"

"The President has asked me to be Chief Economist of the United States, and I have reached the pinnacle of all my dreams and desires. See here."

He held out to me an impressive envelope with "White House" embossed in the upper left. I opened it and, as I did so, I heard a strange sort of *zing-g-g,* as though a bullet had buzzed its way past my ear, and I caught a strange flash of light in the corner of my eye.

Vissarion was sprawled sideways on the bench, a splotch of

blood on his shirt front, clearly dead. Some passersby stopped in astonishment; others screamed or gasped and hurried on.

"Call a doctor!" I called out. "Call the police!"

They came eventually, and the verdict was that he had been shot, right through the heart, by a gun of uncertain caliber, fired by some psychopathic sniper. They never caught the sniper, or even found the bullet. Fortunately there were witnesses willing to testify that I had been holding a letter in my hand at the time and was clearly innocent of any evil deed, or I might have had an uncomfortable time of it.

Poor Vissarion! He had been chairman for exactly one year, as he himself had feared he would be, and yet it was not Azazel's fault. Azazel had said that Vissarion would not be killed by anything on Earth, but as Hamlet wisely said, "There are more things in heaven and earth, Horatio, than there are in earth alone."

Before the doctors and police arrived, I had noted the small hole in the wood of that part of the bench that had been behind Vissarion. With my penknife, I picked out the small dark object embedded in it. It was still warm. Months later, I had it quietly looked at at the museum and I was right. It was a meteorite.

In short, then, Vissarion had been killed by nothing on Earth. He was the first person in history known to have been killed by a meteorite. I kept it absolutely quiet, of course, for Vissarion was a very private man and would have hated to achieve notoriety in this way. It would have drowned out all his great works of economics and I couldn't allow that.

But on every anniversary of his elevation and of his death— like today—I sit and think: Poor Vissarion! Poor Vissarion!

George mopped at his eyes with his handkerchief and I said, "And what happened to the next person to succeed to the chairmanship? He must have held office for a half year, and then the next one for three months, and then the next—"

George said, "There is no need to flaunt your knowledge of higher mathematics at me, old fellow. I'm not one of your poor suffering readers. None of that ever happened. The irony of it is that the club altered the law of nature on its own."

"Oh? And how did they do that?"

"It struck them that the name of the club, the CDR, the Club of Diminishing Returns, was an ill-omened named that controlled the length of tenure of the chairman. They simply inverted the initials, therefore, and changed CDR to CRD."

"And what does CRD stand for?"

"The Club of Random Distribution, of course," said George, "and the next chairman has now been in office for ten years and is still going strong."

And as the waiter returned with my change, George caught it in his handkerchief, put both handkerchief and bills into his breast pocket with a flourish, got up and, with a debonair wave of his hand, walked off.

The Mind's Construction

I was moved to philosophic utterance that morning. Shaking my head in mournful reminiscence, I said, "There's no art to find the mind's construction in the face. He was a gentleman on whom I built an absolute trust."

It was a rather chilly Sunday morning and George and I were seated at a table in the local Bagel Nosh. George, I remember, was finishing his second large sesame bagel, this one liberally interspersed with cream cheese and whitefish.

He said, "Is that something from a story of the type you habitually put together for the less discriminating editors?"

"It happens to be Shakespeare," I said, "It's from *Macbeth.*"

"Ah, yes, I had forgotten your penchant for petty plagiarism."

"It is not petty plagiarism to express yourself in an appropriate quotation. What I was saying was that I had a friend whom I had considered a man of consideration and taste. I had bought him dinners. I had, on occasion, lent him money. I had praised his appearance and character fulsomely. And mind you, I did this entirely without any consideration for the fact that he was a book reviewer by profession—if you want to call it a profession."

George said, "And despite all these disinterested actions of yours, the time came when your friend reviewed one of your books and he proceeded to slam it unmercifully."

"Oh?" I said, "Did you read the review?"

"Not at all. I just asked myself what kind of review a book of yours could possibly get, and the correct answer came to me in a flash."

"I didn't mind his saying it was a bad book, mind you, George —at least I didn't mind it any more than any other writer would mind such a brainless statement—but when he went on to use phrases like 'senile dementia' I felt that was going too far. Saying that the book was meant for eight-year-olds but that they would be better off playing tiddledywinks was hitting below the belt." I sighed and repeated, "There's no art—"

"You said that already," said George at once.

"He seemed so pleasant, so friendly, so grateful for little favors. How could I know that underneath it all he was a vicious, libelous hellhound."

George said, "But he was a critic. How could he be anything else? You train for the post by maligning your mother. It is really unbelievable that you should have been fooled in so ridiculous a fashion. You are worse than my friend Vandevanter Robinson ever was, and he, I'll have you know, was once spoken of as a possible candidate for a Nobel Prize for Naïveté. His story is a curious one—"

"Please," I said, "the review came out in the current *New York Review of Books*—five columns of bitter spleen, venom, and gall. I am in no mood to listen to one of your stories."

I thought you would be [said George], and you are perfectly right. It will take your mind off your own inconsequential troubles.

My friend Vandevanter Robinson was a young man whom anyone would have judged to be of great promise. He was handsome, cultured, intelligent, and creative. He had been to the best schools, and he was in love with a delightful young creature, Minerva Shlump.

Minerva was one of my goddaughters and was devoted to me, as was only right. A person of my moral fiber, of course, is quite averse to allowing young ladies of outstanding proportions to hug one and attempt to climb into one's lap, but there was something so endearing about Minerva, so innocently childlike, and, most of all, so resilient to the touch, that I allowed it in her case.

Naturally I never allowed it in the presence of Vandevanter, who was quite unreasonable in his jealousy.

He explained this failing of his once in accents that touched my heart. "George," he said, "from childhood it was my ambition to fall in love with a young woman of superlative virtue, of untouched purity, of—if I may use the expression—a porcelain-like gleam of innocence. In Minerva Shlump, if I may be allowed to breathe that divine name, I had found just such a woman. It is the one case in which I know I cannot be deceived. Were I ever to find out my trust was abused, I would scarcely know how to continue to live. I would become an embittered old man with no consolation but such paltry items as my mansion, my servants, my club, and my inherited wealth."

Poor fellow. He was not deceived in young Minerva—as I well knew, for when she wriggled delightedly on my lap. I could easily tell her utter lack of any trace of vice. But it was the only person, or thing, or concept, in which he was not deceived. The poor young man simply had no judgment. He was, though it may seem unkind to say so, as stupid as you are. He lacked the art to find the mind's—Yes, I know you said that already. Yes, yes, you said it twice.

What made it particularly hard for him, of course, was that Vandevanter was a rookie detective on the New York police force.

It had been his life's ambition (in addition to finding the perfect damosel) to be a detective; to be one of the keen-eyed, hawk-nosed gentlemen who are the terrors of evil-doers everywhere. With that end in mind, he majored in criminology at both Groton and Harvard, and read assiduously those important research reports committed to paper by authorities such as Sir Arthur Conan Doyle and Dame Agatha Christie. All that, together with the unremitting use of family influence, and the fact that an uncle of his was Borough President of Queens at the time, led to his appointment to the force.

Sadly, and quite unexpectedly, he was not a success at this. Unsurpassed at the ability to weave an inexorable chain of logic while sitting in his armchair, making use of evidence gathered by others, he found himself utterly incapable of gathering the evidence himself.

His problem was that he had this incredible urge to believe whatever someone told him. Any alibi, however sieve-like, baffled him. Any well-know perjurer had but to offer his word of honor and Vandevanter found himself incapable of doubting him.

This became so notorious that criminals from the lowliest purse-snatcher to the highest politician and industrialist refused to be questioned by anyone else.

"Bring us Vandevanter," they would cry out.

"I will spill my guts to him," the purse-snatcher would say.

"I will apprise him of the facts, as carefully arranged in the proper order by none other than myself," the politician would say.

"I will explain that the hundred-million-dollar government check just happened to be lying about in the petty-cash drawer and I needed a tip for the shoeshine boy," said the industrialist.

The result was that whatever he touched got away. He had an exonerative thumb—an expression invented for the occasion by a literary friend of mine. (Of course you don't remember inventing it—I'm not referring to you. Would I be so mad as to think of you as 'literary'?)

As the months passed, the case load in the courts grew less, and innumerable grieving burglars, muggers, and assorted felons were restored to their friends and relations without a stain on their reputations.

Naturally it did not take long for New York's Finest to understand the situation and to penetrate the cause. Vandevanter had been on the job not more than two and a half years when it dawned on him that the camaraderie he had been accustomed to was fading, and that his superiors were wont to greet him with a puzzled frown. There was virtually no talk of promotion, even though Vandevanter would mention his Borough President uncle at what seemed like appropriate moments.

He came to me as young men in trouble are wont to do, seeking refuge in the wisdom of a man of the world. (I don't know what you mean, old man, by asking me if I knew of anyone I could recommend. Please don't distract me with non sequiturs.)

"Uncle George," he said, "I believe I am in a spot of difficulty." (He always addressed me as Uncle George, impressed as he was by the dignity and splendid nobility lent me by my well-kept white locks—so different in nature from your own dubiously unkempt mutton chops.)

"Uncle George," he said, "there seems to be an unaccountable reluctance to promote me. I remain a rookie detective, zero-class. My office is right in the middle of the corridor and my key to the lavatory doesn't work. I don't mind this in itself, you understand, but my dear Minerva in her unspoiled artlessness has suggested that this may mean I am a failure and her little heart almost breaks at the thought. 'I don't want to marry a failure,' she says, her little lips pouting. 'People will laugh at me.' "

I said, "Is there any reason why you should be having this trouble, Vandevanter, my boy?" I asked.

"None at all. It's a complete mystery to me. I admit I haven't solved any cases, but I don't think *that's* the problem. No one can be expected to solve them all, you know."

"Do any of the other detectives solve at least a few?" I asked.

"Yes they do, now and then, but their manner of doing so shocks me to the core. They have an unlovely sense of disbelief, a most deplorable skepticism, a distasteful way of staring at some accused person in a supercilious manner and saying, 'Oh, yeah!' or, 'Says you!' It just humiliates them. It just isn't the American way."

"Is it possible the accused might be telling lies and that they *should* be treated with skepticism?"

Vandevanter puzzled over that for a moment. "Why, I believe that might be so. What a horrible thought!"

"Well," I said, "let me think about this."

That evening I called up Azazel, the two-centimeter demon who, on an occasion or two, has been of use to me with his mysterious powers. I don't know if I've ever mentioned him to you, but—Oh, I have, have I?

Well, he appeared on the little ivory circle on my desk about which I burn the special incense and recite the age-old incantations—the details, however, are secret.

When he appeared, he was wearing a long, flowing garment; or at least it seemed long and flowing in comparison to the two centimeters that measured him from the base of his tail to the tips of his horns. He had one of his arms raised high and he was speaking in his shrill way while his tail twitched from side to side.

Clearly, he was in the midst of something or other. He is a creature who is somehow preoccupied with unimportant detail. I never seem to get him when he is quietly at rest or in dignified repose. He is always engaged in some petty concern of no moment and is furious at having me interrupt him.

On this occasion, however, he became aware of me and at once lowered his arm and smiled. At least, I think he smiled for it is hard to see the details of his face, and once, when I used a hand lens to help me make them out, he seemed unaccountably offended.

He said, "It's just as well; I welcome the change. I have the speech well in hand and I'm certain of success."

"Success at what, O Great One? Though success in anything you do is certain." (He seems to have a fondness for this sort of orotundity. He resembles you oddly in this respect.)

"I am running for political office," he said with satisfaction. "I expect to be elected grod-catcher."

"May I ask, humbly, that you relieve my ignorance by informing me of what a grod might be?"

"Why, a grod is a small domestic animal much esteemed as a pet by my people. Some of these animals lack a license, and a grod-catcher is expected to gather them up. They are small creatures of fiendish cunning and resolute defiance and it takes someone of might and intelligence to succeed at the task. There are people who sneer and say, 'Azazel couldn't be elected grod-catcher,' but I intend to show them I can. Now what can I do for you?"

I explained the situation and Azazel seemed surprised. "Do you mean to say that on your miserable world it is not possible for people to tell when other people make statements that do not coincide with objective truth?"

"We have a device called a 'lie detector,' " I said. "It measures blood pressure, electrical conductivity of the skin and so on. It can detect lies, although it also detects nervousness and tension and calls them lies as well."

"Naturally, but there are subtle glandular functions that exist in any species intelligent enough to misrepresent truth, or is this something you wouldn't know?"

I avoided answering that question. "Is there any way to make it possible for zero-grade detective Robinson to detect that glandular function?"

"Without one of your crude machines? Using the functioning of his own mind?"

"Yes."

"You must realize you are asking me to deal with one of the minds of your species. Large but infinitely crude."

"I realize that."

"Well, I shall try. You will have to take me to him or bring him to me and, in either case, allow me to study him."

"Certainly."

And it was done.

Vandevanter came to me perhaps a week later, a look of concern on his patrician face.

"Uncle George," he said, "a most unusual thing has happened. I was questioning a young man involved in the robbery of a liquor store. He was telling me in the most affecting detail that he just happened to be passing the store, deep in thought over his poor mother who was suffering from a headache which had struck her after she had consumed half a bottle of gin. He stepped into the store to ask if it was, after all, wise to consume gin too soon after having disposed of a similar quantity of rum, when the owner, for no reason he could tell, pressed a gun into his hands and then began shoving the contents of the cash register at the young man who, confused and astonished, accepted it, just as a policeman walked in. He said he thought it was intended as compensation for the pain his dear mother had experienced. He was telling me all this when it came over me in the oddest way that he was—uh—fibbing."

"Indeed?"

"Yes. It is the most amazing thing I ever experienced." Vandevanter's voice fell to a whisper. "Not only did I know, somehow, that the young man had the gun with him when he entered, but that his mother did not have a headache. Can you imagine someone fibbing about his *mother?*"

Close investigation proved Vandevanter's instinct to be correct in every particular. The young man *had* been telling an untruth about his mother.

From that moment on, Vandevanter's ability sharpened steadily.

Within a month he had become a keen, hard-eyed, remorseless machine for the detection of falsehood.

The Department watched in gasping amazement as accused after accused failed in the attempt to hoodwink Vandevanter. No tale of having been deeply immersed in prayer at the time the poor box was rifled could stand up against his shrewd questioning. Lawyers who had been investing orphans' funds in the renovation of their offices—entirely through oversight—were quickly discomfited. Accountants who had accidentally subtracted a telephone number from the item labeled "Tax due" were trapped in their own words. Drug dealers who had merely picked up a five-kilo packet of heroin in the local cafeteria thinking it was sugar substitute were instantly tied in logical knots.

Vandevanter the Victorious they called him, and the Commissioner himself, to the applause of the assembled body of police, awarded Vandevanter a key that fit the lavatory door, to say nothing of moving his office to one side of the corridor.

I was congratulating myself that all was well and that Vandevanter, his success assured, was now ready to marry the lovely Minerva Shlump, when Minerva herself appeared at the doorway of my apartment.

"Oh, Uncle George," she whispered faintly, her lithe body swaying. She was clearly on the point of fainting. I lifted her and held her close to me for five or six minutes while I considered exactly into which chair I might lower her.

"What is it, my dear?" I asked, after I had slowly disencumbered myself of her, and smoothed her clothing lest it be disarranged.

"Oh, Uncle George," she said, and tears overflowed her lovely lower lids. "It's Vandevanter."

"Surely he has not shocked you with unwonted and improper advances?"

"Oh, no, Uncle George. He is far too refined a person to do that before marriage, although of course I have carefully explained to him that I understand the hormonal influences that sometimes overpower young men and that I was certainly fully prepared to forgive him in case of an untoward event. Yet, despite my assurances, he remains in control."

"What is it, then, Minerva?"

"Oh, Uncle George, he has broken our engagement."

"That is unbelievable. No two people are better suited. Why?"

"He says I'm a teller of—of—inexactitudes."

My reluctant lips formed the word: Liar?

She nodded. "That vile word did not cross his lips, but that is what he meant. It was only this morning that he looked upon me with his dear glance of melting adoration and said, 'Loved one, have you always been true to me?' And, as I always do, I said sentimentally, 'As true as the sunbeam to the sun, as the rose petal to the rose.' And then his eyes grew narrow and hateful and he said, 'Aha, your words are not in accord with verity. You have told a taradiddle.' It was as though I had been struck with a heavy blow. I said, 'Vandevanter, my own, what are you saying?' He answered, 'What you heard. I have been mistaken in you, and we must part forever.' And he left. Oh, what am I to do? What am I to do? Where will I find another success?"

I said thoughtfully, "Vandevanter is usually right about such things—in recent weeks, at any rate. Have you been untrue to him?"

A faint flush mantled Minerva's cheeks. "Not really."

"How unreally?"

"Well, some years ago, when I was but a slip of a girl, aged seventeen, I kissed a young man. I held him tightly, I admit, but that was only in order to keep him from escaping, and not out of any personal affection."

"I see."

"It was not a very pleasurable experience. Not *very*. After I met Vandevanter, I was astonished to find how much more gratifying his kiss was than the one I had earlier experienced with the other young man. Naturally, I was intent on reexperiencing that gratification. Through all my relationship with Vandevanter, I have periodically—entirely in a mood of scientific inquiry—kissed other young men in order to assure myself that not one, not *one*, can match my own Vandevanter. In doing so, I assure you, Uncle George, I granted them every advantage in style and form of kissing, to say nothing of grip and squeeze, and *never* did they match Vandevanter in any way. And yet he says I am untrue."

"How ridiculous," I said. "My child, you have been wronged." I kissed her four or five times and said, "There, that does not gratify you as Vandevanter's kisses do, does it?"

"Let's see," she said, and kissed me four or five more times with great skill and ardor. "Of course not," she said.

"I shall go see him." I said.

That very night, I presented himself at his apartment. He was sitting moodily in his living room, loading and unloading his revolver.

"You are," I said, "doubtless considering suicide."

"Never," he said with a hacking laugh. "What reason have I to commit suicide? The loss of a trifling jade? Of a storyteller? She is well done with, say I."

"You say wrong. Minerva has always been true to you. Her hands, her lips, and her body have never made contact with the hands, the lips, and the body of any man but yourself."

"I know that is not so," said Vandevanter.

"I tell you it *is* so," I said. "I have spoken with the weeping maiden at length and she has revealed to me the innermost secrets of her life. Once she blew a kiss at a young man. She was five years old at the time; he, six; and she has agonized over that moment of amorous madness ever since. Never has such a scene of ribaldry been repeated and it is only that moment that you detected in her."

"Are you telling the truth, Uncle George?"

"Consider me with your unfailing and penetrating glance, and I will repeat what I have just said and then you tell *me* if I am telling the truth."

I repeated the tale, and he said, wondering, "You *are* telling the exact and literal truth, Uncle George. Do you suppose that Minerva will ever forgive me?"

"Of course," I said. "Humble yourself to her and continue your keen pursuit of the dregs of the underworld through every liquor store, corporate boardroom, and City Hall corridor, but never, never turn your keen eyes on the woman you love. Perfect love is perfect trust and you must trust her perfectly."

"I will, I will," he cried out.

And he has done so ever since. He is now the best-known

detective on the force and has been promoted to the rank of Half-Class Detective with an office in the basement right next to the laundry machine. He is married to Minerva and they live together in ideal peace.

She spends her life testing the superior gratification of Vandevanter's kisses over and over in an ecstasy of happiness. There are times when she will willingly spend the entire night with some likely man who seems suitable for investigation, but always the result is the same. Vandevanter is the best. She is now the mother of two sons, one of whom bears a slight resemblance to Vandevanter.

And so much for your claim, old man, that my labors and those of Azazel always lead to disaster.

"As it happens, though," I said, "if I accept your story, you were lying when you told Vandevanter that Minerva had never touched another man."

"I did it to save an innocent young maiden."

"But how is it that Vandevanter did not detect the lie?"

"I presume," said George, wiping the cream cheese from his lips, "that it was my air of unassailable dignity."

"I have another theory," I said. "I think that neither you, nor your blood pressure, nor the electrical conductivity of your skin, nor your subtle hormonal reactions, can any longer tell the difference between what is true and what is not; and neither can anyone else who must depend on the data derived from studying you."

"Ridiculous," said George.

The Fights of Spring

We were looking across the river at the college campus on the other side, George and I, and George, having dined to repletion at my expense, was moved to a lachrymose nostalgia.

"Ah, college days, college days!" he moaned. "What can we find in life thereafter to compensate for your loss?"

I stared at him in surprise. "Don't tell me you went to college!"

He favored me with a haughty glare. "Do you realize I am the greatest president the fraternity of Phi Pho Phum ever had?"

"But how did you pay the tuition?"

"Scholarships!" he said. "They were showered on me after I showed my prowess in the food fights celebrating our victories in the coed dormitories. That, and a well-to-do uncle."

"I didn't know you had a well-to-do uncle, George."

"After the six years it took me to complete the decelerated program, he wasn't any longer, alas. At least not as much. What money he could save from the wreck, he eventually left to a home for indigent cats, making several remarks about me in his last will and testament that I scorn to repeat. Mine has been a sad and unappreciated life."

"Sometime in the distant future," I said, "you must tell it all to me, omitting no detail."

"But," continued George, "the memory of college days suffuses all my hard life with a glow of pearl and gold. I felt it in its full force of few years back when I revisited the campus of old Tate University."

"They invited you back?" I said, almost succeeding in stifling the unmistakable note of incredulity in my voice.

"They were about to, I'm certain," said George, "but I returned, actually, at the request of a dear comrade of my collegiate years, old Antiochus Schnell."

Since you are clearly fascinated by what I have already said [said George], let me tell you about old Antiochus Schnell. He was my inseparable pal in the old days, my fidus Achates (though why I waste classical allusions on a nincompoop like you I'll never know). Even now, though he has aged much more drastically than I have, I remember him as he was in the days when we swallowed goldfish together, filled telephone booths with our cronies, and removed panties with deft twists of the wrists to the delighted squeals of dimple-cheeked coeds. In short, we savored all the lofty pleasures of an enlightened institution.

So when old Antiochus Schnell asked me to see him on a matter of great moment, I was there at once.

"George," he said, "it's my son."

"Young Artaxerxes Schnell?"

"The same. He is a sophomore at old Tate University, but things are not going well with him."

My eyes narrowed. "Has he fallen in with a worthless crowd? Is he running into debt? Has he foolishly allowed himself to be entrapped by an elderly beer-hall waitress?"

"Worse! Much worse!" said old Antiochus Schnell in broken syllables. "He has never told me so himself—hadn't the face for it, I suppose—but a shocked letter from one of his classmates, written in the strictest confidence, has reached me. George, old friend, my poor son—let me say it straight out without searching for euphemisms—is studying calculus!"

"Studying calc—" I couldn't bring myself to say the awful word.

Old Antiochus Schnell nodded forlornly. "And political science, too. He's actually attending class and he has been seen studying."

"Great heavens!" I said, appalled.

"I can't believe it of young Artaxerxes, George. If his mother should hear of it, it would be her end. She's a sensitive woman, George, and not in good health. I conjure you in the name of our ancient friendship to go to old Tate and investigate the matter. If the boy has been lured into scholarship, bring him to his senses, somehow—for his mother's sake and his own, if not for mine."

With tears in my eyes, I wrung his hand. "Nothing shall deter me," I said. "No consideration on earth shall swerve me from this holy task. I shall spend the last drop of my blood, if necessary—and speaking of spending, I will need a check."

"A check?" quavered old Antiochus Schnell, who has always been a quick man at slapping the wallet shut.

"Hotel room," I said, "meals, drinks, allowance for tips, inflation, and overhead. It's for your son, old fellow, not for me."

—I finally got that check and did not wait long after having arrived at Tate before arranging to meet young Artaxerxes. I barely took the time to have a good dinner, an excellent brandy, a long night's sleep, and a leisurely breakfast before I was calling on him in his room.

It was quite a shock entering that room. On every wall there were shelves filled not with bric-a-brac to catch the eye, not with nutritious bottles replete with the vintner's art, not with photographs of winsome lassies who had unaccountably lost their clothes—but with *books*.

One book lay unashamedly open on his desk, and I do believe he had been fingering it just before I had arrived. There was a suspicious dustiness about his right index finger, and he clumsily tried to hide it behind his back.

But Artaxerxes himself was an even greater shock. He recognized me, of course, as an old friend of the family. I had not seen him for nine years, but nine years had not changed my noble carriage or my fresh and open countenance. Nine years before, however, Artaxerxes had been an unimpressive boy of ten. Now he was an unrecognizable but entirely unimpressive youth of nineteen. He was barely five feet five, wore large, round glasses, and had a caved-in appearance.

"How much do you weigh?" I asked impulsively.

"Ninety-seven pounds," he whispered.

I stared at him in heartfelt pity. He was a ninety-seven-pound weakling. He was the natural butt of scorn and derision.

And then my heart softened as I thought: Poor boy! Poor boy! With a body like that, could he take part in any of the activities essential to a well-rounded college education? Football? Track? Wrestling? Chug-a-lugging? When other youngsters cried out: 'We've got this old barn, we can sew our own costumes—let's put on a musical play of our own' what could *he* do? With lungs like that, could he sing anything but a faint soprano?

Naturally he was forced, against his will, to slide into infamy.

I said softly, almost tenderly, "Artaxerxes, my boy, is it true you are studying calculus and political economy?"

He nodded. "Anthropology, too."

I stifled an exclamation of disgust. I said, "And is it true that you attend classes?"

"I'm sorry, sir, but I do. At the end of this year, I will make the Dean's list."

There was a telltale tear in the corner of one of his eyes, and in the midst of my horror I found myself able to extract hope from the fact that at least he recognized the sink of depravity into which he had tumbled.

I said, "My child, can you not, even now, turn away from these vile practices and return to a pure and unsullied college life?"

"I cannot," he sobbed. "I have gone too far. No one can help me."

I was clutching at straws now. "Is there not a decent woman at this college who can take you in hand? Surely the love of a good woman has wrought miracles in the past and can do so again."

His eyes lit. I had clearly touched a nerve. "Philomel Kribb," he gasped. "She is the sun, moon, and stars that beam down upon the sea of my soul."

"Ah!" I said, detecting the emotion hidden behind his controlled phraseology. "Does she know this?"

"How can I tell her? The weight of her contempt would crush me."

"Would you not give up calculus to wipe out this contempt?"

He hung his head. "I am weak—weak."

I left him, determined to find Philomel Kribb at once.

It did not take long. I quickly determined at the registrar's that she was majoring in advanced cheerleading, with a strong minor in chorus-line dramatics. I found her in the cheerleading studio.

I waited patiently for the intricate stomping and melodious shrieking to end, and then had Philomel pointed out to me. She was a blond girl of middle height, glowing with health and perspiration, and possessing a figure that caused my lips to purse in approval. Clearly, buried under Artaxerxes's scholarly perversion, there beat a dim realization of a collegiate's proper interests.

After she had emerged from her shower and donned her colorful and skimpy collegiate dress, she came to meet me, appearing as fresh and bright as a dew-sprinkled field.

I got to the heart of the matter at once, saying, "Young Artaxerxes considers you the astronomical illumination of his life."

It seem to me her eyes softened a bit. "Poor Artaxerxes. He needs so much help."

"He could use some from a good woman," I pointed out.

"I know," she said, "and I'm as good as they come—or so I am told," and here she blushed prettily. "But what can I do? I cannot go against biology. Bullwhip Costigan endlessly humiliates Artaxerxes. He sneers at him in public, pushes him about, knocks his silly books to the ground, all to the cruel laughter of

the assembled multitude. You know how it is in the ebullient air
of springtime."

"Ah, yes," I said feelingly, remembering the happy days and
the many, many times I had held the contestants' coats. "The
fights of spring!"

Philomel sighed. "I have long hoped Artaxerxes would stand
up to Bullwhip somehow—a footstool would help, of course,
considering that Bullwhip is six foot six, but for some reason
Artaxerxes will not. All that studying,"—she shuddered—
"weakens the moral fiber."

"Undoubtedly, but if you helped him out of this slough—"

"Oh, sir, he is, deep underneath, a kindly and thoughtful
young man and I would help him if I could, but the genetic
equipment of my body is paramount and it calls me to Bullwhip's side. Bullwhip is handsome, muscular, and dominating,
and these qualities naturally impress their way into my cheerleader's heart."

"And if Artaxerxes were to humiliate Bullwhip?"

"A cheerleader," she said, and here she drew herself up
proudly, offering an astonishing display of frontal obtrusiveness,
"must follow her heart, which would inevitably recede from the
humiliatee and advance toward the humiliator."

Simple words that came, I knew, from the soul of the honest
girl.

My course was plain. If Artaxerxes ignored the trifling deficit
of thirteen inches and a hundred-ten pounds, and ground Bullwhip Costigan into the mire, Philomel would be Artaxerxes's
and would convert him into a true-blue male who would age
gracefully toward a lifetime of useful beer swigging and TV football watching.

Clearly it was a case for Azazel.

—I don't know if I have ever told you of Azazel, but he is a
two-centimeter being from another time and place whom I can
call to my side through secret spells and incantations to which I
alone have the key.

Azazel possesses powers far beyond ours, but he is otherwise without redeeming social qualities, for he is an exceedingly self-ish creature who consistently places his own petty concerns over my important needs.

This time, when he appeared, he was lying on his side, his tiny eyes closed and his little whip lash of a tail slowly caressing the empty air before him with soft, languorous strokes.

"Mighty One," I said, for he insists on being addressed so.

His eyes opened and he at once emitted ear-piercing whistles at the upper range of my hearing. Very unpleasant.

"Where is Ashtaroth?" he called out. "Where is my own precious Ashtaroth who, at this very moment, was in my arms."

Then he noticed me and said, grinding his tiny teeth, "Oh, it's you! Are you aware that you called me to your side at the very moment when Ashtaroth—But that is neither here nor there."

"Nor yon," I said. "Still, consider that after you've helped me out a bit, you can return to your own continuum half a minute after you left. Ashtaroth will then have had time to grow disturbed over your sudden absence, but not yet furious. Your reappearance will fill her with joy, and whatever was being done can be done a second time."

Azazel thought for a moment and then said, in what was for him a gracious tone, "You have a small mind, primitive worm, but it is a devious one and that can be of use to us who are of giant mentalities but who are hampered by a candid and luminously straightforward nature. What sort of help do you need now?"

I explained the plight of Artaxerxes and Azazel, considered it and said, "I could increase the power output of his muscles."

I shook my head. "It is not a matter of muscle alone. There are skill and courage, which he badly needs."

Azazel said indignantly, "Do you want me to sweat my tail off increasing his spiritual qualities?"

"Have you anything else to suggest?"

"Of course I have. Am I infinitely superior to you for nothing? If your weakling friend cannot assault his enemy directly, what about effective evasive action?"

"You mean running away very speedily?" I shook my head. "I don't think that would be very impressive."

"I didn't speak of flight; I mean evasive action. I need only greatly abbreviate his reaction time, which is simply done by one of my vast attainments. In order to avoid having him waste his strength needlessly, I can have such abbreviation activated by adrenal discharge. It will be operative, in other words, only when he is in a state of fear, rage, or other strong passion. Just allow me to meet him briefly and I will take care of it all."

"Certainly," I said.

In a matter of a quarter of an hour, I visited Artaxerxes in his dormitory room and allowed Azazel to peep at him from my shirt pocket. Azazel was thus able to manipulate the young man's autonomic nervous system at close range, and then to go back to his Ashtaroth and to whatever foul practices he wished to indulge in.

My next step was to write a letter cleverly disguised in a collegiate hand—block lettering in crayon—and slip it under Bullwhip's door. There was not long to wait. Bullwhip put a message on the student bulletin board summoning Artaxerxes to meet him in the taproom of the Guzzling Gourmet, and Artaxerxes knew better than to refuse.

Philomel and I came, too, and remained at the outskirts of a crowd of jolly collegiates anxious to see the excitement. Artaxerxes, his teeth chattering, carried a weighty tome entitled *Handbook of Chemistry and Physics*. Even in this extreme crisis he could not rid himself of his addiction.

Bullwhip, standing tall and with his muscles, under his carefully torn T-shirt, rippling in a manner fearsome to behold, said, "Schnell, it has come to my attention that you have been telling lies about me. Being a true-blue college lad, I will give you a chance to deny this before I shred you. Have you told anyone you once saw me reading a book?"

Artaxerxes said, "I once saw you looking at a comic book, but you were holding it upside down, so I didn't think you were reading it, so I never told anyone you were."

"Did you ever say that I was afraid of girls and talked big about what I couldn't do big?"

Artaxerxes said, "I heard some girls say so once, Bullwhip, but I never repeated it."

Bullwhip paused. The worst was yet to come. "Okay, Schnell, did you ever say I was a closet nerd?"

Artaxerxes said, "No, sir. What I said was you were positively absurd."

"Then you deny everything?"

"Emphatically."

"And admit it's all untrue."

"Vociferously."

"And that you're a dirty liar, pants on fire?"

"Abjectly."

"Then," said Bullwhip through clenched teeth, "I won't kill you. I'll merely break an obscure bone or two."

"The fights of spring," called out the collegians, laughing as they made a ring about the two combatants.

"This will be a fair fight," announced Bullwhip, who, although a cruel bully, followed the collegiate code. "Nobody is to help me and nobody is to help him. It is to be strictly one-on-one."

"What could be fairer?" chorused the eager audience.

Bullwhip said, "Take off your glasses, Schnell."

"No," said Artaxerxes boldly—whereupon one of the onlookers removed the glasses for him.

"Hey," said Artaxerxes, "you're helping Bullwhip."

"No, I'm not. I'm helping *you,*" said the collegiate, who was now holding the glasses.

"But now I can't see Bullwhip clearly," said Artaxerxes.

"Don't worry," said Bullwhip, "you will feel me clearly." Without more ado, he swung his hamlike fist at Artaxerxes's chin.

It whistled through the air and Bullwhip swung half around, for Artaxerxes had faded back at the approach of the blow, which missed him by a quarter of an inch.

Bullwhip looked astonished. Artaxerxes looked flabbergasted.

"That does it," said Bullwhip. "Now you'll get it." He moved forward and his arms pumped in alternation.

Artaxerxes danced right and left with a look of extreme anxiety on his face, and I really feared he might catch cold from the wind of Bullwhip's mighty flailing.

Bullwhip was clearly tiring. His mighty chest heaved. "What are you doing?" he demanded querulously.

Artaxerxes, however, had by now realized that he was, for some reason, invulnerable. He therefore walked toward the other, and, lifting the hand that was not holding the book, slapped Bullwhip's cheek soundly, saying, "Take that, you *nerd.*"

There was a synchronized sharp gasp from the audience and Bullwhip went into a frenzy. All one could see was a powerful piece of machinery lunging, striking, and whirling with, at its center, a dancing, swaying target.

After interminable minutes there was Bullwhip, breathless, face streaming with perspiration, and utterly helpless with fatigue. Before him stood Artaxerxes, cool and untouched. He had not even dropped his book.

He shoved that book, now, hard into Bullwhip's solar plexus, and when Bullwhip doubled up, Artaxerxes brought it down, even harder, on Bullwhip's skull. The book was very badly damaged as a result, but Bullwhip collapsed in a state of blissful unconsciousness.

Artaxerxes looked about myopically. He said, "Will the scoundrel who took my glasses return them *now.*"

"Yes, sir, Mr. Schnell," said the collegiate who had taken them. He smiled spasmodically in a placatory effort. "Here they are, sir. I have cleaned them, sir."

"Good. Now scram. That goes for all you nerds. Scram!"

They did so, standing not upon the order of going but hurtling over one another in their anxiety to be elsewhere. Only Philomel and I lingered.

Artaxerxes's eye fell upon the panting young girl. With a

haughty lift of his eyebrows, he crooked his little finger. Humbly she came to him, and as he turned on his heel and left, she, just as humbly, followed him.

It was a happy ending all around. Artaxerxes, filled with self-confidence, found he no longer needed books to give him a spurious sensation of worth. He spent all his time in the boxing ring becoming collegiate champion. He was worshipped by all the young coeds, but in the end he married Philomel.

His boxing prowess had given him so clear a reputation for collegiate worth that he had his choice of positions as junior business executive. His keen brain made it possible for him to see where the money lay, so he managed to procure the toilet-seat concession for the Pentagon, to which he added the sales of items such as washers that he bought at the hardware store and then sold to government procurement agencies.

It turned out, though, that his studies in his early nerdish days have stood him in good stead after all. He claims that it takes calculus for him to work out his profits, political economy to get his deductions past the IRS, and anthropology to deal with the executive branch of the government.

I stared at George with disbelief. "Do you mean to say that this case of you and Azazel interfering with some poor innocent ended *happily?*"

"Certainly," said George.

"But that means you now have an extremely rich acquaintance who is beholden to you for everything he has."

"You express it perfectly, old fellow."

"But then, surely, you can put the bite on him."

And here George's brow darkened. "You would think so, wouldn't you? You would think there would exist gratitude in the world, wouldn't you? You would think there would be individuals who, when it is carefully explained to them that their superhuman evasive abilities resulted entirely from the arduous labors of a friend, would see fit to shower rewards upon that friend?"

"You mean Artaxerxes doesn't?"

"That's right. When I approached him at one time with a request that he let me have ten thousand dollars as an investment in a scheme of mine that would surely pay back a hundredfold—a paltry ten thousand dollars which he makes whenever he sells a dozen cheap screws and bolts to the armed forces—he had me thrown out by a flunky."

"But why, George? Did you ever find out?"

"Yes I did, eventually. You see, old chap, he takes evasive action whenever his adrenaline flows, whenever he is in a strong passion, such as anger or rage. Azazel explained that."

"Yes. And so?"

"And so, whenever Philomel considers the family finances and feels a certain libidinous ardor steal over her, she approaches Artaxerxes, who, detecting her intention, feels his own adrenaline flow in passionate response. Then, when she lunges at him in her girlish enthusiasm and abandon—"

"Well?"

"He evades her."

"Ah!"

"In fact, she can never lay a hand on him any more than Bullwhip could. The longer this goes on, the more his frustration level rises and the more his adrenaline flows at the mere sight of her—and the more efficiently and automatically he evades her. She, of course, in weeping despair is forced to find solace elsewhere, but when *he* tries an occasional adventure outside the strict bonds of matrimony, he cannot. He evades every young woman who approaches him, even when it's a mere matter of business convenience on her part. Artaxerxes is in the position of Tantalus—the stuff is forever available, to all appearances, and yet forever out of reach." George's voice grew indignant at this point. "And for this piddling inconvenience, he has me thrown out of the house."

"You might," I said, "get Azazel to remove the curse—I mean the gift you wished upon him."

"Azazel has a strong objection to operating on a particular

individual twice; I don't know why. Besides, why should I do additional favors for someone who is so ungrateful for favors already done him? In contrast, look at you! Occasionally you, even though a well-known niggard, will lend me a fiver—I assure you I keep track of all those occasions on little scraps of paper I have here and there, somewhere in my rooms—and yet I have never done you a favor, have I? If you can be helpful without a favor, why can't he with one?"

I thought about that, and then said, "Listen, George. Let's keep me without a favor. Everything is all right with my life. In fact, just to emphasize that I don't want a favor, how about a tenner?"

"Oh, well," said George, "if you insist."

Galatea

For some reason unknown, especially to myself, I occasionally use George as the repository for my innermost feelings. Since he has an enormous and overflowing fund of sympathy, all of which is reserved for himself, this is useless, but I do it anyway, now and then.

Of course my own fund of self-pity was overflowing at the moment so perhaps I couldn't help myself.

We were waiting for our strawberry shortcake after a substantial lunch at the Peacock Alley, and I said, "I am sick and tired, George, of having critics make no effort to find out what it is I am trying to do. I am not interested in what *they* would do if they were I. After all, they can't write, or they wouldn't waste their time being critics. And if they *can* write, after a fashion, the only function their criticisms offer them is a chance to chip away at their superiors. What's more—"

But the strawberry shortcake arrived and George seized the opportunity to take over the conversation, something that he would have done at about that point even if the dessert had not arrived.

"Old boy," he said, "you must learn to take the vicissitudes of life calmly. Tell yourself, for it is true, that your miserable writings have so little effect on the world that what reviewers may say, if they bother to say anything at all, is totally without consequence. Thoughts of this kind will greatly relieve you and prevent your developing an ulcer. You might particularly avoid such maudlin speech in *my* presence, as you would if you had the sensitivity to realize that my work is far more important than yours and the reviews I receive are, on occasion, far more devastating."

"Are you going to tell me you write, too?" I said sardonically, digging into the cake.

"No," said George, digging into his. "I am that far more important individual, a benefactor of humanity—a berated, unappreciated benefactor of humanity."

I could swear that a suspicion of a tear slightly dampened his eyes. "I don't see," I said kindly, "how anyone's opinion of you can possibly sink so low as to be considered an underappreciation."

"I ignore the sneer," said George, "since it originates with you and will tell you that I am thinking of that beautiful woman, Elderberry Muggs."

"Elderberry?" I said, with a touch of incredulity.

Elderberry was her name [said George]. I do not know why her parents should have named her so, though it might well have commemorated a tender moment in their prenuptial relationship. It was Elderberry's own suggestion that both her parents were a bit tiddly with elderberry wine during the activities that gave her her start in life. She might not have had the chance for such a start otherwise.

In any case her father, who was an old friend of mine, asked me to be godfather at her christening and I could not refuse him. A great many friends of mine, impressed by my noble appearance and by my ingenuous and virtuous countenance, can only feel at ease in church with me next to them, so that I have had a great many godfatherships to my credit. Naturally I take these things seriously and feel the responsibility of the post keenly. I therefore remain as close to my godchildren as possible in later life, all the more so when they grow up to be as supernally beautiful as Elderberry.

He father died at just about the time Elderberry turned twenty and she inherited, as it happened, a substantial sum of money which, naturally, increased her beauty in the eyes of the world generally. I am, myself, above making a great to-do over mere trash such as money, but I did feel it necessary to guard her from fortune hunters. For that I made it my business to cultivate her society to an even greater extent, and frequently dined at her home. After all, she was very fond of her Uncle George, as you can well imagine, and I, for one, certainly can't blame her for that.

As it further happened, Elderberry did not quite need the nest egg her father had left her, for she turned out to be a sculptor of renown, producing works whose artistic value could not be questioned since they commanded high prices at the marketplace.

I myself did not quite understand her output, for my taste in art is quite ethereal and I cannot expect to appreciate the things she created for the delectation of that portion of the crass multitude who could afford her prices.

I remember on one occasion asking her what a particular piece of sculpture represented.

"As you see," she said, "the work is labeled 'Stork in Flight.'"

I studied the object, which was cast in the finest bronze, and said, "Yes, I noticed the label, but where is the stork?"

"Here," she said, pointing to a small cone of metal that arose from a rather amorphous bronze base and came to a sharp point.

I regarded it thoughtfully, then said, "Is that a stork?"

"Certainly it is, you old clotpoll," she said (for she always addressed me in affectionate terms), "it represents the tip of the stork's long bill."

"Is that enough, Elderberry?"

"Absolutely," said Elderberry. "It is not the stork itself I am attempting to represent, but the abstract notion of storkness which is exactly what this brings to mind."

"Yes it does," I said, slightly bemused, "now that you mention it. Still, the label says that the stork is in flight. How does that come about?"

"Why, you ninny-puss," she exclaimed, "don't you see this rather amorphous bronze base?"

"Yes," I said, "it rather forces itself on my attention."

"And you won't deny that the air—or any gas, if it comes to that—is an amorphous mass. Well, then this rather amorphous bronze base is a crystal-clear representation of the atmosphere in the abstract. And you see that on this face of the base there is a thin straight line, absolutely horizontal."

"Yes. How clear it is once you point it out."

"That is the abstract notion of flight through the atmosphere."

"Remarkable," I said. "Luminously clear once it is explained. How much will you get for it?"

"Oh," she said, waving one hand negligently as though to emphasize the nothingness of it all. "Ten thousand dollars, perhaps. It is so simple and self-evident a thing, I would feel guilty charging more. It is more a *morceau* than anything else. Not like that," and she waved toward a mural on the wall constructed of gunnysacks and pieces of cardboard, with the whole centered about a broken eggbeater that seemed to have something that looked like dried egg upon its lower reaches.

I looked at it respectfully. "Priceless, of course!" I said.

"I should think so," she said. "That's not a new eggbeater, you know. It has the patina of age. I got it out of someone's rubbish bag."

And then, for some reason I could not fathom, her lower lip began to tremble and she quavered, "Oh, Uncle George."

I was instantly alarmed. I seized her capable left hand, with its strong, sculptor's fingers, and squeezed it. "What is it, my child?"

"Oh, George," she said, "I get so tired working out these simple abstractions just because they represent the public's taste." She put the knuckles of her right hand to her forehead and said tragically, "How I wish I could do what I *want* to do; what my artist's heart tells me I must do."

"What is that, Elderberry?"

"I want to experiment. I want to move off in new directions. I want to try the untried, dare the undared, produce the unproduceable."

"Then why don't you do that, my child? Surely, you are rich enough to indulge yourself."

And she suddenly smiled and her whole face beamed with loveliness. "Thank you, Uncle George," she said, "thank you for saying that. Actually, I *do* indulge myself—now and then. I have a secret room in which I place my little experiments, those which only the educated artistic palate can possibly appreciate. Those which are caviar to the general," she added, coining a phrase.

"May I see them?"

"Of course, *dear* Uncle. After what you have said in encouragement of my aspirations, how could I deny you?"

She lifted a thick curtain under which one found a secret door that was scarcely visible, so closely did it fit into the wall. She pushed a button and it opened electrically. We passed in and, as the door closed behind us, brilliant fluorescents lighted the windowless room we had entered and made it as bright as day.

Almost at once I saw before me the representation of a stork, made of a rich stony material. Every feather was in place, the eyes were bright with life, the bill a little open, the wings half outspread. To my eyes it seemed ready to launch itself into the air.

"Good heavens, Elderberry," I said. "I have never seen anything like this."

"Do you like it? I call it 'photographic art,' and I think it is beautiful in its way. Thoroughly experimental, of course, and critics and public alike would laugh and sneer and fail to see what I am trying to do. They honor only simple abstractions which exist entirely on the surface and which anyone can understand, nothing like this which can appeal only to the subtle and to those who are content to allow comprehension to dawn slowly."

After that, I was privileged to enter her secret room now and then, and to study the occasional bit of exotica that formed under her strong fingers and educated chisel. My admiration at a woman's head that looked exactly like Elderberry's own was profound.

"I call it 'The Mirror,' " she said, dimpling shyly. "It pictures my soul, don't you think?"

I agreed enthusiastically.

It was that, I think, which finally induced her to allow me to see the innermost secret of all.

I had said to her, "Elderberry, how is it that you do not have any—" I paused and then, scorning euphemisms, completed the sentence with "any boyfriends?"

"Boyfriends," she said with a look of deep scorn, "Pah! They flock around, these would-be boyfriends you speak of, but how can I look at them? I am an artist. I have in my heart and mind and soul a picture of true manly beauty that no mere flesh and blood can duplicate and that, and that alone, can win my heart. That, and that alone, *has* won my heart."

"*Has* won your heart, my child?" I said softly. "Then you have met him?"

"I have . . . But come, Uncle George, you shall see him. You and I shall share my great secret."

We returned to the room of photographic art, and there another thick curtain was pulled aside so that we stood before an alcove I had never seen before. There in the alcove was the statue of a man, six feet tall and nude, which was, as far as I could see, anatomically correct to the last millimeter.

Elderberry pushed a button and the statue slowly turned on its pedestal, its smooth symmetry and perfect proportions evident from every angle.

"My masterpiece," breathed Elderberry.

I am not myself a great admirer of manly beauty, but reflected

in Elderberry's lovely face I saw a panting admiration that made
it clear she was suffused with love and adoration.

"You love that statue," I said, cautiously avoiding the imper-
sonal 'it.'

"Oh, yes," she whispered. "I would die for him. While he
exists, I find all other men deformed and hateful. I could never
let any man touch me without a sensation of disgust. I want only
him. Only him."

"My poor child," I said, "the statue is not alive."

"I know. I know," she said brokenly. "My poor heart is shat-
tered over that. What shall I do?"

I murmured, "How sad! It reminds me of the tale of Pygmalion."

"Of whom?" said Elderberry, who like all artists was a simple
soul who knew nothing of the wide outer world.

"Of Pygmalion. It is a story of ancient times. Pygmalion was a
sculptor just like you except, of course, that he was a man. And
he carved a lovely statue as you did, except that, because of his
peculiar manly prejudices, he carved a woman, whom he called
Galatea. The statue was so beautiful that Pygmalion fell in love
with it. You see, it is just like your case, except that you are a
living Galatea and the statue is a graven—"

"No," said Elderberry energetically, "don't expect me to call
him Pygmalion. That is a rough, crude name and I want something poetic. I call him," and her face lit up with love again,
"Hank. There is something about the name of Hank, so soft, so
musical, that speaks to my very soul. But what happened to
Pygmalion and Galatea?"

I said, "Overcome by love, Pygmalion prayed to Aphrodite—"

"To whom?"

"Aphrodite, the Greek goddess of love. He prayed to her and
she, out of sympathy, gave life to the statue. Galatea became a
living woman, married Pygmalion, and they lived happily ever
after."

"Hmm," said Elderberry, "I suppose that Aphrodite doesn't really exist, does she?"

"No, not really. On the other hand—" But I went no further. I didn't think that Elderberry would be able to understand me if I spoke of my two-centimeter demon, Azazel.

"Too bad," she said, "because if anyone could bring Hank to life for me, if anyone could change him from cold, hard marble to warm, soft flesh, I would give him—Oh, Uncle George, can't you imagine embracing Hank and feeling the warm softness of his flesh under your hands—softness—softness—" She kept murmuring the word in an ecstasy of sensual delight.

I said, "Actually, dear Elderberry, I don't wish to imagine doing it myself, but I can see that you would find it delectable. But you were saying that if anyone could change him from cold, hard marble to soft, warm flesh, you would give him something. Did you actually have some specific something in mind, dear?"

"Why, yes! I would give him a million dollars."

I paused, as anyone would, out of simple respect for the sum and then I said, "Do you *have* a million dollars, Elderberry?"

"I have two million lovely bucks, Uncle George," she said, in her simple and unspoiled way, "and passing out half of them would be fine for me. Hank would be worth it, especially since I could always make more by grinding out a few more abstractions for the public."

"So you can," I muttered. "Well, you just keep your chin up, Elderberry, and we'll see what your Uncle George can do for you."

It was clearly a case for Azazel, so I called up my little friend, who happened to look like a little two-centimeter version of a devil, complete with little nubbins of horns and a twitching spiked tail.

He was, as usual, in a bad humor and he insisted on wasting my time by telling me in rather boring detail just why he was in a bad humor. It appears he had done something of an artistic nature—artistic, at least, by the standards of his own ridiculous world, for though he described it in detail, I couldn't understand it—and it had been frowned on by the critics. Critics are the same the universe over, I should suppose; worthless and vicious, one and all.

At that, though, I think you should be grateful that critics on Earth have *some* minimum dregs of decency about them. If Azazel may be trusted, what the critics said about him was far beyond anything anyone has said about you. The mildest adjective would call for the horsewhip. It was the similarity of your complaint to his that helped bring this episode to my mind.

It was with difficulty that I managed to stem his vituperation long enough to interject a request that he bring a statue to life. He squawked with a shrillness that hurt my ears. "Bring silicate-based material to carbon-and-water life? Why don't you ask me to build you a planet out of excrement and be done with it? How can I turn stone to flesh?"

"Surely you can think of a way, O Mighty One," I said. "Consider, that if you achieve this enormous task, you can report it to your world and then wouldn't the critics feel like a bunch of silly asses?"

"They are far worse than a bunch of silly asses," said Azazel. "If they felt like silly asses that would exceed their worth by a great deal. Such a feeling would *reward* them. I want them to feel like a pack of farfelanimors."

"That is exactly what they will feel like. All you have to do is turn cold into warm, stone into flesh, hard into soft. Especially soft. A young woman I think highly of wants to embrace the statue and feel soft, elastic flesh under her fingertips. It shouldn't be too hard. The statue is a perfect representation of a human being and you just fill it with muscles, blood vessels, organs, and nerves and cover it with skin, and you'll have it."

"Just fill it with all that, eh? Nothing more, eh?"

"But think, you will make the critics feel like farfelanimors."

"Hmm. There's that. Do you know what a farfelanimor smells like?"

"I don't, but don't tell me. And you can use me as a model."

"Model, shmodel," he said peevishly (where he picks up his

expressions, I don't know). "Do you know how complicated even the most rudimentary human brain is?"

"Well," I said, "you don't have to go very far with the brain. Elderberry is a simple girl and what she wants of the statue does not very deeply involve the brain, I imagine."

"You'll have to show me the statue and let me consider the case," he said.

"I will. But remember. Arrange for the statue to come to life while we are watching, and make sure that it is terribly in love with Elderberry."

"Love is easy. That's just a matter of adjusting hormones."

The next day I managed to get Elderberry to invite me to view the statue again. Azazel was in my shirt pocket, peeping out and emitting feeble high-pitched snorts. Fortunately Elderberry had eyes only for her statue and would not have noticed if twenty full-sized demons had stepped up next to her.

"Well?" I said later to Azazel.

"I'll try to do it," he said. "I'll fill him with organs based on you. You are a normal representative of your foul and inferior species, I trust."

"More than normal," I said haughtily. "I am an outstanding specimen."

"Very well, then. She shall have her statue entirely encased in soft, warm, palpitating flesh. She will have to wait till noon tomorrow, your time. I can't hurry this."

"I understand. She and I will be waiting."

The next morning I phoned Elderberry. "Elderberry, my child, I have spoken to Aphrodite."

Elderberry said in an excited whisper, "Do you mean she *does* exist, Uncle George?"

"In a manner of speaking, dear child. Your ideal man will come to life at noon today under our very eyes."

"Oh, my," she said faintly. "You are not deceiving me, are you, Uncle?"

"I never deceive," I said, and I never do, but I will admit I was a little nervous, for I depended entirely on Azazel. But then, he had never failed me.

At noon we were both at the alcove once more, looking at the statue, which stared stonily into space. I said to Elderberry, "Is your watch showing the correct time, dear?"

"Oh, yes. I check it with the Observatory. We have one minute to go."

"The change may possibly be a minute or two late, of course. It's hard to judge these things exactly."

"Surely a goddess ought to be on time," said Elderberry. "Otherwise, what's the good of being a goddess?"

I call that true faith, and she was justified, for on the second of noon, a tremor seemed to course through the statue. Slowly, his color changed from a dead marble white to a warm flesh pink. Slowly, motion animated his frame, his arms lowered to his side, his eyes gained a blue and glistening life, the hair on his head darkened to a light brown and appeared wherever appropriate elsewhere on his body. His head bent and he looked at Elderberry, who was hyperventilating madly.

Slowly, creakily, he stepped down from the pedestal, and walked toward Elderberry, arms outstretched.

"You Elderberry. Me Hank," he said.

"Oh, Hank," said Elderberry, as she melted into his arms.

For a long time they stood frozen in the embrace and then she looked over her shoulder at me, her eyes shining with ecstasy, and said, "Hank and I will remain in the house for a few days as a sort of honeymoon, and then, Uncle George, I will see you," and she twiddled her fingers as though she were counting money.

At that my eyes shone in ecstasy, too, and I tiptoed out of the house. Frankly, I thought it rather incongruous for a fully dressed young woman to be so warmly embraced by a naked young man, but I was sure that almost immediately upon my leaving, Elderberry would manage to correct the incongruity.

I waited ten days for Elderberry to phone me, but she never did. I was not entirely surprised, for I imagined she was otherwise occupied. Still, after ten days I did think there would be a pause for breath, and I further began to think it only fair that since her ecstasy had been fulfilled, entirely through my efforts— and Azazel's—it was only fair that my ecstasy be fulfilled, too.

I went to her place of abode, where I had left the happy couple, and rang the bell. It was quite a while before there was an answer, and I was having an unpleasant picture of two young people having ecstasied each other to death when finally the door opened a crack.

It was Elderberry, looking perfectly normal, if you count an angry look as perfectly normal. She said, "Oh, it's *you.*"

"Why, yes," I said. "I was afraid you had left town to continue and extend your honeymoon." I didn't say anything about honeymooning themselves to death. I felt it would not be diplomatic.

She said, "And what do you want?"

It was not terribly friendly. I could understand that she might not like to be interrupted at her activities, but after ten days surely a small interruption was not the end of the world.

I said, "There's a little matter of a million dollars, my child." I pushed the door open and walked in.

She looked at me with a cold sneer and said, "What you get is bubkes, fella."

I don't know what "bubkes" are, but I instantly deduced it was a good deal less than a million dollars.

I said, puzzled and more than a little hurt, "Why? What's wrong?"

"What's wrong?" she said. "What's wrong? I'll tell you what's wrong. When I said I wanted Hank soft, I didn't mean soft all over, permanently."

With her sculptor's strength, she pushed me out the door and slammed it shut. Then, as I stood there nonplussed, she opened it again, "And if you ever come back, I'll have Hank tear you to pieces. He's strong as a bull in every other way."

So I left. What could I do? And how do you like that for a

critique of *my* artistic efforts? So don't come to me with your petty complaints.

George shook his head when he completed his story and looked so despondent that it really touched me.

I said, "George, I know you blame Azazel for this, but really it's not the little guy's fault. You emphasized the bit about softness—"

"So did she," George said indignantly.

"Yes, but you told Azazel to use you as a model for designing the statue, and surely that would account for the inability—"

George lifted his hand in a stop gesture and glared at me. "That," he said, "hurts me even more than the loss of the money I had earned. I'll have you know that, despite the fact that I'm some years beyond my prime—"

"Yes, yes, George, I apologize. Here, I believe I owe you ten dollars."

Well, ten dollars is ten dollars. To my relief. George took the bill, and smiled.

Flight of Fancy

When I dine with George, I am careful not to use a credit card in payment. I pay cash, since that gives George the chance of exercising his amiable habit of scooping up the change. Naturally, I am careful to see to it that the change brought back is not excessive, and I leave a tip separately.

We had had lunch, on this occasion, at the Boathouse and were walking back through Central Park. It was a beautiful day and just a bit on the warm side so we sat down on a bench in the shade and relaxed.

George watched a bird, seated on a branch in the twitching way birds have, and then followed it with his eyes as it flew away.

He said, "When I was a boy I was outraged that those things could go darting through the air, and I couldn't."

I said, "I suppose every child envies the birds. And grown-ups, too. Yet human beings *can* fly, and they can do so faster and farther than a bird ever could. Look at the plane that circumnavigated the Earth in nine days, nonstop and without refueling. No bird could do that."

"What bird would want to?" said George with contempt. "I'm not talking about sitting in a machine that flies, or even dangling from a hang glider. Those are technological compromises. I mean being in control: flapping your arms gently, then rising and moving at will."

I sighed. "You mean being free of gravity. I once dreamed that, George. I once dreamed that I could jump into the air and stay there by the gentlest maneuvering of my arms, and then come down slowly and lightly. Of course I knew that was impossible, so I assumed I was dreaming. But then, in my dream, I seemed to wake up and find myself in bed. I got out of bed and found I could *still* maneuver freely in the air. And now, because it seemed to me I had awakened, I believed I could really do it. And then I *really* woke up and found I was as much a prisoner of gravity as ever. What a feeling of loss I had, what a keen sense of disappointment. I didn't recover for days."

And, almost inevitably, George said, "I've known worse."

"Is that so? You had a similar dream, did you? Only bigger and better?"

"Dreams! I don't traffic with dreams. I leave that to dabbling scriveners like yourself. I'm talking about reality."

"You mean you were really flying. Am I supposed to believe you were in a spaceship in orbit?"

"Not in a spaceship. Right here on Earth. And not me. It was my friend, Baldur Anderson—but I suppose I had better tell you the story—"

Most of my friends [said George] are intellectuals and professional men, as perhaps you might consider yourself to be, but Baldur was not. He was a taxi driver, without much education but with a profound respect for science. Many an evening we spent in our favorite pub, drinking beer and talking about the big bang and the laws of thermodynamics and genetic engineering and so on. He was always very grateful to me for explaining these arcane matters to him and insisted, over my protests, as you may well believe, on picking up the tabs.

There was only one unpleasant aspect of his personality: he was an unbeliever. I don't mean your philosophical unbeliever who happens to reject any aspect of the supernatural, who joins some secular humanist organization, and who carefully expresses himself in language that no one understands by way of articles published in magazines that no one reads. What harm is there in that?

I mean that Baldur was what in the old days would have been termed the village atheist. He would pick arguments in the pub with people as ignorant of such matters as he was and they would go at it with loud and scurrilous language. It was not an exercise in rarefied reasoning. The typical argument would go as follows:

"Well, if you're so smart, onionhead," Baldur would say, "tell me where Cain got his wife?"

"None of your business," his adversary would say.

"Because Eve was the only woman alive at the time according to the Bible," he would say.

"How do you know?"

"The Bible says so."

"It does not. Show me where it says, 'At this time, Eve was the only dame on the whole Earth.'"

"That's implied."

"Implied, my foot."

"Oh, yeah?"

"Yeah!"

I would reason with Baldur, during some quiet moments. "Baldur," I would say, "there's no reason to argue matters of faith. It won't settle anything, and it just creates unpleasantness."

Baldur would say belligerently, "It's my constitutional right not to go for the phony-baloney stuff and to say so."

"Of course," I said, "but one of these days, one of the gentlemen who are consuming alcoholic beverages here might hit you before he stops to remember the Constitution."

"Those guys," said Baldur, "are supposed to turn the other cheek. It says so in the Bible. It says, Don't make a fuss about evil. Leave it be."

"They could forget."

"So what if they do. I can handle myself." And indeed he could for he was a large and muscular man with a nose that looked as though it had stopped many a punch and fists that looked as though they had exacted exemplary vengeance for such acts.

"I'm sure you can," I said, "but in arguments over religion, there are usually several persons in opposition and only one of you. A dozen people acting in concert might well reduce you to something approaching a pulp. Besides," I added, "suppose you do win an argument over some religious point. You might then cause one of these gentlemen here to lose his faith. Do you really feel you should be responsible for such a loss?"

Baldur looked troubled, for he was a kindly man at heart. He said, "I never make any remarks about real tender parts of religion. I talk about Cain and about Jonah not being able to live three days in any whale and about walking on water. I don't say anything *really* lousy. I don't ever say anything against Santa Claus, do I?—Listen, I once heard a guy say right out loud that Santa Claus had only eight reindeer and that there was no Rudolph the red-nosed reindeer ever pulling that sleigh. I said, 'Are you trying to make little kids unhappy?' and I popped him one. And I don't let anyone say anything against Frosty the Snowman, either."

Such sensitivity touched me, of course. I said to him, "How did you ever get to this state, Baldur? What turned you into such a rabid unbeliever?"

"Angels," he said, frowning darkly.

"Angels?"

"Yeah. When I was a kid, I saw pictures of angels. You ever see pictures of angels?"

"Of course."

"They got wings. They got arms and they got legs and on their backs they got big wings. I used to read books on science when I was a kid and those books said that every animal that had a backbone had four limbs. They got four flippers, or four legs, or two legs and two arms, or two legs and two wings.

Sometimes they could lose the two hind legs, like whales did, or two front legs like kiwis did, or all four legs like snakes did. But none of them could have more than four. So how come angels have six limbs, two legs, two arms and two wings. They got backbones, ain't they? They ain't insects, or something? I asked my mother how come and she said to shut up. So then I thought of lots of things like that."

I said, "Actually, Baldur, you can't take those representations of angels literally. Those wings are symbolic. They simply indicate the speed with which angels can move from place to place."

"Oh, yeah?" said Baldur. "You ask those Bible guys anytime if angels got wings. *They* believe angels got wings. They're too dumb to understand about six limbs. The whole thing is dumb. Besides, it bothers me about angels. They're suppose to fly, so how come *I* can't fly? That ain't right." His lower lip thrust out and he seemed to be on the point of tears. My soft heart melted and I looked for some way to console him.

"If it comes to that, Baldur," I said, "when you die and go to heaven, you'll get wings along with a halo and a harp and then you'll be able to fly, too."

"You believe that junk, George?"

"Well, not exactly, but it would be comforting to believe it. Why don't you try?"

"I'm not going to, because it ain't scientific. All my life I've wanted to fly—personally, just me and my arms. I figure there must be some scientific way to fly by myself, right here on Earth."

I still wanted to console him so I said incautiously, having had perhaps half a drink above my abstemious limit, "I'm sure there is a way."

He fixed me with a censorious and slightly bloodshot eye. "Are you kidding me?" he said. "Are you making fun of an honest childhood desire?"

"No, no," I said, and it suddenly occurred to me that he had had perhaps a dozen drinks too many and that his right fist was twitching in a most unpleasant way. "Would I make fun of an honest childhood desire? Or even of an adult obsession? I just happen to know a—a scientist who might know of a way."

He still seemed belligerent to me. "You ask him," he said, "and let me know what he says. I don't like people who make fun of me. It ain't kind. I don't make fun of you, do I? I don't mention that you never pick up a tab, do I?"

That was treading on dangerous ground. I said hurriedly, "I'm going to consult my friend. Don't worry, I'll fix everything up."

On the whole, I thought I had better do so. I did not want to cut off my supply of free drinks, and I wanted even less to be the object of Baldur's resentment. He did not believe in the biblical admonitions that he love his enemies and bless them that curse him and do good to them that hate him. Baldur believed in popping them in the eye.

So I consulted my otherworldly friend Azazel. Have I ever told you that I have—I have? Well, I consulted him.

Azazel was, as usual, in a terrible temper when I brought him in. He held his tail at an unusual angle, and when I inquired about it he broke into a frenzy of very shrill commentary on my ancestry—matters concerning which he could not possibly have known anything.

I gathered he had been accidentally stepped on. He is a very small being, about two centimeters tall, from the base of his tail to the top of his head, and even on his own world I suspect that he can only succeed in being underfoot. He was certainly under someone's foot on this occasion, and the humiliation of having been too small to be noted had reduced him to frenzy.

I said soothingly, "If you had the ability to fly, O Mighty One to whom all the universe pays homage, you would not be subject to the clodhoppers of clodhoppers."

That rather cheered him up. He kept muttering the final phrase to himself, as though he were memorizing it for future use. Then, he said, "I *can* fly, O Ugly Mass of Worthless Flesh, and I would have flown if I had taken the trouble to note the presence of the lower-class individual who, in his clumsiness, fell up against me. —In any case, what is it you want?" He rather snarled as he asked this, though the high pitch of his tiny voice made it sound more like a buzz.

Smoothly I said, "Although you can fly, Exalted One, there are people on my world who cannot."

"There are no people on your world who *can*. They are as gross, as swollen, as clumsy as so many shalidraconiconia. If you knew anything about aerodynamics, Miserable Insect, you would know—"

"I bow to your superior knowledge, Wisest of the Wise, but it had crossed my mind that you might manage a small amount of antigravity."

"Antigravity? Do you know how—"

"Colossal Mind," I said, "may I have leave to remind you that you have done this before?"*

"That, as I recall, was only a partial treatment," said Azazel. "It was barely enough to allow a person to move along the tops of the heaps of frozen water you have on your horrid world. You are now asking, I take it, for something more extreme."

"Yes, I have a friend who would like to fly."

"You have peculiar friends." He sat down on his tail as he frequently did when he wished to think, and, of course, jumped up with a thin shriek of agony, having forgotten the contused state of his caudal extremity.

I blew on his tail, which seemed to help and mollify him. He said, "It will take a mechanical antigravity device, which, of course, I can get for you, together with the complete cooperation of your friend's autonomic nervous system, assuming he has one."

"I believe he has one," I said, "but how may he achieve the cooperation?"

Azazel hesitated. "I suppose that what it amounts to is that he must *believe* he can fly."

* See "Dashing Through the Snow."

I visited Baldur two days later in his unassuming apartment. I held out the device to him and said, "Here."

It was not an imposing device. It was the size and shape of a walnut and if one put it to one's ear, one could hear a very faint buzz. What the power source was I could not say, but Azazel assured me it would not run down.

He also said it had to be in contact with the skin of the flier, so I had put it on a small chain and made a locket of it. "Here," I said again, as Baldur shied away from it suspiciously. "Put the chain around your neck and wear it under your shirt. Under your undershirt, too, if you have one."

He said, "What is it, George?"

"It's an antigravity device, Baldur. The latest thing. Very scientific, and very secret. You must never tell anyone about it."

He reached out for it. "Are you sure? Did your friend give you this?"

I nodded. "Put it on."

Hesitatingly, he slipped it over his head and, with a little encouragement from me, he opened his shirt, let it fall down behind his undershirt, and then buttoned up again. "Now what?" he said.

"Now flap your arms and you'll fly."

He flapped his arms and nothing happened. His eyebrows hunched in lowering fashion over his small eyes. "Are you making fun of me?"

"*No.* You've got to *believe* you're going to fly. Did you ever see Walt Disney's *Peter Pan?* Tell yourself, 'I can fly, I can fly, I can fly.'"

"They had some kind of dust they sprinkled."

"That's not scientific. What you're wearing is scientific. Tell yourself you can fly."

Baldur favored me with a long, hard stare, and I must tell you that although I am as brave as a lion, I felt a bit anxious. I said, "It takes a little time, Baldur. You've got to learn how."

He was still glaring at me, but he flapped his arms vigorously and said, "I can fly. I can fly. I can fly." Nothing happened.

"Jump!" I said. "Give it a little head start." I wondered nervously if Azazel had known what he was doing this time.

Baldur, still glaring and still flapping, jumped. Up he went in the air about a foot, remained there while I counted three and then slowly descended.

"Hey," he said eloquently.

"Hey," I responded in considerable surprise.

"I sort of floated there."

"And very gracefully," I said.

"Yeah. Hey, I *can* fly. Let's try again."

He did, and his hair left a distinct greasy spot where he hit the ceiling. He came down rubbing it.

I said, "You can only go up about four feet, you know."

"In here, I can. Let's get outside."

"Are you crazy? You don't want people to know you can fly. They'll take that antigravity thing away from you so scientists can study it, and you'll never be able to fly again. My friend is the only one who knows about it now and it's secret."

"Well, what am I going to do?"

"Enjoy yourself flying around in the room."

"That's not much."

"Not much? How much could you fly five minutes ago?"

My powerful logic was, as usual, convincing.

I must admit that as I watched him move about freely and gracefully within the rather unfragrant air of the limited confines of his not very large living room, I had a distinct urge to try it myself. I was not sure he would give up his antigravity device, however, and, what was more, I had a strong suspicion it would not work for me.

Azazel consistently refuses to do anything for me directly, on what he calls ethical grounds. His gifts, he says in his idiotic fashion, are meant only to benefit others. I wish he didn't feel that way, or that others did. I have never been able to persuade the beneficiaries of my beneficence to enrich me noticeably.

Baldur finally came down upon one of his chairs and said complacently, "You mean I can do this because I believe?"

"That's right," I said. "It's a flight of fancy."

I rather liked the phrase but Baldur is wit-deaf, if I may invent a term. He said, "See, George, it's much better to believe in science than in heaven and all that junk about angel wings."

"Absolutely," I said. "Shall we stop off for dinner and then have a few drinks?"

"You bet," he said—and we had an excellent evening.

And yet, somehow, things did not go well. A settled melancholy seemed to cast its pall over Baldur. He abandoned his ancient haunts and found new watering holes.

I didn't mind. The new places were a cut about the old ones and usually produced excellent dry martinis. But I was curious and asked.

"I can't argue with those dumbheads no more," said Baldur glumly. "I get the craving to tell them I can fly like an angel, so are they going to worship me? And would they believe me? They believe all that crud about talking snakes and dames turning into salt—fairy tales, just fairy tales. But they wouldn't believe *me.* Not on your life. So I just got to stay away from them. Even the Bible says: 'Hang not out in the company of jerks, nor sit in the seat of the scornful.' "

And periodically he would burst out and say, "I can't just do it in my apartment. There's no *room.* I don't get the *feel.* I got to do it in the open air. I got to climb into the sky and go swooping around."

"You will be seen."

"I can do it at night."

"Then you'll crash into a hillside and be killed."

"Not if I go up real high."

"Then what'll you see at night? You might as well fly around in your room."

He said, "I'll find a place where there are no people."

"These days," I said, *"where* are there no people?"

My powerful logic always won the day, but he got more and more unhappy, and finally I didn't see him for several days. He wasn't at home. The taxi garage out of which he worked said he had taken a two-week vacation that was coming to him, and no, they didn't know where he was. It wasn't that I minded missing out on his hospitality—at least I didn't mind much—but I was worried what he might be doing on his own with all this madness about swooping through the air.

I found out eventually, when he returned to his apartment and telephoned me. I scarcely recognized his broken voice, and of course I came to him at once when he explained that he needed me badly.

He sat in his room, dispirited and heartsick. "George," he said, "I never should've done it."

"Done what, Baldur?"

It poured out of him. "You remember I said I wanted to find a place where there was no people."

"I remember."

"So I got an idea. I took some time off when the weather forecast said there would be a bunch of bright, sunny days, and I went and hired a plane. I went down to one of those airports where you can get a ride if you pay for it—like a taxi, only you fly."

"I know. I know," I said.

"I tell the guy to head out to the suburbs and fly around all the hick places. I said I wanted to look at the scenery. What I was gonna do was look around for some real empty places, and when I found one I'd ask what it was and then some weekend I'd come out there and fly like I really wanted to fly all my life."

"Baldur," I said, "you can't tell from up in the sky. A place may look empty from up there, but be full of people."

And he said bitterly, "What's the use of telling me that *now.*" He paused, shook his head, then went on. "It was one of those real old-fashioned planes. Open cockpit in front and open passenger seat in back, and I'm leaning way out so I can watch the ground and make sure there are no highways, no automobiles, no farmhouses. I take off my seat belt so I can watch better—I mean, I can fly, so I'm not scared of being high in the air. Only I'm leaning way out and the pilot don't know I'm doing that and he makes a turn and the airplane sort of leans in the direction I'm looking out, and before I can catch hold of something, I fall right out."

"Good heavens," I said.

Baldur had a can of beer at his side and he paused to gulp at it thirstily. He wiped his mouth with the back of his hand and he said, "George, did you ever fall out of an airplane without a parachute?"

"No," I said. "Now that I think of it, I don't think I have ever done that."

"Well, try it someday," said Baldur; "it's a funny feeling. I was caught all by surprise. For a while I couldn't figure out what happened. It was just open air everywhere and the ground was sort of turning around and then moving up and going over my head and around and I kept saying to myself, What the heck's going *on.* Then after a while I can feel a wind and it's blowing stronger and stronger, only I can't tell exactly from what direction. And then it sort of percolates in my head that I'm falling. I just says to myself, Hey, I'm falling. And as soon as I say that, I can see I am, and the ground looks like it's below and I'm going down fast and I know I'm going to hit and covering up my eyes isn't going to do me any good.

"Would you believe, George, all that time I never thought I could fly. I was too surprised. I could've been *killed.* But now when I'm almost down there, I remember, and I say to myself: I can fly! I can fly! It was like skidding in the air. It was like the air turning to a big rubber band that's attached to me on top and is pulling back so that I slow down and slow down. And when I'm about treetop high I'm going real slow and I'm thinking: Maybe now is the time to swoop. But I feel sort of worn out and there's just a tiny way to go so I straighten out, slow down some more, and land on my feet with the tiniest, tiniest bump.

"And, of course, you're right, George. Everything looked empty when I was way up there, but when I got down to the ground there was a whole crowd of people gathered around me and there was a kind of church with a steeple nearby—which I guess I didn't make out from way up, what with the trees and all."

Baldur closed his eyes, and for a while he contented himself with breathing heavily.

"What happened, Baldur?" I asked finally.

"You'll never guess," he said.

"I don't want to guess," I said. "Just tell me."

He opened his eyes, and said, "They'd all come out of the church, some real Bible-believing church, and one of them falls to his knees and lifts up his hands and yells, 'A miracle! A miracle!' and all the rest do the same. You never heard such a noise. And one guy comes up, a short, fat guy, and says 'I'm a doctor. Tell me what happened.' I can't think what to tell him. I mean, how do you explain how come you're shooting down from the sky? They're gonna holler I'm an angel soon. So I tell the truth. I say, 'I accidentally fell out of an airplane.' And they all start hollering, 'A miracle' again.

"The doctor says, 'Did you have a parachute?' How'm I going to say I had a parachute when there ain't none around me, so I say, 'No.' And he said, 'You were seen falling and then slowing up and landing gently.' And then another guy—it turned out he was the preacher of the church—said in a kind of deep voice, 'It was the hand of God upholding him.'

"Well, I can't take that, so I said, 'It was *not*. It was an antigravity thing I got.' And the doctor says to me, 'A what?' I said, 'An antigravity thing.' And he laughs and says, 'I'd go for the hand of God, if I were you,' like I'm coming up with a gag.

"By that time the pilot has landed his airplane and come up and he's white as a sheet, saying, 'It wasn't my fault. The damn fool unbuckled his safety belt,' and he sees me standing there and he damn near faints. He said, 'How did you get here? You didn't have no parachute.' And everyone starts singing some kind of psalm or other and the preacher takes the pilot's hand and tells him it's the hand of God and I've been saved because I'm meant to do some great work in the world and how everyone in his congregation who was here this day were now surer than

ever that God was on his throne and working away like anything
to do his good work, and all sorts of stuff like that.

"He even got *me* to thinking about it; I mean, that I was being
saved for something great. Then newspaper people came and
some more doctors—I don't know who called them—and I was
asked questions till I thought I would go crazy, but the doctors
stopped them and carried me off to a hospital for an examina-
tion."

I was stupefied at this. "They actually put you in a hospital?"

"Never left me alone for a minute. The local paper had me in
headlines and some scientist came over from Rutgers or somewhere and he kept asking me about it. I said I had this antigravity and he laughed. I said, 'Do you think it was a miracle,
then? You? A scientist?' And he said, 'There are lots of scientists
who believe in God, but not one scientist who believes antigravity is possible.' Then he said, 'But show me how it works,
Mr. Anderson, and I may change my mind.' And, of course, I
couldn't make it work, and I still can't."

To my horror, Baldur covered his face with his hands and
began to weep.

I said, "Pull yourself together, Baldur. It *must* work."

He shook his head and said in muffled tones, "No, it don't. It
only works if I believe and I don't believe no more. Everyone
says it's a miracle. No one believes in antigravity. They just
laugh at me and the scientist said the thing was just a piece of
metal with no power source and no controls and antigravity was
impossible according to Einstein, the relativity guy. George, I
should've done like you said. Now I'll never fly again, because I
lost my faith. Maybe it wasn't never antigravity and it was all
God, working through you for some reason. I'm beginning to
believe in God, and I've lost my faith."

Poor fellow. He never did fly again. He gave me back the
device, which I returned to Azazel.

Eventually Baldur quit his job, went back to that church near
which he came down, and he now works as a deacon there. They

take care of him very kindly because they think the hand of God was upon him.

I looked at George intently, but his face, as always when he tells me of Azazel, bore a look of simple candor.

I said, "George, did this happen recently?"

"Just last year."

"With all this fuss about a miracle, and newspapermen and headlines in the papers and the rest?"

"That's right."

"Well then, can you explain how it is that I've never seen anything about it in the papers?"

George reached into his pocket and extracted the five dollars and eighty-two cents that represented the change he had carefully collected after I had paid for lunch with a twenty and a ten. He isolated the bill and said, "Five dollars says I can explain that."

I didn't hesitate a moment, and said, "Five dollars says you can't."

He said, "You only read the New York *Times,* right?"

"Right," I said.

"And the New York *Times,* with due regard to what it considers its intellectual readership, places all reports of miracles on page thirty-one in some obscure place near the advertisements for bikini bathing suits, right?"

"Possibly, but what makes you think I wouldn't see it even in a small, obscure news item?"

"Because," said George triumphantly, "it is well known that except for some scare headlines, you see nothing in the newspaper. You go through the New York *Times* looking only to see if your name is mentioned anywhere."

I thought awhile, then let him have the other five dollars. What he said wasn't true, but I know it's probably the general opinion, so I decided there was no use arguing.